WHEN IT RAYNES

12/15 FR

Chambers of the Heart

CHAMBERS OF THE HEART
BOOK 1

WHEN IT RAYNES

C.D. CAIN

BInk

Bedazzled Ink Publishing • Fairfield, California

978-1-939562-94-4 paperback
978-1-939562-95-1 ebook

Cover Design
by

TreeHouseStudio

Bink Books
Bedazzled Ink Publishing, LLC
Fairfield, California
http://www.bedazzledink.com

CHAMBER 1

For Mamaw and Papaw,
you'll always have my respect for showing me the person I
needed to be and loving me for the person I was. I love you both
so very much.

Acknowledgements

Getting this book into the hands of readers has been a wonderful experience for me. I have been marveled by the generosity of others that have given freely of their time whether it was to offer a proofreading, words of encouragement, or even at times a swift kick in the tail to get me in gear. I will forever be indebted to each of you.

Along the way I have met a few pretty great authors who unselfishly gave me a piece of what little free time they had. Melissa, you never failed to answer any of my questions no matter the hectic schedule of your own life. Please know it didn't go unnoticed. RJ, you gave me several good kicks in the tail to keep me on track. I hope you are pleased with the end result. Cindy, what can I say? You helped me throughout it all and gave me the chance to have my very first public reading. I believe we are up to a case of wine I owe you at this point. Sandra, it's finally out and yes BC is still editing. Mardi, I couldn't imagine a better friend to debut with this year. As we have said, this year . . . our debut books brought us together. I hope for our friendship to grow for many years to come.

To my GCLS Writing Academy classmates, we did it! I am very proud to be among such a great group of women. I hope our support of each other's craft of writing continues to flourish over the years to come.

Thank you Bedazzled Ink Publishing for taking the chance on a little ole southern gal who had a dream to write. Casey, you are the voice in my head that whispers "nasty dangling participle." Maybe one day I'll lose those little buggers. Ann, thank you for a brilliant cover. You nailed my every vision for the design.

I can never thank my beta readers enough for their encouraging feedback and edits of the things I never saw. Eh, Jane, Lori, Tracy, and Shannon, I look forward to working with you on Chamber Two.

And lastly but never leastly to Geanie, you have been my rock for twenty-two years now. You are my balance . . . my center and I will always love you.

"Life is all memory except for the one present moment that goes by so quick you can hardly catch it going."
—Tennessee Williams, *The Milk Train Doesn't Stop Here Anymore*

CHAPTER 1

I SAT AGAINST a tall cypress tree as I stared out across the water, focusing not on the dance of the red-and-white cork as it bobbled with the current's flow but rather beyond it to see everything . . . to feel everything . . . to remember *everything*. The elevated roots of its massive trunk cradled me as if holding me in its arms. I wanted to burn into my soul the cool dampness of the morning fog against my skin as it hovered above the water's surface.

I prayed the song of the bayou with its chorus of ripples softly lapping at the surface, smacking fish, and croaking frogs would play over and over again in my head in the years to come. The cypress knees had been a place I came to for comfort—for shelter.

In three months I would leave my southern Louisiana home. In three months I would begin my life. No longer would I be confined to the restrictions of proper southern etiquette or the narrow-minded southern values of which I had been bred. In a few short months I would be free from the views that had been passed down to me and be freely able to develop my own. Up until this point, I knew not what they were as I had been raised not to challenge the beliefs of those around me. To challenge was to disobey. To disobey was unheard of, Sugar. After all this was the south! No, my views were but beliefs passed down along the southern bloodline—for at least the next three months anyway.

"Penny for 'em." Memaw's piercing blue eyes held me in their stare.

"Who says I'm thinking anything?"

"I's do, cuz I can read them eyes of yours," she said.

Adelaide "Addie" Cormier was the name given my grandmother. Although I suspect that was my great grandfather's doing as Memaw's mother was full Native American. Memaw had the bluest eyes I had ever seen, probably highlighted even more against the contrast of her long white hair and darkened skin.

"Honey child, they always been the one thing you couldn't

hide. You weren't but a babe fresh to this world when you looked deep through me with those eyes of yours. Couldn't've been more than a couple of days old . . . but 'em eyes . . . 'em eyes showed a soul as old as mine."

"Thankfully you're the only one that can read them, Meems." That was what I called her usually. It was my playful nickname for her as if Memaw wasn't a nickname enough.

We were inseparable. I spent each moment possible, soaking up everything she would share with me. I was captivated by the culture that existed within her. Our bond was strong enough to speak without words. Our personalities were so equal that we figured they skipped a generation with mother. A birth certificate proved my mother was born of Memaw, but not much else did. Her soul was unsettled . . . confined . . . completely without freedom. Memaw was as unrestricted as her loose white hair flowing about her. Mom was wound tighter than a tick as they say. Or so she was in the days I remember her most.

"Not forever. One day someone gonna learn 'em." MeMaw winked at me before looking back to realize her cork was now submerged under the water. She flicked her wrist and the pole in her hand, sending the empty hook flying into the air. "Dadgummit! Damn little bastards stealing my bait."

The sun reflected off of the shiny gold band that slipped above the collar of her shirt as she bent over to get another cricket from the box. She rubbed the black leather cord between her fingers and brought the wedding band to her lips before tucking it back under her collar. She had her heart stolen by Papaw early in life only to lose him in a car accident long before I was born. Never again would her heart skip a beat for another man. She wore a token of black fabric about her on days she missed him most—a piece of satin woven into her long, white braid or, like today, a string of black leather tied loosely around her neck. Her expression changed, giving no doubt her thoughts drifted to him.

"We're not going to have enough bait to last us until noon if you keep feeding them like that."

She looked at me with a half grin. "You best be worrying 'bout the end of yo' line and not meddling with mine." She pointed at the absent cork that had been bobbling atop the water in front of me.

"Dammit!" I yelled in response to her laughter.

She was chuckling so hard I was afraid she was going to fall off of the overturned paint bucket she was sitting on.

"If you bust your butt you know I'll have to laugh."

"Laugh at this," she hollered as she fought the fish stretching out her line.

She fought it to shore, removed the hook, and tossed the bream into the cooler between us.

She peered into the cooler. "Hmmm . . . that's four for me and," she pretended to count the catch of the day, "ummm . . . none for you. You gonna get mighty hungry watching me eat up some fried fish."

I felt a strong tug at my line. "Oh, I believe I'll be okay." I pulled the fish to the side of the bank and turned to Memaw to gloat . . . She was bringing yet another one up to the shore.

We continued to catch fish after fish for the next several minutes. They seemed to hop on the line as soon as we threw our hooks back out into the water. Memaw shook the bait basket vigorously to jiggle the few remaining crickets from the upper lid so she could snag one in her arthritic grip.

"You ready for yo' shindig tomorrow?" Memaw asked as she flipped her hook in between a circle of grayish brown cypress knees poking through the surface of the water.

"Would it matter if I wasn't?" I said.

"Knowing my daughter . . . not one darn bit."

"Charlie Grace wouldn't miss the chance to throw a party."

She looked over her shoulder at me. "Your momma proud of you, Rayne. Don't be fixin' your mind to nothing else."

"She'd been prouder if I had snagged a husband in college instead of a degree. All I ever heard from her was," I changed my tone to mock my mother's, "find a man, get married, and have some grandchildren." I kicked at the Louisiana red clay caking the bottom of my once white tennis shoes. "Not once, Meems . . . not once did she ask me how school was going for me . . . what I wanted to do with my time. Nope, it was either about boys or sorority crap. Always dragging me to one mother-daughter function after another."

"Sis, don't pay her no mind at'oll," Me Maw said. "She prizes her happiness as what others be thinking of her. She gets her happiness picturing what 'em people think of her. What she sees of herself through their eyes . . . not her own."

"Guess I burst her bubble then. I didn't have time to date, Meems."

"Uh huh, baby girl."

"What?" I asked. "What does that mean?"

"Oh, nothing. Just saying."

"I didn't, Meems. I spent my time studying and playing intramural sports. Plus you know I shadowed down in the emergency room on weekends."

"That's what I know. Your momma done bragged all over town 'bout you working so hard."

I knew she was right. I had heard through the socialites I would run into from time to time about the things Charlie Grace had said. No doubt she enjoyed the bragging rights. But it did not get her any closer to her dream of orchestrating a grand wedding. I knew her hunger for more would grow. She would eventually become ravenous on it until I became united with a man befitting of our family. Up until that point, it seemed my attentions were held by anything other than the opposite sex.

"I agreed to go on a few dates this summer before I leave," I said as I rested the fishing pole across my lap to raise the cork up my line. I hadn't gotten a nibble in several minutes and figured the fish had gone deeper in the water as the day warmed in the early afternoon sun.

Memaw smirked at me as she copied my depth on her own line. "Oh, did you now?"

"I did, but her definition of few and my definition are most likely not one in the same."

She chuckled hardily. "I don't be doubting that at'oll."

For as long as I could remember, I had spent the summers with Meems. I wasn't about to change that the summer before I left for Alabama.

"You don't s'pose there is any way she has a quiet party planned for tomorrow night do you?"

Memaw didn't answer with words but rather in an expression she gave. One I had come to know well and generally meant in the most simplest of terms, "Have you lost yo' damn mind?"

"Yep . . . didn't think so," I said.

She patted the thighs of her denim coveralls then lifted the lid of the cooler.

"Whoooweee . . . Sis, we done caught us some titty bream today!" she said, using one of her many terms not found in Webster's dictionary.

It was her description for fish too large for her hand to reach around them. So, instead they had to be secured firmly between her arm and her breast to remove the hook.

"We found us a right fine bream hole today." She was so excited her plump little feet lifted off the ground. She turned to me with a widened grin. "We got us a mess fo' sure. But I'm sweating more than that hooker Janice sitting in church. Let's get under some air, clean these here fish, pop a couple of cold ones, and fry us up a mess?"

I stood from my bucket and rubbed the numbness out of my aching butt. "Sounds like a plan to me, Meems." I grabbed the cooler.

The walk down the levee with nothing but the weight of a bag of ice wasn't quite as taxing as the walk up with the cooler now loaded half full of fish. I was thankful Memaw had parked her nineteen-eighty Chevrolet Silverado pickup truck on the lowest part of the levee she could find. She tossed the two five gallon paint buckets and tackle box over the top of the tailgate before lowering it for me to lift the chest into the bed.

"One day I'll have us a boat," Memaw said as she walked around to the driver's side door of the canary yellow truck. The door screamed a horrendous screech as she opened it. You could hear someone a mile away getting into Memaw's truck. "Sis, turn your air on."

I climbed in on the passenger side. "Are you ever going to get the air fixed?" I rolled down my window.

"Hell no. It highway robbery what 'em boys trying to charge me. I won't pay 'em one red cent to do nothing for me."

She bounced us around on the front seat of the truck as she drove down the bumpy road that ran alongside the levee. We drove down the path of road made by years of tires traveled before us. The long stalks of Bahia grass stretched up tall between the two worn dirt paths.

"I remember seeing you pedaling your bike 'cross a road much like this. You remember dat?" Memaw took her eyes off the road long enough to look at me and smile. "That when you and your momma used to live on the other side of 'em woods from me. You be riding that bike so hard you nearly knocked everything out of that there wicker basket you had tied to your handlebars. Every Sunday afternoon here you'd come on that bike. Tweren't nothing I liked more than to see you riding down that road as fast as your little legs could pedal. 'Em pigtails were bouncing all over the place."

"I hated those damn things nearly as much as the stupid dresses she made me wear. She'd put those dang things in my hair every Sunday and she always used some kind of ribbon to tie around them. Ten minutes after church I was back in my t-shirt and jeans." I looked down at my clothes, realizing my style hadn't changed much over the years.

"IT'S A GONNA be a hot one this year, Sis," Memaw called out over her shoulder as she stood in front of the fish cooker that she had welded from old metal grating. It had a large cooking surface attached to a deep pot that was now filled with spattering hot grease.

I watched her diligently work the fish into her homemade batter of seasoned corn meal, flour, and several dashes of pickled jalapeno pepper juice. Sweat dampened the hair of the back of her neck, causing the strands to spring into small curls—much like the ones I found on my own head.

"It sure is, Meems. Hard to believe it's this hot in early May."

"Grab me a cold one, eh, girlie," she said.

I walked to the refrigerator in the corner of her screened back porch. I had no idea how this thing was still working. It must have been older than me. It had only one door . . . not the common ones now with a door for the freezer and a separate one for the refrigerated part. No, this one had a big white door enclosing both so that when you opened it a burst of cold air against the stagnant humidity encircled you like an Arctic breeze. I was always happy to volunteer the beer retrieval on a hot summer day.

I pulled the long silver handle toward me to unfasten it from the clasp and the hinges let out a loud screech. I giggled as I remembered Memaw's voice ringing through the air, "Sis, bring me one too." That was what she yelled from inside the house when I tried to sneak outside and grab one of the amber-colored bottles for myself when I was a young girl. There was no way to open that door quietly and even less of a chance of pulling one past Memaw.

"I LOVE THAT sound," I mumbled as I closed my eyes to focus my senses on the gentle patter of rain falling on the tin roof above us. "I could sleep for days to a sound like that." We had returned to the porch after dinner to watch the rainfall.

"I love the smell, Sis." Memaw inhaled in a deep breath.

I joined her, taking in a breath of my own. There was a distinct smell to the rain as it turned to vapor suspended over the hot asphalt drive. I wondered if this too would be something else I would miss from my Louisiana home.

"I'm scared, Meems."

"What you scared of?" From the corner of my eye, I could see her expression filled with concern.

I flicked at the corner of the blue ribbon label on my beer bottle. Its adhesion had been loosened by the condensation along the sides of the glass. I paused to consider her question. There wasn't a short easy answer I could give her . . . or maybe there was. Her tender blue eyes were transfixed on me.

"Honestly . . . everything."

"Aw, baby girl, that normal. It normal to feel this way. You going out into a wide big world. You 'bout to live Rayne's life. Course you scared. Would be worried if you weren't."

"Maybe I should've waited a year? Maybe I'm moving too fast? I could've stayed here with you. I . . . I could've taken a year off."

"Time don't wait around for nobody. You follow the road in front of you. Don't go looking for no hills to pass. They gone be there sho' 'nough. Don't need to go chasing after 'em."

I looked out into the backyard at the pecan tree I used to climb as a young girl, the plum tree I made myself sick from eating too many of the tiny fruits, and the well house I ran into with my Big Red three-wheeler. An involuntary sigh escaped me—the times of my youth and the protections it afforded me had passed.

"Sis?" I felt her long fingers caress the top of my hand. "You gone be just fine. I'm so proud of you. Don't go missing something you ain't yet left. We got all summer together."

I looked at her face as it glowed in the moonlight. Her smile was contagious. I grinned at the thought of spending the next three months with her.

CHAPTER 2

"ARE YOU GOING in?"

Startled, I turned around to see Jacques standing behind me. "I haven't decided yet."

"She'd be awfully upset if you didn't. Pert near pissed off I'd imagine." His smile hinted at his joking manner but I knew his words were filled with truth.

I had been five years of age when Charlie Grace first met Raymee Jacques Doucet. He was known to me simply as Jacques, pronounced Jack, which is what I had called him growing up . . . not Father or Dad—just Jacques. I don't remember a time he ever tried to get me to refer to him as anything else, not that I wouldn't have. He never asked. I suppose it was a sign of respect not wanting to try to substitute another man's place in my life. Yet he was truly the only father figure I had ever known.

"I don't doubt that one bit. I'll be in shortly . . . just delaying the inevitable as always." I had never been one to enjoy the social limelight, not like mother. That was always Charlie Grace's desire.

"It won't be that bad. Charlie Grace took it down a notch or two after Addie lit into her."

I chuckled out loud. "Meems jumped on Mother?"

Jacques returned my laughter in a hushed tone. "She sure did. She told your mom that this wasn't one of her damn debutante balls. She reminded her you didn't like all that crap. Charlie Grace walked around with her tail feathers ruffled for a long time after but she finally came around. I think you'll be happily surprised."

I learned early in my young life that it was much easier to play the part Mother wished rather than argue. I wasted more time belaboring my defense than I would have if I'd just done her wishes to begin with. I found a balance in setting false pretenses in order to fit into each of the social events presented to me. I became a chameleon, in essence caught somewhere in between the confirmed daughter of a would be socialite upholding a correct social standing and a hellion running circles around Memaw on the banks of the bayou. During my undergraduate studies that chameleon transformed into a social butterfly flapping its wings with insurmountable precision. But now that I had graduated, I was hoping those days of pretense were few and far between.

I sighed. "I sure hope you're right."

Jacques stepped past me toward the entrance doors to Lagniappe. He turned back to me before walking fully inside. "I'm real proud of you Rayne. Real proud."

"Thanks, Jacques." I gave him a wide smile.

I stood underneath the black awning of the restaurant, studying the silhouetted shapes of mingling guests. Our treasured Lagniappe had been the venue of choice for many of Mother's celebrations. The restaurant was named for its meaning, "a little something extra." It had a prime location on the busiest corner of downtown. Its outer wall and large double entryway doors were nearly full-length glass which gave an unobstructed view for those looking in as well as those looking out . . . except for events like tonight when Charlie Grace would lower the cloth shades for privacy. I swallowed hard before pulling the door open to follow Jacques inside.

"I was beginning to think you were gonna stand 'round out there all night," Memaw said as she walked up to me. "Thought I was about to have to drag yo' tail in here. Good thing Jacques got you to come to your senses."

"Hi, Meems," I said, accepting the hug she offered. "He looks handsome tonight doesn't he?"

"He sure do."

Jacques had made his way through the crowd to whisper something into the bartender's ear. He did look nice in his khaki pants and burgundy button-down shirt. His hair was the same style I had always known it to be—cut close around the ears and neck with the bangs brushed back off his forehead. The once black hair was now a healthy mixture of black and gray. His head fell back in a hardy laugh.

I turned back to Memaw. "He looks happy."

"Why shouldn't he be? You the only daughter that boy gone ever have. He proud of you," she said, smiling as she tapped the end of my nose. "But not as proud as me."

I took her hands and lifted them up and away from her body.

"Speaking of looking nice tonight . . . you look right snazzy yourself."

"What this ole thing?" She brushed my compliment away with her hand. She motioned at the new royal blue dress she was wearing. "Cora picked it out. Like I done said . . . ain't every day I get to celebrate a doctor's graduation."

"Ha! That hasn't happened yet."

"It will." Memaw winked at me. "It will."

"Wow. This place looks great." I peered around the groups of conversing guests.

White linen cloths adorned the small four-top tables located in a scattered fashion throughout the room. Crystal vases filled with turquoise stones and red with yellow center hibiscus flowers were on the center of each table. Dimly lit chandeliers and candles of varied sizes illuminated the room. The walls were salt and peppered with black-and-white photos taken during my college years.

"You sho' 'nough right about dat. My girl done put on a shindig," Memaw said as she took in the surroundings. "We in high cotton tonight!"

"She has indeed, Meems," I said. "You would think I had married into royalty with this affair."

"Don't go puttin' ideas in her head or she may just catch ya with yo' pants down," she said with a crooked grin. "Speak of the devil. Here she a comes now."

Mom walked toward us—no glided toward us. The hem of her linen skirt swayed to and fro with her steps. She looked absolutely gorgeous. She didn't reflect her forty-three years as one would have never guessed she was any older than her mid-thirties. The ivory-colored dress contrasted her natural sun-kissed brownish skin beautifully. She kept her hair a professionally highlighted blond in a usual style about two inches below her shoulders. But tonight she wore it pulled up with well-placed dangles hanging along the sides of her face.

"Mom, you look absolutely stunning," I said as she stopped before me. "And this place looks amazing. You even remembered my favorite flower."

"Why of course I did, dear." Her eyes sparkled in the glow of the chandelier above us—a grayish color of the brilliant blue found in Memaw's. "The hibiscus is such a beautiful flower. It's always been your favorite. Mom has planted one in her garden every year just for you," she said in her sophisticated southern flair.

Memaw's eyes flashed. It was true, her landscaping had always been found with a few hibiscus planted throughout the beds. Occasionally one plant would be lost to the frost if we had an uncharacteristically cold winter but usually the warm climate of the south was a natural environment for its foliage.

"Lagniappe holds many surprises for us this evening," Mother said with too much sparkle flashing in her eyes. She had the expression of a woman trying to suppress a secret she impatiently wished to expose.

"Wow. Mother you look as if you are about to burst," I said. "I'm now afraid of what little surprises you have hidden under your sleeves."

"Why, honey, I am simply celebrating my only child's accomplishments."

"There has never been anything *simple* when it comes to your celebrations . . . or you for that matter," I replied with the same crooked grin Memaw had worn a few moments earlier.

"Come with me, Rayne. You need to attend to your guests rather than hiding over here by the door. We can discuss the simplicities of my life at a later date," Mother said, tugging at my arm. "You'll excuse us won't you, Mom?"

"Yep, ya'll have fun now," Memaw said, giggling.

I shook my head at Memaw as Mother dragged me deep into the crowd. We stopped to greet the guests with common pleasantries as we made our way around the room. That wasn't the part I minded so much because honestly Mother did most of the talking for me. I simply shook my head in agreement as if her words were true. No, that wasn't what bothered me the most. It was the hugs. Why these ladies thought they needed to hug me was unknown to me. Sure they had either seen me growing up around town or had at least heard of me but a hug? Seriously? I didn't know them well enough for all of that. The short side hugs of greeting were somewhat tolerable but those full-frontal, holding on for what seemed an eternity was quite near painful if you asked me.

I was finally able to return to Memaw nearly thirty minutes later. I found her sitting at an empty table closest to the door.

"Gawd, I didn't think I would ever escape," I said, handing her a glass of beer. "Here, brought you something. Sorry, they wouldn't let me have the bottle. Apparently Mother wanted all drinks served in glassware as it is more proper that way."

Memaw took the glass and inspected its bubbles. "Figures as much. Damn fools don't know how to pour a good beer without making it taste flat. I'll just bet they ruint a perfectly good drink."

I sat down in the chair next to her. "That's why I talked them into letting me pour them." I clinked the rim of my glass against hers. "Look at these things." I held up the small card placed in front of the silverware. It was a replica of my diploma. "Rayne Amber Storm, Bachelors of Science in Biology. Geesh. Cheesy enough?"

Memaw took the card from my hand and tucked it gently into her purse. "I kinda liked 'em."

"Don't make me laugh. My cheeks are still hurting from holding my smile so long while walking around with Mother."

"Best plant you another one cuz here she comes again," she said, motioning her head toward the center of the room.

"Please tell me she is *not* bringing him over here." I sighed. "What is he doing here anyway?"

"Hello, Rayne. I was hoping to catch you before I left," Brother Dan said as he stood by the table.

"Rayne, honey, wasn't it nice of Brother Dan to come out this evening?" Mother asked.

"Aw shuckin', Charlie Grace, I wouldn't have it any other way. We are right proud of our little Rayne." Brother Dan smiled his best Sunday smile. You know, the one he gave right before he passed out the offering plates.

I never believed his smiles were genuine. They seemed fake as if given with the intent of wanting something in return. I wondered if his true reason for attending tonight was because he was promised some form of donation for the church. He was the preacher of Mother's Southern Baptist Church. With this being his only source of income I was often left questioning his excessive wardrobe complete with a thickened gold chain around his neck.

"Well, anyway, I best be going. I've got a sermon to prepare for. Rayne congratulations on your graduation. I'm sure I'll be seeing you and your lovely Mother tomorrow morning at church to celebrate the word of the Lord, our Savior." He used his famous sermon dialect as he said those last few words.

"We'll be there, Brother Dan," Charlie Grace answered, once again speaking for me.

"Good night, Brother Dan. Thank you for coming," I said. I realized my tone was flat but I was too drained to give him much more.

"You are very welcome." Brother Dan turned toward Memaw. "Sister Adelaide we sure would like to see you tomorrow morning serving the Lord."

"I serve the Lord just fine, Dan," she said.

"Nothing like worshipping in a house of God though."

I could tell Brother Dan's persistence was wearing thin on Memaw because she pursed her lips.

"Didn't you say you were leaving?" she said and then pointed at the carryout bag in his hand. "Wouldn't want yo' dinner to get cold now would we?"

"Aw yes, of course. Guess I'll be saying good night then." He paused to tip his head toward Mother and me. "Ladies." He gave a side glance at Memaw. "Adelaide."

Memaw returned his head tip. Her lips still tightly pursed. "Dan."

As soon as the door closed behind Brother Dan, Mother glared at Memaw. "I have no idea why you must be so crass."

"I won't be judged by the likes of him," Memaw said.

"He wasn't judging you for Pete's sake. He was inviting you to church. There's a difference you know."

"Oh, I know," Memaw said. "I'm a wondering if you do."

"I don't have time for this, Mom. I need to attend to my guests. Rayne, I have us a table over there." She motioned over her shoulder to the table where Jacques was sitting. "Dinner shall begin in a few moments."

"I'm good here with Meems," I said.

"Ugh." Charlie Grace tightened her hands into a fist as she grunted. "I swear you two are going to be the death of me one day." She turned on her heel and walked away.

Lagniappe's menu was nothing short of sinfully delectable. Those attending were lavished with a four course meal straight from a Cajun kitchen. Mother reserved her prize chef from New

Orleans to host the affair. For an appetizer, he served pan grilled green tomatoes atop mini crawfish pies followed by a satsuma salad. The main course was shrimp and andouille sausage with Asiago grits. As if anyone had room for the dessert, he completed the meal with pineapple-apple bread pudding with bourbon sauce.

The room was filled with the sounds of pleased guests clinking their forks on nearly empty dessert plates. Many released soft moans of both pleasure and utter discomfort after devouring the meal.

A *clink clink clink* sound rose above the crowd. Charlie Grace stood in the center of the room, tapping a dessert fork on her half-empty champagne flute.

"My dearest guests," she said with distinct clarity.

"Here we go, Sis. Hold on to yo' britches," Memaw whispered in my ear.

"I would like to thank each of you for coming to join us in celebrating Rayne's graduation from our fine university," Charlie Grace continued in her thickest southern flair. "As many of you've noticed from the hangings about the room, she graduated summa cum laude with a perfect four-point-zero grade point average. She was an active member of multiple groups and president of her sorority. What most of you don't know, is my dahlin' has been accepted into UAB's Medical School. She'll be starting this fall." She focused her moistened gray eyes on me. No, focused them inside of me. "Rayne, I'm so very proud of you. I've never been able to give you everything you deserved. Nor have I been able to give you all of your wants. But, baby girl, you will live your dreams. In that, I have no doubts. I'll watch in admiration and love as you walk this life you have before you."

Tears had not yet fallen from my moistened eyes as I was transfixed by Charlie Grace's speech. Memaw's hand gently squeezed mine, comforting me before the first tear dampened my cheek.

Charlie Grace held up a single key on a Lagniappe key chain. "I believe there's something to help get you to Alabama in the parking lot." She jiggled the key and gave me an exaggerated wink.

I loathed these kinds of moments deep down to my center. The moments when all eyes were focused on me, when every head was turned in my direction. Everyone sat waiting—waiting for my reaction. Lacking the callus calculations of Mother, I could do nothing more than show the swirl of emotions forming in the pit of my stomach. The social butterfly desperately sought the ability to return to her cocoon. Yet one sat next to me. One that could cease the frantically flapping wings.

"Easy girl," Memaw whispered into my ear.

They were but two simple words softly spoken. They were two simple words of stability . . . of unconditional love. Yet they were enough to give me the strength I needed to meet Charlie Grace in the center of the room.

"I love you, Rayne," she said softly as she took me in her embrace. "I'm so very proud of you."

"You never stop surprising me," I whispered as I leaned in to kiss her cheek. "So . . . this was the reason for the twinkle in your eyes all night?"

"Well . . ." she said slyly and with a small wink. She snuck her arm around mine and motioned me to the door. "Let's go have a look, shall we?"

With her arm around mine, she led me through the now open patio doors and out onto the outdoor dining area. The crowd followed behind us. My eyes fell upon a black Jeep. Its gloss reflected the shine of the street light hanging above it. It sat alone in a now empty parking lot. Well, it sat *nearly* alone. The driver side door of the glistening beauty was opened giving sight to a gray interior. Standing in that doorway was Grant Thibodeaux.

"Grant?" I mumbled out loud.

Mother released my arm to hand me the key. "Well," she said in that same sly tone, "perhaps there was more than one reason for the twinkle." And yes, this too was followed by a wink.

"Mother . . . Grant?" I stumbled for a coherent sentence. "What's Grant doing here?"

"Why delivering your Jeep from his father's dealership, of course."

"Oh . . . but of course, why would I've thought anything else at ten o'clock in the evening? I'm sure these are normal business hours for delivery."

"Come, dear, don't waste any further time standing here debating the hours for which it is common practice to deliver a vehicle. You have roads that need to be traveled," she said as she motioned me away toward my graduation prize . . . toward both graduation prizes.

Grant Thibodeaux . . . the closest I ever came to breaking my noncommittal relationship status. He possessed all the right checks to the boxes: handsome, funny, intelligent, and compassionate. But the most important of those, he was easy. Grant was easy to be around, never asking too much, never asking at all. I could give him as much or as little as I wished. Both of which he took in stride. He stood in the doorway of my new means of transportation. I wondered which was to be Charlie Grace's ultimate graduation surprise—perhaps both.

A soft hand upon my arm stopped my approach to the trophies awaiting me.

"Baby girl, don't you be forgittin' me in the morning. I've gotta give ya my present," Memaw said with that ever present sparkle shining in pools of blue.

"Aren't you going to come take a look at the new wheels, Memaw?"

She looked over her shoulder at Grant and chuckled. "No dear. Not tonight. You take her out for a spin. I'll see ya in the morning." She hugged me and the smell of brown sugar and honey scented my nose. I took in another deep inhalation before letting my thoughts wander away . . . Grant.

I turned back and noticed the crowd dispersing about the parking lot. I noted for the future I should be more careful to read the evening's program as it surely stated at the end, "Kindly disperse to leave the love birds to their evening."

Mother, angrily ran through my mind as the sense of irritation built. I was growing tired of her continued exploits at ending my single status. There he stood in his starched white shirt in contrast with the shiny black paint. The cutest boy in high school had grown to be a very handsome young man. And . . . he was standing in the way of my Jeep. I smiled. *Let's go check her out.*

"Rayne, you're a beauty before my eyes," Grant said. His voice had deepened since I had heard it last.

Am I? Am I a beauty? I cannot say I ever took notice of such things throughout my life. Others would make comments here and there. But to me, the mirror never seemed to hold quite the same reflection as what they described.

Tonight I had dressed as Mother requested. She always wished for us to be outfitted in a similar fashion—another example of her knack for the dramatic. I wore a linen skirt and loose-fitting linen button-down shirt. My accessories were a bit less extravagant than her choices. I wore a simple gold cross that sat at the notch of my neck. I had worn it nearly every day since it was given to me.

"Hello. It's been a few years. What? High school?" I tried to sound excited to see him. And why shouldn't I be excited? "I think you've grown since I've seen you."

He collected me in a hug, filling the air between us with the scent of his aftershave. We had grown to be adults over the last four years. His growth was more than half a foot taller than mine. Nevertheless our bodies were built in the same athletic tone. He had gone to a university in South Louisiana on a track scholarship. Memories of Mother's incessant reviews of his athletic accomplishments filled my head.

"Tell me. Just how did the dear Mrs. Lagniappe rope you into this evening's shining event?" I said.

"As if she would've had to hog tie me to see you, Rayne. She just asked is all. Dad said your mother stole this Jeep right outta from under him with," he made quotation marks with his fingers, "those eyes of hers." He paused and then winked. "Must be genetic with the Storm women." Giving no time for my response, he stepped away from the driver's side door. "Let's take her for a drive. I'll do my duties in giving you a proper once over with her."

"First thing I want to know is how to take the top off."

"A woman after my own heart," he replied slyly.

A chuckle escaped my lips as his perverse hidden meaning was not entirely lost on me. I responded with nothing more than a raised eyebrow.

He laughed and cleared his throat. "You can actually mostly fold this top back. Come to this side and I'll show you." He walked around to the other side of the Jeep and stood on the step bar. I did the same on my side. "Just follow my lead."

I followed his instructions until we were able to fold the soft top back. Grant patted the hard material with his hand. "See not too bad. I'm sure you could do it alone with some practice. Your mom figured you'd want the top off the majority of the time so she told Dad to get you the soft top. You know, that way you won't be stuck if the weather turns on you. But she also ordered you a hard top if you wanted it for long trips or when the weather turned cold."

Giddiness overtook the residual frustrations of Mother's attempts at matchmaking. The vehicle before me was what I had wanted since I was a child. I longed for the openness to arrive at my destination without closing out the world around me. Tonight I would drive with a view of the blanket of stars above me. I climbed in and turned to the patio. Mother was there, watching me. She shyly waved as I ignited the engine's hum. With one last glance, I drove toward the street lights and away from Lagniappe.

GRANT INSTRUCTED ME on the nuances of my new black beauty with salesman-like precision. He had spent his summers at his father's dealership while I slipped off to the water's edge. She was a beauty stocked with four-wheel drive and power windows. But most of all—I looked up into the night sky—she had freedom!

"She had this special ordered, you know," Grant said, breaking the silence of my meditation with the stars.

"I'm sorry."

"Your mother. She had this planned for months. Dad said she has been to the dealership at least once every other week, making sure it was just right. He told me he never once saw or talked with Jacques. She did the whole thing . . . even down to the payment."

"She does have her moments, doesn't she?"

The uncomfortable silence hung in the air between us. The silence when one person awaited the opportunity to say what was truly on their mind . . . and the other awaited in hopes that they never did!

"Thank you again for bringing it to me," I said. "It was very sweet of you. Is your vehicle back at the restaurant?"

"No, it's at the dealership. You can drop me there if you don't mind." He paused to look out the window. "But, Rayne, it wasn't purely unselfish on my part. I . . . well . . . I . . . wanted to see you. I *want* to see you. Please, let me take you to dinner one night next week. Any night. I'm in town until the end of the summer."

In that moment he looked like the cute little boy I remembered from our younger years. His expression was filled with nervous intent. His deep brown eyes were searching mine for an answer. His matching brown hair was tousled from the blowing of the

night air into the cab of the Jeep. Yes, he had indeed become a
fine-looking young man.

"Yeah, that sounds good. I'll be spending tomorrow with
Memaw but how does Monday sound?"

CHAPTER 3

HERE I SAT again in the crowded pews of Mother's Southern Baptist Church. Once again Brother Dan's sermon sang no song of truth for me. He stood upon his stage, animated in his drive to preach right and wrong. I never felt quite right under that roof. Never felt like I belonged in the same pew as those who sat around me. Sure I looked the part, dressed in my Sunday best complete with dress and shining shoes. My makeup and hair complemented the rest. The problem was I never fit the part. Something . . . something was never right.

"Hear me now, my congregation, for I'm speaking the Lord's word." He slammed the palm of his hand against the leather-bound Bible he held in his grip. "This world is filled with heathen ways. All around us the sinners are trying to corrupt us, my brothers and sisters. Look around you!" His voice crescendoed from a whisper to a full-blown scream. "The devil's serpents slither pass and rub against you. You see them everywhere. Tempting you with their poisonous alcohol . . . their fornication!"

The vessels of his neck bulged as his voice grew louder and louder. He paced back and forth across his stage, flailing his arms about in wild mannerisms. His swept-back feathered hairstyle was surely secured with hair spray as it never fell upon his forehead even with his most forceful foot stomp.

"The *homosexuals* marching in the streets are nothing more than an abomination of God's word!" He stomped his foot forcefully against the raised wooden platform, causing me to startle in my seat.

I looked around at the faces of those intently listening to him. Their heads nodded in agreement. "Amen" could be heard from different voices in the crowd.

Brother Dan slumped across the podium. "Brothers and sisters, I'm weak. Weak with the filth that surrounds you. As the choir begins to sing, if you feel the Lord our God calling on your heart this morning. Calling on you to repent the evilness lurking in your

heart . . . come forward and let me pray with you." He walked to
the edge of the stage.

I sat steadfast in the pinewood pew. Benediction—that was what
they called this part of the sermon. It was the most uncomfortable
moment at the end of each service when Brother Dan would call
the sinners forward, coaxing them with the words of being called
forward by the spirit of God.

I felt his eyes piercing their blackness through me when he
rested them upon me. "Come my sisters . . . come my brothers . . .
let me pray for a cleansing of your soul. I feel the sins plaguing
you from the inside out." Did he see? Did he see the thoughts in
me wishing their release? If he did, could he shed light into them
for my own recognition?

AFTER CHURCH I escaped up to my bedroom before anyone
else arrived home from the service. I hadn't been inside longer
than ten minutes before I found myself comfortable in jeans and
t-shirt, free of the Sunday dress.

I caught my reflection in the mirror as I walked past it. I hadn't
really aged much over my college years. I didn't gain the freshman
forty like so many of the girls in my sorority had. My favorite size-
five jeans from high school fit me just fine. I also hadn't changed
my hair. It was still a light golden brown found in the same cut
of my late teenage years. Wisps of curls flowed erratically about
my face with the length hanging an inch below my chin. There
was no order to the style, which suited me fine. No order meant
no time wasted to style my hair. A good towel drying, some hair
product, a few passes with the blow dryer, and I was done. I was
momentarily distracted by the floating dust particles caught in
the light of the sunshine bursting through my window. That was
until I heard the echoes of Charlie Grace's shoes clicking on the
kitchen floor—each step a louder tap than the one before. They
were evidence to her growing impatience downstairs. No doubt
an inquisition awaited me as I had deliberately delayed coming
downstairs earlier in the morning until I knew she and Jacques had
already left for church.

"How long have ya'll been home?" I asked Mother as I entered
the kitchen.

"Rayne! I thought you were going to stay up there the rest of the day. Sit down. I was just putting on another pot," she said as she tilted her head.

I knew she was anxious to know if I was going to be forthcoming in the details of last night's surprise visit. A strong cup of coffee may entice me to stay a little longer. Strong black coffee was the norm of any Louisiana kitchen. I had been drinking it since the age of two. Honestly, I didn't know of many youth in my generation that hadn't had coffee milk from a toddler cup—one part coffee, two parts milk and three parts sugar. No matter the kitchen I had ever visited, there was always a pot on the stove. Of course with Memaw, this was a literal term as she used an old-style percolator on the stove top. She timed the heat settings with an egg timer. Distract her in conversation and you would be drinking a nice, hot black cup of syrup. Mother had since advanced to the fancy Italian version complete with espresso side. Although an espresso had nothing on the strength of Memaw's coffee. That stuff would put hair on your chest.

"So dear . . ." Mother gave a characteristic pause. "How was your evening?"

"Mother," I said through a smile, "before we get into all of that, can I please say thank you without you blowing it off as if it's nothing?" I walked to her and took her hands. "Thank you for everything. For the wonderful dinner . . . the speech . . . and especially for the Jeep. It's what I have always wanted. I love it. And I love you."

"Oh, honey, that was nothing. Now tell me about Grant." She squeezed my hands with excitement and released them. "My, didn't he grow to be a handsome young man?"

I wasn't surprised in the least as to how quickly she dismissed my comment. I rolled my eyes as I noticed the gleam in hers. I had no doubts her head was filled with visions of grandchildren. Hell, I nearly saw them too. There, all four of them sitting under the Christmas tree dressed in red and white and waiting impatiently to dig into the mountain of presents at their feet.

"Don't you roll your eyes at me young lady," she said.

"I'm sorry," I said, shaking the images free. "Yes, Grant is a very nice-looking young man. And before you get your panties in a wad, yes . . . we did have a nice chat. Yes . . . I'll be seeing him again. No . . . we don't want a summer wedding in the sweltering heat. Yes . . . we'll name our first born after Memaw, male or female."

She swatted me on the butt with the hand towel she had been pretending to use to wipe off the counter. "I didn't raise a smartass."

"Aw . . . but didn't you?" I winked at her as I popped a piece of her banana nut bread into my mouth and picked up my mug of coffee. "Okay, gotta run. I'm s'posed to pick up Memaw in fifteen. You know how she gets when I'm late."

"*What*? I thought you were going with me to the Forsythe Lake Ladies League meeting today? We're planning the Independence Day events for this year," she said in a surprised tone.

"Ha. Whatever gave you the notion I'd do such a dreadful thing? In fact, I think I said I'd never be a part of that group of well-kept snobs. Those women's noses are stuck so far up in the air they would drown if caught out in the rain."

"Rayne Amber Storm. You should be ashamed of yourself, talking of my society that way. We have made many contributions to this town. Many contributions," she repeated, waving her arms in the air. "You'll need these connections I've made for you when you come here to practice."

"You're a saint indeed, what with your selfless offerings to my career and all. But today I'll be with Memaw. Give the ladies cheek kisses for me." I stopped at the door and looked back at her. "Oh, please take an umbrella just in case. Who knows? You could save a life today."

I darted through the door before she could make any further argument.

The sound of her yelling, "Smartass!" followed me out onto the porch steps.

"I DO DECLARE, Sis, I got but a few years left'n in me and done wasted one waitin' on you," Memaw said as she walked out of her house and locked the door behind her.

"Hey. Wait a minute. Don't I even get a cup of coffee? Are we really in that big of a hurry?"

"Try being on time and you can try talking me outta my good grounds." She never missed a beat, walking toward the driveway.

"Oh, Lawd. You mean I'm a gonna be riding in a car with no roof?"

"Where exactly are we going anyway?" I asked, smiling at her pretend disgruntled state. Deep down I knew she would have been disappointed had I shown up any other way. Well, except of course the part about being on time.

"You drive and I'll instruct."

The drive was quite perfect. The warming sun shined down onto our shoulders as a refreshingly, cool breeze sifted through the exposed top of the Jeep. Our words were few as we watched the scenery unfold around us. The two hours' drive was filled with plentiful sights of pastureland with a few homes scattered here and there. Memaw's directions continued until we found ourselves turning onto an old gravel road. I could hear the crunch of the pebbles under my tires as we drove through the stillness of the canopy of overhanging limbs above us. The narrowed road was nearly camouflaged by the greenery—its width barely enough for a single vehicle to pass.

"Just a little farther, Sis. Go down this road a piece." Her eyes were filled with child-like excitement. "There! Turn in that driveway on the right." She pointed her arthritic finger down the rock-strewn road to a single drive on the right. It sat alone at the edge of large fields devoid of any planted crop. In fact, it seemed like the crops hadn't been harvested in years. Weeds filled the center of the land. The acreage extended as far as I could see. A dense forest of trees bordered the large plot.

A small home with cypress wood siding stood at the end of the road. Its roof was composed of shingles of faded black laid in a simple pattern. An end-to-end screened porch ran along the front of the house. The yard was covered mostly in dirt with a few scattered blades of grass. It stood alone on the road. In fact, very alone as I hadn't noticed a home in the last several miles we had traveled.

Memaw hopped out of the Jeep as if springs gave bounce to her feet. She certainly didn't move like any other woman in their early seventies.

"Come, baby girl, lemme show you 'round," she said.

Her smile was as bright as the sun's glare casting off the Jeep's black paint. She led me through the covered front porch. The

squeaking of the rusted hinges echoed in the silence around us.
Two concrete steps sat in front of the main door. One large nearly
empty room greeted us as we walked in.

She walked to the center of the room where a wood-burning
space heater sat. "Look, they don't make them like this anymore."
She ran her palm over the top of the dark iron and kicked at a
collection of bark pieces and ash that had been left scattered
around the legs of the stove. "Ain't she a beauty?"

"Ummm . . . yeah," I answered hesitantly.

Memaw walked to the back wall, which appeared to be the
kitchen. She patted the wooden plank board that was secured
waist high along the wall.

"Countertop needs a little work," she said.

The two-by-four wood planks that secured the board against
the wall shook a little under the strain. Cuts had been made in the
wood for the refrigerator, single sink, and small stove but there
were no appliances, cabinets, or drawers. She walked to the small
hallway splitting two bedrooms and through the bathroom door at
its center.

"Look. There is a full bath over here." She turned around in the
small bathroom space. Its pink ceramic tile was visible through
the doorway.

My tour guide described each area with excitement. As wrapped
up as I was in watching her joy, I was still left wondering what we
were doing there and exactly whose cabin we were invading. She
eagerly led me through the back door located next to the kitchen.
Her words became difficult to interpret as she was several steps
ahead of me and calling out over shoulder.

"Hurry up, Sis. This the best part," she called. "Listen. Do you
hear it?"

Memaw was at the edge of a wood line of cypress and pine
trees, her head tipped upward as if listening beyond where she
stood. Tall brush and grass grew nearly halfway up the tree trunks,
forming a living fence along the borders of the yard. Standing next
to her, I tried to hear the sound beyond the silence. Then . . . there
it was—the soft sounds of water hitting against a bank.

A small trail broke through the living fence to lead us further
down the embankment. Louisiana red clay swallowed my shoes
deeper and deeper into its suction with each step I took. Memaw's

pace slowed once she reached a clearing. Before her was an expanse of clear bayou water—not the muddied versions I had come to know. Curtains of moss hung from tree branches over our heads. Some of the stands of moss extended so far below the branches their tips were wet with the water's surface.

"You a'ready?" she asked, gesturing to a canoe pulled onto the bank next to us.

"Ready for what, Memaw? What are we doing here?" I said.

"Aw hell, Sis. I'm a only asking you to take a float with me. Now git your tail in here." She swung her leg briskly over the side of the canoe and maneuvered her way to the back.

Shaking my head in defeat of her request, I pushed the vessel away from the shore and jumped into its hull. The quicksand effect of the red mud suctioned my flip-flop off my foot as I tried to gain extra strength in sending us further into the water. The air around us was calm . . . serene.

As I rowed us toward the middle of the open water, I marveled at the expression on Memaw's face. She was smiling as she held her head up to the blueness of the sky above us. I lifted my face to let the sun warm my skin. My eyes closed as my thoughts traveled back to the morning in church. I never felt a place in those pinewood pews, not like I did here. Here, floating on the bayou speckled with cypress knees is where I heard God's gentle voice amidst the choir of croaking frogs, chirping crickets, and the rippling sound of a water's current against our boat. This was my church. This was where my beliefs were free to spread into my own. This was where I belonged.

"I've never thought of you as my granddaughter," she said. "You know dat? I gotta remind myself that you ain't my daughter every day I wake up. My time with you is the best I've known all my days."

"Me too, Memaw. Me too." I slowly rowed the canoe along the still water. "But you're starting to worry me. Here we are in some stranger's boat after traipsing through some stranger's house. Please, tell me you aren't demented already? I don't think I could handle it."

"Stranger? They always did say you were'n a little strange but I told them to hush with that. You were born of this world and the next." She smiled and raised her hand to show me a single key. "Happy graduation, baby girl. This all yours now. The house comes with one-hundred-eighty acres to do with what you want. The ground's still fertile but no one crops it no more. I know you won't live here but this'll be your heart. This'll be your escape." She leaned over and put the key in my hand. "You my heartbeat, sweet girl." A single tear trickled down her cheek. She swallowed hard as if she was trying to force words through a tightened throat.

Words found no way to my lips as a lump formed in my throat. Any coherent communication was lost in a swirl of mixed emotions—excitement . . . astonishment . . . overwhelming joy . . . disbelief. But one emotion conquered them all—love . . . unconditional . . . *love*. Matching tears fell upon my cheeks, stinging the skin along their way. I searched her face until the tears came faster. I searched my heart for words worthy enough to share.

She cupped her hand against my cheek and wiped away a fresh fallen tear with her thumb. "I know, Sis. I know." She gave me a wink and tapped the back of my hand, ending the need for any further words. Our hearts communicated without them.

Over the next hour, we floated along the bank as Memaw told me the details of her purchase. The borders of the land included the asphalt road we had originally turned off of, the bank of the bayou, and the farm land. Solitude could be a plentiful commodity if I wished it to be grown on my land. She had spoken to no one of her purchase; therefore, the secret would be mine to tell.

Walking back through the cabin had an all new meaning to me. It was no longer a stranger's home we had trespassed in. No, this was now my escape—my serenity. Once again found in the arms of Memaw. She was my rescue. In her home, I found my structure. In the ways of her life, I found the woman I most desired to become. In her arms, I found my acceptance.

Plans of the cabin's transformation dominated our conversation on our way home. Our voices carried high over the wind that blew between us. We would divide our time between harvesting Memaw's garden and the home on the bayou we yearned to cultivate together. At her back door were, once again, little to no words worthy to be spoken. My heart was still too full to let them find their way to my voice.

A strong hug of duration was all I could do to express the

emotions she had caused me to feel. Brown sugar and honey filled my senses. I drove away in reflection and my fingers rubbed the small gold cross hanging at the base of my neck. Memaw had once again touched my soul.

CHAPTER 4

CHARLIE GRACE WOULD know nothing of my escapes with Memaw. I would keep our destination hidden from her. It would be a place known only to Memaw and me. She wasn't very troubled with my disappearances. Her sugar high was met with the first appearance of Grant at our door. Once more I imagined visions of grandchildren at her feet circling her mind as she saw him arrive for our first date.

I was pleasantly surprised he had not chosen a night for a show; but rather made plans quite perfect for me. He took me to a local pizza joint to dine on the outdoor patio. We shared a crawfish, shrimp, and andouille pizza along with a pitcher of their daily draft beer. My reservations of the evening diminished with each mug I drank.

In times long before ours, the downtown streets had been laid with cobblestone bricks. New businesses occupied old run-down and vacant buildings which was one of Charlie Grace's influences in the town's future renovations. She explained it would be an example of a quaint little town filled with southern charm for the would-be tourists turning off of the interstate. The pizzeria occupied one of the four corners flanking a small center garden. The patio we dined in was beneath an overhang of flowering crepe myrtle branches.

"Seriously, not one guy stole your heart in college?" Grant asked as he extended his hand to me.

He motioned to a dimly lit footpath. He didn't release it as we made our way to a bench next to the fountain in the center of the garden. I felt my palm moisten within his grip.

"I dunno. I was always too busy in school to seriously date anyone. A relationship would've been a huge distraction," I said, hoping my words would be accepted for truth. I didn't want to explain to him, or anyone, why I had never wanted a relationship. Honestly, I wasn't even sure if I knew the real reason. Having a boyfriend had not been one of my priorities.

"That was your excuse in high school. Don't you want to share your life, your dreams with someone special?"

"I do. I do share my life. I will know when it is time to settle down. But my plate is pretty full right now."

"What if I say that time is now?"

"Then I'd say pretty poor timing. I leave for Alabama at the end of the summer to start med school at UAB this fall. There's no way I'll have time for a long distance relationship."

"True. It's a hard program," he said. "It'd be nice to find someone with common interests to share that time with. Y'know, someone to hang out with that understands how busy you are."

"Yep, it would." I looked up at the stars, hoping for the conversation to change topics. "But I'm glad you understand."

"Oh . . . yeah, totally."

Thank God, I thought.

"I suppose it's a good thing I am starting there this fall too." He looked at me and smiled.

Dammit, I screamed loudly in my head, leaving a pounding echo in its wake. Charlie Grace had scored again. She would surely be on a sugar high overload, knowing her plans had been successfully orchestrated. *Damn her!* She was always one step ahead of me. I don't know why the lack of coincidence in her actions continued to surprise me.

My surprise would have been nearly comical to me had I not noticed Grant's lips suddenly appearing inches from mine. His kiss was soft . . . hesitant . . . but wishful. They were easy repetitive touches upon my lips—easy. A wisp of his tongue urged acceptance of his robotically gliding tongue against mine. I felt his hand slide up the back of my neck to pull me closer against him. The kiss was not much different than I had experienced before. It felt like more of an invasion to my space more than anything else . . . easy not exciting.

"I intend to make you mine before this summer is over," he whispered against my lips.

"Do you?" I said.

"Indeed I do, Miss Storm."

CHAPTER 5

DATES WITH GRANT became sandwiched in between my times spent with Memaw. I would delegate a few nights of the week to spend with him but for the most part I spent my time studying the ways of Mother Earth with Memaw.

Earlier in the spring we had deliberated over the bible of our garden, the *Farmer's Almanac*. We stood under the stars to read their unspoken words. Under the instruction of both we planted our crops. Memaw would inevitably take handfuls of dirt about our explorations and gently release the granules from her hand as she chanted words I had not yet learned to interpret. Words were spoken to the herbs, vegetables, and fruit. She would tell me, in her delicate form of expression, "Don't overlook Mother Nature, Sis, or she'll jump up on you and bite you in the ass."

"I think that is my favorite picture of Mother," I said, looking at the small bookcase where the wedding day photo rested.

It showed an unrecognizable Charlie Grace. Her hair was fixed in a common style of the sixties as she wore a wedding dress with a hem resting well above her knees. Both were quite uncommon to the sophisticated Charlie Grace I had grown up seeing. But what was most foreign about her in that photo was her smile. It was a smile I had seen quite infrequently in my life with her.

"Mine too, Sis," Memaw said as she let the freshly shelled peas fall from her hand into the empty pot on her lap. "When that boy left her, it was as if her aura done packed up in his suitcase and went right along with him."

"She's so cold . . . so indifferent to any kind of feelings. Like she's numb to anyone's love."

"She wasn't always like dat. Nope . . . not always. My baby girl had dreams. Yo' daddy . . . well, he done made her change those dreams when he came along. That boy had him some kinda charm to him. He made her forget all of 'em dreams for a while." The pressure cooker on the stove whistled its release, and she looked up at the clock. "You keep a shelling. I'm a gonna go get these jars out to start cooling."

I looked down to see the growing purple stain on my fingertips. The rising sun had found us elbow deep in the garden. The rest of the afternoon we spent either shelling, shucking, peeling, stewing, or canning what we had picked that day. I grew up having no doubts that Memaw could have lived off of her own harvest, never having to visit a grocery had she not wanted. Each year her crop was plentiful enough to carry her through to next year's planting.

"You think she'll ever be happy again?" I asked loudly enough for her to hear me in the nearby kitchen. "She looked so happy in this picture. Her smile looks . . . I don't know . . . *real.* I don't think I've ever seen that on her."

"Sure you have, Sis," she said as she used her tongs to lift the mason jars filled with stewed tomatoes. "Look at the picture next to it."

I looked at the frame next to the wedding photo. It was a picture of Mother holding me. I was probably no more than six months old when it had been taken.

"Now that's a smile," Memaw said, standing behind me with her hands on my shoulders. "That girl couldn't stop looking at you."

"Time sure has a way of changing things."

"Not so much," she said, smiling. "You just gotta look a little deeper sometimes."

I lingered a few seconds longer on the photo before looking back into the kitchen. "I sure hope you are going to cook a pot of those peas you are blanching because the smell is driving me insane. I'm about to starve to death."

"I happen to be fixin' some already," she said, swatting me with the dish towel that had been resting on her shoulder.

IN THE LIGHT of my headlights panning across the front of my house, I saw Memaw's last expression held in her eyes as I told her good night. These days of summer before I was to leave for school were quite treasured for us, which made it more and more difficult to break away from her to fit in time with Grant. I knew my visits home would seem nearly impossible with the program demands of medical school and the miles that separated us. I could sense this knowledge was ever so present in Memaw's thoughts as well.

I could see it in the sadness of her eyes. A sadness her smile could not hide. So much so I spent the drive home wondering what career I could have if I were to never leave for medical school. She would have tanned my hide had she known I even let that thought waver in my mind.

"It's about time," Charlie Grace said. She was sitting on the bottom step of the staircase, holding a half-full glass of wine. "Where have you been?"

"Ummm . . . if you remember I'm not fifteen anymore. But if you must know I was at Memaw's."

"For Christ's sake, Rayne. You spend all waking days over there."

"I'm tired," I said, brushing past her to walk up the stairs. "I'm going to bed."

"Grant was here. He just left," she said gruffly.

"What did he want?"

Charlie Grace turned her body to face me. "It's Saturday night. I suppose he wanted to take his girlfriend out."

"Ugh. Gawd . . . don't call me that."

"And why not? What is so wrong with that?"

I leaned against the wall of the staircase. "Please, I don't want to fight. We didn't have plans tonight. He knows I'm spending time with Memaw."

"He wanted to surprise you with dinner. That poor boy's face fell when you weren't here." She sipped her wine. "You're going to lose that boy if you don't pay him more attention. He is a fine catch. Going to be a doctor one day."

"Yeah and so am I, Mother. Or have you forgotten that. Or do you just not give a damn."

"Oh hell, you don't have to take that tone with me and you will not swear at me, young lady. All I'm saying is there are plenty of women with their sights on him."

"I'll call him tomorrow." I walked up the stairs and away from her.

I was in no mood to have yet another discussion over making Grant Thibodeaux my future husband. Although, if I were honest with myself, I really didn't want anything to happen to the relationship I was developing with him. Up until this surprise visit, Grant had accepted my distance . . . my distractions. He hadn't pushed me to give him more than I initiated. It would be nice to have the ease of us continue through the summer and even into medical school.

I'll call him tomorrow.

OVER THE NEXT month, Memaw and I spent more time tucked away at our cabin on the bayou. The weed-and-dirt-filled yard was the first thing we tackled. Once the brush was cleared away from the edge of the bank, we found the slope of the levee to be a fairly easy walk. The home itself was also present with hidden treats and treasures. Beautiful pinewood floors were buried beneath the old, dank green-and-gold carpet.

One Saturday midmorning, Memaw and I ventured to Antique Alley as our first calling for furnishings. Like many towns, our downtown had added eclectic shopping areas to its buildings in hopes of boosting the economy by attracting travelers passing through. Memaw was a common shopper to the area as she could turn old junk into furniture worthy of any diverse home. An old whitewash wicker set sitting in front of This and That Antiques was the first to catch her eye.

The shop was owned by Mrs. Imogene Gentry Bell. A child of one of the town's founding families. She had married Singleton Bell III when she was barely a teenager. The families had arranged the marriage of their eldest children many years prior to their union. His ancestors had started the First Parish Bank and her ancestors had invested the majority of their oil and gas money into this bank. They were both products of our town's history.

Their marriage was now into its fortieth year even though they had barely met each other prior to their nuptials. The antique shop was but one of many of Imogene's hobbies. She could be found milling about the shop or the bakery nearly every other day. Both were a part of the downtown area Mother had so proudly developed. This little part of Louisiana was surely more than a small nestled area of brick pattern streets. But you wouldn't have known it by the attitudes of the patrons who visited these shops. We were like our own Chinatown of California or Little Italy of

Boston. Many of the shop owners' daily ritual was to drink coffee at Mrs. Bell's bakery, Sugar Bakers, before dispersing to their respective businesses.

"Why I do declare, if it isn't the future Dr. Rayne Storm in my presence!" Mrs. Bell always spoke with exclamation. Although, I wasn't sure who she was trying to impress with her exaggerated mannerisms as the shop was empty other than us.

"Good morning, Mrs. Bell. It's good to see you. Let's not jinx the doctor thing, huh? I haven't even started med school yet."

"Oh dahling, there isn't a shadow of doubt in any of our minds that you'll show those folks up in Alabama a thing or two about a thing or two. Ya'll just don't forget you bleed purple and gold like the rest of us!" Her southern drawl was a definition of perfection. Even Scarlet O'Hara would have been envious. "What brings you to my fine little establishment today?"

"Memaw's looking for some patio furniture to redo. She liked that set you had out front. What are you asking for it?"

"Oh yeah, that's a real dandy of a set. It's a full set too! It comes with the love seat, two chairs, and two ottomans. I could let her have the whole setup for three-hundred-and-fifty dollars. A right steal that is!" She straightened one of the hundred rooster figurines lining the shelf.

"Three-hundred-and-fifty dollars?" Memaw shouted from the aisle over. "Have you lost your cotton pickin' mind, Imogene? Your tom cat done pissed his mark all over that furniture outside. It'll take me months to get the stench out."

"Adelaide Cormier, how dare you use such language in front of me? There's no need to be foul in my presence! Besides, you're absolutely incorrect. Mr. Snuggles has not been near that furniture!"

"Oh, is that so? Well then, Mrs. Imogene Bell, how about us prim-and-proper lady folk have us a nice glass of tea out front, sitting on those dandy chairs you got out there. I'll be sure and pick out the best seat for your high-priced fanny to sit on." Memaw winked.

"I have much too much work to do to loaf around with you all day, Addie," Mrs. Bell said as she again repositioned the same rooster figurine.

"I'll give you two hundred dollars and not a penny more."

An hour later, Mrs. Bell rang us up for not only the wicker

patio set but also four matching cushions, two queen size iron bed frames, two nightstands, two dressers, and a living room set inclusive of a sofa, love seat, chair, and coffee table.

"Your total comes to eight-hundred-seventy-five dollars. Lord knows I should have worked at the bakery today than to be subject to the likes of you, Addie! The boys will deliver this by ten a.m." With that she had concluded her business with Memaw which freed her to direct her attention solely on me. "Rayne, honey, when are you going to come with your poor momma to our Ladies' League Meeting? She has been so disappointed not to have you there. Don't you know your momma would like to show you off? Plus imagine the contacts she is setting up for you when you return home to start your practice. Why, you won't want for nothing. With our group you'll have yourself right fine realtors, contractors, loan officers. Whatever you'll need. She's working very hard to ensure your success as a prominent young business woman of our community."

"Why, Mrs. Bell, I didn't realize the amount of suffering she had endured on my account. God bless her soul." I mimicked her perfect drawl.

"Young lady, don't you let 'country is as country does' over there," she tilted her head toward Memaw, "let you forget you are a southern lady."

"I know who I am, Mrs. Bell, but thank you. Thank you for the invitation to join y'all. I'll try to come with Mother before the Independence Day Festival."

"See that you do," she said. "See that you do."

Pleasant farewells were exchanged between us. Her expression was more relaxed in the apparent decision for me to attend the next meeting. Although I had made no discernible declaration as to which meeting I would attend, I knew without a doubt in her mind it was to be the next one held. We made a few more purchases down the alley before celebrating our finds with red velvet cupcakes topped with cream cheese icing and two cups of fresh brewed coffee at Sugar Bakers.

"I don't believe I've ever tasted no sweeter cupcakes," Memaw said with a smile.

Yes, not only had Memaw swindled some pretty fine furniture off of Mrs. Bell but she had also talked her into free cupcakes and coffee at the bakery.

CHAPTER 6

I WENT TO more Ladies' League meetings than I had originally intended but I won't pretend they were dreadful. The meetings were held at six o'clock every other Thursday evening. This time corresponded nicely with cocktail hour or so I learned after the first meeting. The liquor bottle was handled more than the community business which made for rather amusing entertainment for me. Memaw got a pretty big kick out of it too when I shared with her stories of the night's activities. The nights I wasn't with Memaw or at the meetings I found myself in the company of Grant. He kept true to his nature, holding me to no commitments or pressures.

Grant was enjoyable company on the nights we found ourselves alone. We talked of our future plans and dreams—both being very much the same as the other's. He too wished to return back home to practice. Our views of marriage and family were where we differed most. He wanted marriage the moment he found love. I had never honestly considered a legal decree to bind me to someone. The notion had simply not entered into my plans. Yet he gave no efforts to try to change me in my future designs. He listened with a smile or a nod, giving no adverse comments.

The Independence Day Festival brought about a record crowd that July. People from several different parishes came. The Ladies' League believed it was due to the Internet blog and website Grant had designed. They called him their "entry into the age of technology" or at least that was how they referred to him the night he showed them his progress. Although, I wasn't quite sure the cocktail hour left the ladies with many memories the next day. Grant, however, was scarred for life. Those women had given him an all new definition to the word "cougar." He told me afterwards he was waiting for them to break out dollar bills from their purses. He even mentioned a few bruises appeared on his bum the day after the meeting.

During the festival, the local police department blocked traffic from passing through the downtown streets. Multiple genres of bands from Zydeco to Country to Southern and Christian Rock had set up stages along the corners. Patrons danced in the streets before them. Above the crowds were huge canopies of red, white, and blue lights. Booths with every kind of craft or food imaginable lined the streets. I had been chosen to peddle sweets from Sugar Bakers. An occasional breeze would break up the humid air, bringing with it smells of grilled sausage and peppers. The scent stirred the hunger inside of me even more.

"You look like you need a break," Grant said as he walked up to the booth. "Think you've paid your penance yet?"

Mrs. Bell had already started shooing me out of the booth. "Go, dear! Go have a good time with your fella. I've got this all taken care of!"

"Perfect timing," I said as I looped my hand through the arm offered me, "I'm starving. The smell of those sausages is driving me crazy."

"Then sausage dogs with extra peppers it is."

We mingled along the booths, nibbling bites between our conversations. I couldn't resist buying a plaque with two key hooks that read "Home." It was made from a shellacked, cross-section piece of cypress branch. I thought it would be perfect to hang on the wall next to the door of Memaw's and my little cabin. After all it had become the place I called home.

"I hope you don't think Charlie Grace is going to let you hang that in her house," he said, interrupting my daydreams of a peaceful cabin sitting atop a bank of Louisiana clay.

"She wouldn't have it." I laughed. "No, I have something else in mind."

We continued to walk along the booths lining the streets, visiting with people who stopped us along our way. The sound of a frottoir caught our attention as we stepped from the curb. A band playing contemporary Cajun music stood upon a stage in the middle of the street. They had drawn a large crowd in front of them. The lead singer wore the frottoir as a vest and scratched a rhythmic tune with spoons along its corrugated metal. Behind him, his band was composed of a steel guitar, drums, accordion, triangle, and a fervently played fiddle. Lyrics were sung in French as to traditional Cajun style.

We walked closer to the syncopated rhythms, where a crowd of onlookers watched several couples who had chosen to dance. The center of the dance area was occupied by one couple performing an energetic Cajun jitterbug, while the perimeter was left open for the traveling dancers doing the Mamou Two-Step with its quick/ quick, slow/slow steps.

The center couple was nearly a blur with their fast pace hobble step and underarm turns. They moved like liquid motion as if they had danced together for years. And they had. Charlie Grace appeared escalated into a world of freedom found in a rhythmic beat. The smile I had dreamt would always possess her covered her face. It was the smile that made her seem alive. It was the smile I remembered from the wedding day photo.

"Aaaaaaa EEE eeeee!" the lead singer shouted into the microphone at the conclusion of the song and raised his spoons towards Mom and Jacques who stood center of the makeshift dance floor in front of their stage.

"Mother!" I called to get her attention as she and Jacques made their way through the cheering crowd.

"Hello, dear. I thought you were at the Sugar Bakers booth helping Mrs. Bell," she said delicately, using her index finger to wipe the droplets of perspiration from her lip and nasal bridge.

"Grant was my knight in shining armor, rescuing me from a torture of slow starvation."

"That's right, Mrs. Doucet. Just call me Lancelot," Grant said.

Mother cocked her head and raised an eyebrow.

"Ummm . . . what I meant to say was," he corrected quickly, "that's right, *Charlie Grace.*"

"Mother, I had no idea you and Jacques danced like that. I had no idea you *would* dance like that."

"Well, I surely don't know why you find it so hard to believe that I dance," she said.

"You young'uns want to come watch the fireworks with us?" Jacques said, breaking into our conversation before our usual banter began. "They're scheduled to start in about thirty minutes or so."

"No thanks, Mr. Doucet. I was hoping to steal Rayne away for a little bit. But we really should get goin' if that's okay with y'all?" Grant looked at me as if searching for approval.

"Of course it is, Grant. You two have a wonderful night," Charlie Grace answered quickly for me.

Grant held my hand excitedly. His smile had a flash of boyish impishness behind it as he led me down a vacant street away from the festival activities. We walked until the sounds of the street party were barely audible. He pushed our way through a path of overgrown shrubbery until we were at the bottom of a levee.

"It's right over this levee," he said, looking back over his shoulder with that same mischievous smile.

We climbed over the levee to find a completely secluded area in front of us. The only sound was the rippling water of the river's current. It made a sloshing sound as it broke against muddy soil. The dampness of the breeze being carried over the water cooled the humidity around us. Grant led me down the embankment until we came upon a blanket spread across the grass. Its three corners were anchored down by a small cooler and two burning gas lanterns.

"Do you like it?" he asked.

"I love it. I didn't know this place existed."

"Yeah, I found it when I was a kid. I used to come here all of the time. I would sneak off after school and ride my bike over here. Would spend all afternoon. Not a soul ever knew where I was. This past visit home I realized it was still a hidden little spot." His smile beamed.

"I bet it was," I said.

He motioned for me to sit down. "Here have a seat." He sat next to me, opened the cooler, and pulled out two beers.

"Mmmmm." I moaned as I took a swallow from the amber-colored bottle coated with slivers of ice chips. "Now that is some good stuff."

The sky lit up in an explosion of colors above us. He was right. This was the perfect spot to watch the fireworks. The show was directly over our heads. We sat back on our elbows and watched the colors flash in the sky. The reflection of the bursting lights shining off of the water's surface gave us twice the show. "Oooooh" and "Aaaaaah" escaped our breath in unison. The finale was the best part with booms so loud the ground shook beneath us.

I watched the glowing light of the firework's embers fade as they fell into the water. My thoughts wandered back to the perfection of the day. The festival had been a success in both revenue and fellowship for my hometown. I had witnessed smiles and laughter of those townspeople I dearly treasured. I was even rewarded with the pleasure of watching Charlie Grace lifted to a moment of happiness as her feet musically floated along the asphalt streets. And here I sat in a nightfall's peace.

My reflections were broken with lips upon mine. His kiss was shy . . . timid as the ones we had shared over the months. His hastened breath was warm against my lips, making his longings for the kiss to deepen all the more evident. He pulled his lips from mine and his eyes searched my expression. I watched them dart from my eyes to my lips and then back as if trying to read my thoughts for a response. The wants of his desire were evident in his stare and needed not to be expressed with words.

Perhaps it was the perfection of the day. Perhaps it was the perfection of the scene surrounding me. Whichever it was to be— it was surely one that found me slowly lying back on the blanket and pulling him onto me for another kiss.

The initiation of my affection heightened our awareness of each other's bodies. The heat of his body was warming as his full weight became known to me. His heart beat fast and steady against my chest. His kiss became more urgent than any I had known before. His hands explored the body that laid beneath him. Mirroring movements with movements, we found ourselves scantly clothed under the stars above. His touches were soft for the strength found in his hands. His movements were initially slow . . . gentle . . . seeming to consider my own pleasure equal to his. Moans escaped his lips as our bodies found a rhythm together. His breath was labored in my ear as his excitement increased. The quickening pace of his body halted abruptly as he found himself exhausted and spent upon my chest.

My ears were filled with whispers of sweet affections while my eyes focused on the sky above. Its blackness had previously been abound in an explosion of illuminated colors. Those were to be the only night's fireworks experienced for me.

CHAPTER 7

THE NIGHT ON the levee seemed to end my successful reign of avoiding romantic entanglements. Charlie Grace was overjoyed in her daughter's coupling. I began to wonder if she remembered my name was still Rayne Amber and not Rayne and Grant. We spent time with our families together as a couple, soaking up as much quality time as we could before our med school endeavors were to begin.

More than a few nights we found ourselves alone in my upstairs childhood bedroom free to again venture into the explorations of each other's bodies. In not one of those times did my body feel anything more than the ache of remorse. I never felt the way I remember my friends talking after they had started sleeping with their boyfriends. My body didn't feel the satiety they had described. Instead, all I felt was sheer and utter wrongness for our acts.

My tears ran freely one night as I laid tucked away in the solitude of my room. My pillow held the whispers of questions I didn't dare ask out loud. Had Charlie Grace's Baptist rulings actually sunk in? Was it the guilt of premarital sex coursing through my veins that caused such turmoil? Hell, Grant went to church more than I did and he seemed fine with our secret trysts.

I rationalized my thoughts into the notion that I wouldn't feel the guilt in our love making when we were able to be together under a different roof. I rationalized it was the guilt that hindered my enjoyment of being with him. Yet something deeper, darker in me harbored other thoughts. Thoughts I didn't even dare whisper into my pillow. Thoughts that wondered if maybe there was never to be someone to make me feel the things I had heard my friends speak of.

The days of August passed by rapidly. Mother arranged a private affair at Lagniappe the Friday before Grant and I were scheduled to leave for Alabama. As per her usual flair, the dinner reserved for "Rayne and Grant" had been planned to perfection.

It rang as a smaller celebration with a specific selection of attendees, those of family and friends only. The evening was composed of dinner and cocktails on the veranda. Grant had become comfortable in expressing his public affection toward me. His arm persistently tucked around my waist, occasionally squeezing his fingers gently into my side or kissing my temple as we mingled with those around us. His presence had become a new strength to me . . . an extra solace.

"I do declare, Charlie Grace, we are two proud mommas tonight," Mrs. Thibodeaux said as she sat across our reserved table.

The table was strategically placed in the center of the restaurant so each of the invited guests could easily make their way to congratulate Grant and me on our departure for UAB. Of course it was just large enough to seat Grant, myself, and our parents. Thereby preventing any distractions from those who would try to horn in on Charlie Grace's parade.

"That we are, Nadine," Charlie Grace said.

"We'll be the talk of the town once these two get hitched. My . . . my, two doctors in the family. Lands sake alive I never would'a imagined," Nadine said, waving her martini so briskly that she nearly sloshed the olive out over the side of the glass.

"Did you hear ol' Vaughn caught a mess of crappie down on Bartholomew last week?" Mr. Thibodeaux said as if he was completely oblivious to the conversation at the table.

In all honesty, he most likely was. Ned Thibodeaux must have grown accustomed to tuning Nadine out. No doubt this was a necessity to surviving thirty years of marriage with her. Nadine was the type of woman you used as a town bullhorn. If you wanted something known or announced to the general public, you told her. It was spread particularly fast when you reported it as being a secret to be kept between the two of you. Hell, she was more marketable than the local television station.

"What the hell, Ned? Can't you see we're a having a conversation over here?" Nadine scolded.

"Oh . . . sorry, dear." Ned looked at Nadine and then held his head down as if reading the menu in front of him.

"I heard about that. Heard he caught them on shiners too," I said.

Mr. Thibodeaux's eyes flashed brightly as he looked up to smile at me.

"Leave it to my daughter to talk of fishing before nuptials."

"My Grant doesn't mind being a fish caught in her net." Nadine giggled.

Oh Gawd. Someone shoot me now.

"I S'POSE THE next time I see you will be in Alabama. Are you sure you won't follow me up tomorrow?" Grant asked, as he placed a lingering kiss on my forehead. We had found our way to his car to say our good-byes.

"No, I can't. There's one more person I need to see," I said.

Both a sense of happiness and sadness filled my heart at once. It would be a bittersweet visit with Memaw as I would be spending my last night with her and had no idea when I would be able to come back to visit. I would be leaving our cabin at first light.

"Give the old broad a hug for me."

"I will. But only if I don't call her that first or she may decide to send me back with a message." I paused with a wink. "Do you really want a knee to that certain area?"

Grant grabbed below his waist as if to protect himself. "Ouch! Okay, scratch that idea."

"Off you go. I have at least another two hours to listen to Charlie Grace's rants before I can go to bed. I'll see you at school." With that I met his lips to mine and whispered, "Save me a seat."

"I love you, Rayne," he said with hurried breath against my lips.

His expression of love was not novel to me. He had spoken those words multiple times before while holding me in his arms.

I shared feelings of love for Grant—more so than I had ever felt before for a man. I loved the warmth and compassion in him. So yes on some plane, I loved him. Nevertheless, not once had I spoken those words in return. Honestly, I was unsure of what the underlining meaning would be had I told him. True to times before, he didn't question my silence. He simply smiled and kissed me on my cheek as he said good-bye.

CHAPTER 8

SERENITY EMBRACED MY body like the warmth of a fleece
blanket on a crisp fall morning as I drove to the bayou home. I left
the Jeep fully exposed to the elements surrounding me, taking in
the sounds and smells of the home I would soon be leaving. A
gentle wind circulated the interior cab, giving a subtle break to
the muggy heat of summer. Days had flown like seconds during
summer. Time had sped so rapidly forward that I found myself
nearly in disbelief to be driving to the cabin for the last time.

An hour earlier, I had left Charlie Grace waving her farewells
from the front door of our home. She was proud in her confidence
of my future success at school. Her stoic expression kept her eyes
free of tears during our good-byes. Only once did she give me a
hint to the feelings she may have felt inside. She helped me carry
my bags to the car without a single sign of heartbreak until she
stopped to pat the overnight bag lying in the passenger seat.

"Be sure to give Mom my love." Her expression remained
fixed but her voice cracked. I wondered if tears fell once she found
herself in solitude.

My thoughts were interrupted with a giggle escaping my
mouth. I had come to the point in the road where I had to cross
an old wood-and-iron bridge. The small body of water it once
spanned over was now a dried-up creek bed consisting mostly of
hardened clay. But it was a necessary passage between the main
highway and the country roads traveling along the cotton fields.
In peak season the asphalt roads, sun-bleached a darkened gray,
ran alongside fields that falsely appeared as if covered with a fresh
blanket of fallen snow.

This was my favorite time of the year to drive down these
roads, which was probably why I didn't mind the bridge so much.
Memaw didn't share my sentiment. She hated that damn bridge
and had no qualms in showing it. She spat and cursed each time
we came to cross it. In her opinion, you were to speed over the
bridge as fast as you could so as to decrease the amount of weight

resting on the framework. She didn't seem to mind the fact that it was bumpy as hell and had no true railing to protect the car from speeding off the side. I made an effort to either take separate cars or always ensure I was the driver.

WE ATE OURSELVES sick with bowls of jambalaya and black-eyed pea corn bread. Memaw did all things imaginable to corn bread. Of course, there was your garden variety plain white or yellow corn bread. She also made the well-known Mexican corn bread with jalapenos and cheese but the ones I loved most had meals tucked away inside of them. Tonight's special was white corn bread filled with black-eyed peas, hamburger meat, jalapenos, and cheese. The bread was so moist and thick I had to use a fork to eat it. Our dessert was Pabst Blue Ribbon beer and conversation out on the front porch. Background music was orchestrated by croaking frogs and chirping crickets.

"You know, Meems, I don't smell cat piss at all," I said as I patted the arm of the wicker chair.

She nearly spit her swallow of beer out and laughed. "Serves that Imogene right for trying to swindle an old defenseless lady."

"Oh, there was some swindling going on for sure. The place looks great though. Now look, don't you try to make any big changes while I'm gone. We do this together. Remember that." I had fears that Meems would spend all of her time and money out here alone.

Several minutes went by before she spoke again. "Gonna miss you, Sis."

I was thankful for the darkness of the night. Thankful she couldn't see the tears filling my eyes and slowly breaking the lid's barrier to stream down my face. My heart was a forced pressure trapped in my chest as the breath was slowly choked from me. Images of days in Alabama away from the comfort and companionship of Memaw flooded my thoughts.

We stared into the blind of darkness. The air between us was filled only with silence until we simultaneously cast our sights upward toward the stars.

"So tell me about this fellow that done taken your heart," Memaw said a few seconds later. "Does me some kinda good to know you won't be all alone over there in 'Bama country."

"I don't know that there's much else to tell you about him. You met him. He's kind, gentle, and loves his family. We share the same future goals." I paused, searching for the rest. "So . . . we seem pretty good together, I guess."

"Do you love him, baby girl? Your momma done been hearing wedding bells for weeks."

I stared down at the bottle in my hand. I wiped the condensation off of its neck with my thumb. My brain was trying to answer a question for Memaw that I had not yet been able to answer for myself.

"I fear he hears them too. I love him. I do . . . love him. But you know me, I've never really thought about marriage. I s'pose I should've but I've only gotten as far as finishing medical school and coming back here to start a practice." A deep sigh escaped my breath. "I don't know . . . all my future plans just included me and . . . well . . . you."

"Aw hell, Sis. Ya gonna make an old lady break down to a bawling." She paused, collecting herself. "You know I love ya more than any soul on this earth but you gotta find yourself another kind of love. Your Papaw filled my heart. That man done stole it the day he pulled up on that damn motorcycle. He was a wild one all right. Wild enough to tame this cantankerous woman into settling down. Sis, one day someone gonna do that to you. Gonna ride up into your life and turn it on its heels. There won't be no thinking, no planning . . . it gonna be a doing and that is that."

"But how? How did you know it was Papaw?"

"I just knew'd it. Nottun' complicated about it. I just knew'd it. And you will too."

"I hope you're right, Memaw. I guess it makes sense to be with Grant. But I don't feel all that you say you felt for Pa'. I want to. But I don't. I hope he doesn't ask me to marry him. It would screw everything up. Hey, Memaw." I hesitated, lost again in my reflections, nervous to ask the next question. "Did you ever get butterflies with Papaw?"

"Oh, child . . . *Yes!* And your Pa' knew'd it too. That man had a look to him alright. One look . . . one touch from him and my stomach did belly flops. Lawd, I didn't think I was a gonna make it to my wedding night." She chuckled loudly.

"Ummm . . . *eeeeeew!*" I squealed in mock distaste of her sexual innuendos.

She continued to laugh. "Well hell, how'd you think yo' momma got here. Don't they teach them birds and bees lessons anymore in school."

"Learning about reproduction from Mrs. Crary is a bit different than thinking of you and Papaw."

Her laughter settled after she cleared the tears from her eyes. "Do Grant give 'em to you?"

"Nope," I said, "not even once."

"Aw damn, sweet girl, I was afraid of that. You ever had 'em with anyone?"

"Nope, not even once." I ran my hand through my hair.

"You will, Sis. I promise. You will. Don't settle until you do. Life too short for that nonsense."

"Maybe I'm not cut out to love anyone?" I said with subconscious hopes of her impending argument.

"You're wrong about that one and don't you ever lemme hear that baloney again. You are a precious soul. You love, Sis, and you loves strong. You'll find love one day. But make it be *your* love and not yo' momma's. Lawd knows your pa weren't the fella Daddy would've chosen for me. But you can't tell to your heart what it ain't telling you. And your heart it ain't ever gonna be wrong." She turned her beer upward, downing the last remaining swallow. "You like one of those there seashells. Someone told me once that you could hear the ocean if'n you held your ear up to it. They said you just had to listen for it. Someone gone do that for you one day, Sis. They can hold their ear up to you and listen. That gone be the one for you."

CHAPTER 9

MY FEARS WERE all but notions once school started. Grant and I became engrossed in study groups, exams, research papers, and labs. We were afforded little time to discuss anything not related to the study of the human anatomy. This of course gave us little time for our own physical explorations. Our relationship became one of coexistence and support in a rather intense scholastic program. Both of us had the same determination and drive, giving us an added advantage to our coupling. Neither of us pressured the other to entertain social outings that would interfere with our studies.

The first four years of medical school seemingly passed with hardly enough time for a breath. We had found a groove for which to manage life and school. During my fourth year in residency, I learned I was one of thirty-five students chosen for the accelerated plastic surgery program. The anticipation and excitement of being accepted made the time pass all the more quickly.

I had completed my first year in general surgery and had only two years remaining before I would start my three-year residency in plastic surgery. Grant was starting his second year in general surgery with three remaining before he could move onto finishing up two years in vascular surgery. Well, that was if he were to be accepted into the highly competitive fellowship. Therefore his plans required a much longer stay in Alabama than mine. Plus, there was always the chance he would have to move out of state for the fellowship if the positions were filled at UAB. At least for the time being neither of us were taken any further away from home to complete our goals.

Many of our fellow students were having to move either up north or out west for open residency programs. Grant and I were lucky. Well, lucky and we volunteered for anything the faculty threw at us. A few times we talked of the difference in our anticipated graduation dates. The question as to whether I would stay with him in Birmingham picking up temporary locum work or go back to Louisiana to start my practice lingered in the air between us.

That haunting decision swirled in my thoughts as I sat waiting for grand rounds to begin. Three mornings a week the residents met in the auditorium to discuss case presentations as a group. Thankfully I had presented last week so I wasn't due another go for several more days. The usual faces passed me by as they took their seats around the room. I hardly noticed their distinctions any longer—hardly noticed the expressions upon them. My bright-eyed energy of knowledge had been dimmed by long hours and sleep deprivation.

That was until she walked into the room. Hers was a presence felt as much as it was seen. I was sure in an instant she was someone I had not seen before on campus. She walked with confidence, showing no signs she was new to the room. She paused momentarily until she located an empty seat. Apparently I wasn't the only one to find her captivating as the chatter of the room became mere whispers. Yet she didn't seem to take notice of those being affected around her—her demeanor and stride never hesitated.

She sat close enough to me to remain easily within my gawking range. Stunning was the word that sprang to mind. She had sun-kissed blonde hair with varying highlights which hung inches below her shoulders. Small waves of curls gave it a lack of restriction from conventional form. Her scrubs weren't the royal blue color each of us had been given during orientation. No, hers were a bright green with splattered remnants of stubborn betadine stains. There was an ensign over the left breast pocket but I didn't recognize the lettering.

"Who is that?" I whispered to Grant.

"I heard we were getting a transfer. I'm guessing that's her. Apparently she got the boot from Emory over in Atlanta." That boy spent nearly as much time sucking up to the fellows as he did studying so I wasn't surprised he knew the story. "Must've been something pretty damn bad from what I hear."

The last case had been presented before I realized I had not written one word nor heard one single phrase from the presenters. My attentions hadn't strayed far from the mysterious transfer.

"Hey, check this out." Grant motioned across the room to Tom who was walking up to where the new girl was sitting. "Player is making his move."

I should've known.

Tom was a handsome man—albeit not as handsome in my eyes as he found himself in his own. During his undergraduate years, he was the quarterback of the UAB Blazers. The commanding air was still very much present in his off-the-field actions. Even though I was unable to hear him, I stopped to watch the mannerisms shared between the two of them. His flirtations were cocky and confident. Her smile pleasant and sweet. The words expressed through it must not have been what he expected as his smile quickly faded before he turned to make his exit.

"Fumble on the play, old buddy," I mumbled.

"You got that right." Grant laughed. "Oh no, here comes contender number two."

Apparently Kylie had also been paying attention to the quarterback's play of the day as she took his retreat as a cue. I had not spoken much to Kylie during the years of our education. She seemed to have a group all to her own. Neither of our respective groups had much in common with the other. I would best describe her as handsome and androgynous in appearance. Although her personality prevented me from giving her any compliments beyond those. My opinion was seemingly outside of the norm as I saw her with a diverse collection of women at our social functions.

Kylie stopped the stranger as she was rising from her seat. Fascinated, I watched the stranger speak to Kylie in much the same detached yet polite manner she had used with Tom. It seemed she was not to become a member of either the Tom or Kylie collections.

"And they both crash and burn." Grant made the sound of a crashing plane. "Can't blame them for trying though. She is pretty hot."

Many girls would find it upsetting for their boyfriends to speak in such ways about other women but it never bothered me. And hell . . . he was right, she was pretty hot.

I followed Grant out the door but stopped to look over my shoulder for a final glance. Her blue eyes locked with mine, causing chills to rush to the nape of my neck. Her stare was unwavering as she held me in the azure sea of her eyes. *Yeah pretty hot indeed!*

A smile slinked across her face—not the smile of the past few moments. No, this smile reached the eyes that held me in a trance. I felt a returning smile stretch across my now blushing cheeks.

"You okay there, Rayne," Grant said.

"Huh? I mean . . . what did you say?"

He tugged at my arm. "I said are you okay?"

"Hey, bro. We still on for study group next week?" Tom yelled from down the hallway.

I looked at Grant, shaking my head. He gave me a sideways glance. "I'll catch up with you later, man."

"What the hell is that about?" I said after Tom rounded the corner.

"I've been meaning to tell you that he's been asking to join our study group. I didn't figure you would mind too much. Besides he's an all right guy once you get passed the fact that he's a dick."

"Oh yeah, that makes a lot of sense."

I had realized early in the program that my study habits were not compatible with those of the study group Grant had started during our first year of residency. Shortly after our acceptance into the program, we secured university-assisted duplex housing less than a couple of blocks from the main campus, so this year I had my own place outside of the dorms to study. Finally I had the solitude I craved and wouldn't be forced to study with the boys.

"It's fine," I said. "Besides I've been waiting for a chance to break away and start studying on my own. Tom can now be my excuse."

"Aw, come on. Don't be that way."

"Excuse me."

I hadn't noticed the new girl walking up to us until I heard her voice. I also hadn't noticed Grant and I now stood a good three to four feet apart from each other, nearly taking up the space of the hallway.

"Sure thing. Please, go on through." Grant waved his hand between us, motioning for her to walk pass. "Sorry about that."

"No problem." Her voice had a hint of raspiness to it, not like a smoker's voice but more like the changes that occur right before laryngitis steals your ability to speak.

Eucalyptus mint. I'm not sure if I intentionally breathed in her scent as she walked next to me or if her scent found its way to my senses. But nonetheless, there it was.

"I don't know how she managed to arrange a direct transfer to UAB in the middle of a residency but here she is," Grant said after the girl was far enough down the hall not to hear us. "I'll tell ya, apparently we are happy to have her here because there was a whole damn welcome wagon out to greet her when she showed up. Hell half the faculty was there."

My mind raced with thoughts of how she had come to be at UAB. What had she done to be sent away from Emory? Or had she even done anything at all? What was she like? And why the hell can't I have a sexy voice like that?

CHAPTER 10

A COUPLE OF weeks passed and I hadn't even spoken to the mysterious new student. We had shared a few smiles in passing, but never a verbalized word. I had found myself looking for her, searching for her presence when I walked the hallways. Often I tried to bring her up in conversation with Grant to see if he had heard anything else about her, but he rarely satisfied my curiosity.

I tapped my pen against the chart as my thoughts drifted between studying the morning laboratory values in front of me and wondering about the new blue-eyed student. *What the hell is this woman's story?* I cursed myself for wasting precious time and forced my brain to focus on Mrs. Henderson's results. We had taken her to the operating room two days earlier to take cultures and wash out her wound yet her white blood count was still climbing.

From the corner of my eye, I caught the form of someone walking up to the desk of the nurse's station. She stopped to stand right next to me. *Eucalyptus mint.*

"Hiya, Wendy. Could I get 214's chart?"

"Sure thing, Dr. LeJeune." The young girl smiled broadly before pulling the chart from the rotating rack next to her desk.

The woman turned to me. "Good morning. I'd nearly decided you were never going to speak to me, so I'm closing the gap. I'm Sam Lejeune," she said with a hint of Southern Georgia twang. "And you are?"

I felt my pulse quicken and halt all at the same time. The now rapidly tapping pen became loose in the grip of my sweating palm and my throat tightened to hold me speechless to respond.

"And . . . you . . . are?" A mesmerizing smile played around her lips.

"Rayne . . . Rayne Storm." I hoped I didn't sound as foolish as I felt. This woman was unnerving me of my coherent speech.

"I've always preferred a little thunder with my storm." She

gave me a sly smirk before looking down to open her patient's chart.

I wondered if the glow of my blushing cheeks was blinding the young ward clerk as I watched her eyes dart back and forth between me and the girl beside me. *Sam . . . She said her name was Sam.*

Entranced, I watched Sam flip through the pages of the chart. Her grip of the pen was strong and poised as the fluid strokes of her hand wrote a progress note on the patient's condition. My eyes followed the path of her skin from her hands up her arms to her neck. She wore a leather and brass-colored metal choker that fit snugly against her neckline. It moved slightly up and down in response to the beat of the pulse beneath it—a slow, steady beat not matching the quickened pace of my own.

"Looks like his blood counts are stable, Wendy. Would you tell his nurse I wrote orders to get him prepped for surgery?"

"Sure thing, Dr. LeJeune." The young girl didn't seem to be able to speak to Sam without a huge smile covering her face.

Sam closed the chart and patted the hard plastic as she turned to look at me with a smirk of a smile. "Well . . . Stormy, it was nice to finally meet you."

Stormy? "Uh . . . yeah, you too."

"Same time, same place, Wendy?" Sam said.

She was turned from me so I'm not sure of the look she gave Wendy but it caused the girl to turn into a bundle of giggles.

OCCASIONALLY A CHANGE of scenery helped my studying efforts better than sitting alone in the apartment. The lure of a bed with its comfy pillows and soft sheets merely a few feet away was too tempting of a distraction during the sleep deprivation of residency. Many nights like these I wandered down to the Corner Café.

It wasn't necessarily a small diner but it was surely too small for the customers that frequented it. I'm uncertain if it was a good replica of a sixties diner or if it truly was established during that time. The focal point was a bar lined with stools of circular cushions atop metal posts. Behind the bar was the main cooking area where at least two cooks constantly worked, even in these late hours. Breakfast was served all day with a guaranteed fresh pot of coffee brewing at any given moment. The place stayed packed. If it wasn't the drunken crowd coming in the early hours of the morning to sober up before going home, then it was the horde of students hoping the guaranteed caffeine would keep them awake long enough to study a few more hours. Tonight seemed to be mainly composed of the latter. I was lucky enough to snag a small corner table tucked away from the mainstream of traffic.

"Can I get you another cup of coffee, Miss?"

"No, I'm fine for now but . . ." I said, looking up from my books spread across the table. I was surprised to see Sam instead of the waitress. "Sam?"

"Hiya," Sam said.

I noticed the fullness of her lips as she smiled at me. Many people, like me for instance, had one lip that was plumper than the other. Not Sam. No. Hers were equal and somewhat alluring in this shade of lipstick. *Alluring? Had I just described her lips as alluring?*

Wait a second . . . have I even spoken to her yet or have I just stared stupidly at her lips?

"Hi," I said.

"Fancy meeting you here."

"Uh . . . yeah." I wanted to say more—wanted to be more confident but I was struck void of anything useful to say.

"Looks like you're up to your eyeballs in books. I should probably let you get back to it."

"Oh no, that's okay." My confidence jolted into high gear in the attempt of getting her to stay longer. I felt like I was back in grade school as a shy kid trying to hang out with the cool kid. "A break will do me some good. Are you here studying too?"

She gave me a much broader smile this time. For a minute I thought she may have suppressed a little giggle because her eyes were filled with laughter. "No, I'm here with a friend. I can only do so many nights of cramming before my brain explodes. What will be will be, you know?"

I let out a long exhale and tilted my head back before the remaining breath escaped. "Gawd, I wish I could be that laid back about it."

She raised an eyebrow and craned her neck to the side as she studied me. She bit the corner of her bottom lip as if giving thought to her response. "Maybe I should've taken you out with me instead."

Instead? Instead of who? My mind raced and my throat became dry. *Who was she with? A date?*

Gawd tell me he isn't coming over here.

"Hi, Rayne." Tom stopped at our table. "This week's study group is at Grant's, right?" he asked while watching Sam's reaction from the corner of his eye. I suppose he believed his prey to be one step closer to conquering since she now stood next to someone he knew.

I humored his questioning but was aggravated with his interruption. "Yes, that's right . . . at six-thirty."

"Sam, you should come too," he said, now fully directing his attention toward her. "We've had the same study group for a couple of years now. Grant's place is only a block off campus. I could show you if you wanna walk together. Or I could pick you up?"

Sam gave Tom a sideways glance before focusing her attention directly at me. "Well, I guess I better get back. I'll see you later, eh, Stormy."

"Oh yeah, okay. See ya in grand rounds." *Did I really just say that? See ya in grand rounds? Apparently I am twelve again? Could I have been any more of a dork?* This was one of those moments in life when I desperately wanted to be poised but failed miserably. Yep, that about summed up how I was feeling.

This time she didn't suppress the chuckle I thought she had earlier hid back. She turned on her heel and walked toward the booths lining the wall.

"Yeah, okay, Sam. I'll get with you later about the study group," Tom said to Sam's back.

I strained to see which table she was walking toward but couldn't as Tom blocked my view. For some reason I was curious. Not that it mattered but I wondered who she was with. Was it a date? I caught the slow of her pace but was blocked to see more when Tom shifted his weight.

"What do you think, Rayne? Do you think she likes me?" Tom said.

"What?" I tried to peer around him, and bobbed my head from side to side but it was useless. He had too much girth for me to look past without standing or completely changing my position.

Dammit, move out of the way!

I finally caught a glimpse of Sam's back exiting the door. No one was standing alongside her, nor did she hold the door open for anyone who may have been lagging a few steps behind. The brass bell hanging over the entryway rang a final time as the door closed behind her.

"So?" Tom asked again.

"What? What are you asking me?" I shook my head, frustrated as hell that he was still standing at my table.

"Do you think Sam is into me?"

"Oh, yeah . . . totally smitten."

"I THEN IDENTIFIED and began carefully dissecting the common bile duct with the scissor tip instrument." Grant used the laser pointer to highlight the duct as he presented the recording of the laparoscopic gallbladder surgery he had performed the day before.

I was trying desperately to stay interested in his case presentation but it seemed over the last few weeks most everyone had presented a cholecystectomy, including me.

I looked at Sam who sat next to me at grand rounds. She seemed distracted or in the very least nearly as bored as I was. She took only a few notes and stared off for several moments at a time before looking back at Grant. I felt a gentle tap on my arm and looked to see that infectious smile of hers. She slid the edge of her notebook closer to me.

Diagonally written across the corner of her page was, *How about your digits, Stormy?*

I felt my face flush as the breath caught in my throat. The return of my inconvenient sweating palm nearly prevented me from holding the pen firmly enough to write my cell phone number down.

She smiled and silently mouthed, "Thanks."

Her left eyebrow raised in an arch as she held eye contact with me for a few seconds before broadening her grin and returning her focus to Grant as he finished his case presentation. I also looked back in his direction but all I could concentrate on was trying to slow the heartbeats pounding in my ear.

TEXT MESSAGE FROM Sam, 7:00pm: "where the hell are you"
Text message to Sam, 7:03pm: "Home. Where should I be?"
Text message from Sam, 7:06pm: "Studying @ Grant's"
Text message to Sam, 7:10pm: "I don't study with that group any longer"
Text message from Sam, 7:12pm: "you totally suck leaving me with them!!"
Text message to Sam, 7:14pm: "Nope never said I would be there"
Text message from Sam, 7:40pm: "fine stormy but you owe me BIGTIME"
Text message from Sam, 7:41pm: "bettye jean's coffee thurs @ 6:30"
Text message to Sam, 7:50pm: "Ok. Cya"

CHAPTER 11

THE GROWING ANTICIPATION I felt the days before meeting Sam was foreign to me. I had never felt this anxious waiting to meet up with a new friend. *Friend?* Well, not sure we were quite that but I was hoping. I couldn't keep down the excitement of thinking of the next time I would get to sit and talk with her again. Since the texted invitation, my mind had wandered aimlessly in a circle of anticipation of the time we could talk uninterrupted. I wondered if I would find her to be a drone of endless chatter like the times I had planned to meet with other girls from my classes. Or would I find myself lost in her words as I had been lost in marveling in her mannerisms? The days dragged painfully between our last text and the meeting time at Bettye Jean's.

I was surprised when Sam suggested we meet at Bettye Jean's. With our schedules being what they were, I hardly ventured off campus or the surrounding area for coffee . . . much less down the congested U.S. Highway 280 toward The Summit. Yet here I sat in the parking lot, staring at the small coffee shop next to Saks Fifth Avenue located at the far end of the upscale mall strip.

Seventy-three degree weather was perfect for riding around in a Jeep but the not-so-perfect traffic sitting still under a blaring sun caused a sweat patch to develop at the small of my back. I shook my shirt out as I walked toward the gray-and-cherry wood entrance and wondered if Sam had already arrived.

My eyes adjusted to the dimly lit atmosphere and I could instantly understand why she had chosen this place. Not only was it a neat environment decorated with interior columns designed as bookshelves but it also wasn't over-crowded with inhabitants dressed in varying scrub colors. Most people sat quietly clicking their laptops and drinking their beverages. I found a two-top table closest to one of the book-filled columns and studied the book titles as I nervously tapped to the beat of the jazz music playing overhead.

"Hiya!" Sam said as she appeared next to my table.

I looked up at her, hardly noticing the lingering smell of exhaust fumes in my hair as I turned my head. *Wow.* She looked really different out of her scrubs and in plain clothes. If possible, she was even cooler with a hippish style to her clothing. She looked as if she was lost in the style of the sixties. Her jeans were worn thin in the knees with patches sewn into the material over the thighs and legs. Her top was linen and loose, leaving the imagination to picture a defined body underneath. I wondered if she had found extra time to workout or if she was genetically blessed. Two small white gold hoop earrings glistened as they caught the light of the pendant fixture hanging above the table. In general, she wore minimal make-up—enough to highlight her cheeks and emphasize her eyes. Her lips were the color of a pomegranate drawing my eyes directly to her mouth as she spoke.

"Is this seat taken?" Sam tucked her hair behind her ear. Today, she wore it straightened, exposing the varied layers of her cut.

"As a matter of fact I was waiting for Tom's Flavor of the Month," I said. "I don't suppose you've seen her?"

She gave me a rather strong slap across my shoulder and took the seat across from me. "I'll flavor your month sticking me out all alone with that crew."

"Hey, I never said I was going to be there. I broke free of that group this year because there was no way I could study with them."

"I know, right? Do they really think pizza served up with a side of blaring TV in the background is studying? Shit, I had at least two hours of catching up to do once I got back home."

"Exactly." I picked up my purse. "I believe I was told I owed you a coffee for your evening's sacrifice."

"Damn skippy you do. I'll take the biggest Caramel Macchiato they have . . . double shot, extra froth."

I got up and walked to the counter.

"Oooh, extra caramel too!" she shouted after me.

I returned with the two drinks in hand and sat down.

Sam pulled hers from me and scooped a dollop of froth coated in caramel drizzle into her mouth. "Mmmmmm . . . yummy!" She groaned as she closed her eyes. "And what exactly is that you're having?"

She peered into my cup. Her proximity caused the hairs of my arm to stand on end. The distance between us was close enough for me to smell the remaining scent of peppermint gum she must have discarded moments earlier.

"Black coffee," I said, my voice but a whisper. "Strong black coffee. It's criminal what these shops now do to a good cup of coffee."

"I'm sorry, but aren't girls supposed to be sugar and spice and all that is nice? Well . . . let's say I get my sugar in the form of liquid concoctions." She took another taste of her latte and again followed it with a low humming. "Mmmmmmmmm . . . yep . . . all that is *nice*."

I chuckled at the way she drew out "nice."

Sam sat back as if to fully take me in. Her turquoise shirt made her blue eyes appear as deep as sapphires. Sapphires that now searched me over as she twirled the small stirrer straw in her cup. I watched the bracelets slide up and down on her arm as she lifted and lowered the straw. Some were made of braided leather, others were made of beads.

"Alright, Stormy . . . shoot. What's your story? And please emphasize the dirty parts." She waggled her eyebrows for effect. A small smile played at her pomegranate-colored lips.

"My story?" I asked completely taken off guard by her directness. Perhaps it was her boldness I found enticing.

"Can I get you ladies anything else?" I looked up in gratitude at the girl cleaning the table next to us. Her interruption afforded me a few moments to collect my thoughts.

"Oh, no thanks," Sam looked at the girl's name tag, "Marie. We're just fine here. I'm about to find out what makes this little woman tick. Keep a watch on us though. We may be headed your way for refills. My bet is this lady's full of stories." She smirked, and her left eyebrow cocked up slightly.

Damn, I liked that eyebrow thing she did.

"Well, alrighty then," the girl said. "I'll just leave you two at it."

"Thank you, Marie." Sam turned to me and paused. "You were saying . . . ?"

"Nothing really. I have no story. I'm what you see. Pretty boring actually." I looked down to catch myself tapping the edge of the table.

She looked down at my hand. I quickly tucked it in my lap. She looked back up at me. "You do that a lot you know?"

"Do what?"

"Tap."

"Oh . . . that." I shifted in my chair and looked around the coffee shop. "Why don't we talk about you? I mean, I'm not the one that suddenly appeared at a residency already underway. I do believe that was you and I *do* believe that's the only story here at this table."

"Nice deflection but no dice," she said.

"I'm being honest. But if you insist on being bored to tears . . . I was born and raised in Louisiana. Moved to Birmingham for school. And yep . . . that about covers it."

"There's so much more to you than that, Missy." She sat back and held her cup inches from her mouth as she again studied me. "Looks like you take a bit more prodding to open up. Hmmmmm . . . I think I sort of like that . . . a mystery girl." She took a long sip of her coffee while keeping our eye contact over the lid of her cup. "Okay, so what residency are you going for?"

"I was accepted into plastics."

"Yeah, that's right. Heard you got into their fast track program. That's a tough one. See . . . already there is more to you. Obviously you're pretty damn smart."

"I don't know about that," I said. "Maybe I'm lazy for not going for one of the longer programs."

"And there is something else. You don't take compliments well. Do you?"

I looked down at my cup.

"I'm going to take that as a yes," Sam said. "What do you see yourself doing in ten years? Where will you be?"

"Reconstructive surgery. Not overly keen on the cosmetic side of things. S'pose I'll have to do the bread-and-butter boob jobs but hoping my practice will mostly be reconstructive. I got to shadow a few facial reconstructions after skin cancer removal. It was the closest I've seen to the combination of art and medicine." I bit the inside of my cheek when I realized I had become uncharacteristically talkative.

She seemed to notice as well. Her face lit up with excitement. "Ooooh, are you an artist?"

I laughed. "No, not at all."

"Well, that may pose a problem." Sam chuckled and so did I. "And have you found that certain someone special to be with while you artistically change people's faces?"

"What?"

"With whom will you be sharing this life with?" she repeated.

"Oh, I don't know. Haven't thought about it really."

"I assumed it would be Grant. He seems to think so anyway."

"How do you? I mean . . ." I was unsure why I was so surprised by her knowledge of me being with Grant. "How do you know that?"

"You two are always sitting together at grand rounds. And, well, you remember study group at his place, right? You know the night you ditched me."

"First of all I didn't ditch you and secondly I didn't think my relationship status was a topic of the study session that night."

"Ummmmm." She took a sip of her latte. "Seems I may have stumbled onto a tense topic. Sorry if I offended you, Stormy. Grant seemed pretty taken with you and your futures together. Wanted your take on it."

"It's fine. I'm not offended." But I was quiet. I realized it was the first time I had been uncomfortable with Sam, which in turn made me accept the discomfort I felt in voicing a future with Grant. Why couldn't it simply be my future? Why did it always lead back to Grant and me? Why was everyone so insistent I share my future with someone?

"Seriously, I can tell I hit a nerve. I'm sorry," she said as she set her half-empty latte on the table. "Okay, your turn. Ask away. What is something you want to know about me?"

"I don't really have anything to ask."

"Oh, don't you?"

There's that eyebrow again.

"No, not really."

She leaned across the table and rested on her elbows. "I thought you might be a tad curious as to how I ended up in your little program. Seems there is some gossip rolling around about that topic."

"I heard a few people talking about it."

"It's a pretty juicy story. You better hold onto your panties."

She straightened and sat back. "Don't suppose you've heard of Dr. Edward LeJeune, have you?"

"No, sorry. Can't say that I have."

"Well, dear ol' Dad happens to be a world renowned cardiothoracic surgeon who developed EndoValve, an endoscopic technique for heart valve repair?"

"I'm not really into CT surgery," I said, crinkling my nose.

"You and me both, sista, which pisses the old man off something terrible. Emory decided I was not a student of their caliber so I got the boot. Dr. Dad swooped in to save the career of his future partner. And . . . taa daa . . . here I am." She held her arms out.

"What happened to make them decide that?" I asked.

"You do like the dirt, don't ya?" She chuckled. "I'm beginning to like you more and more each second there, Stormy. Well, seems they frown upon their medical students being caught in a compromising position with one of their faved attendees. In retrospect a more private environment may have been a better choice than the supply closet on Med West."

I laughed too loudly, causing a few heads to turn in our direction. "Ya think?"

"Hey . . . when passion hits, you know?"

Actually I didn't know but I decided not to share that with her. "You said his future partner, but I thought you weren't interested in CT?"

"I'm not." Her sly grin turned into a full sarcastic smile. "That concept doesn't seem to register with Dr. Know-It-All."

My coffee grew cold as I held the ignored cup in my hands. I found myself wrapped in her words with the desire to share my own. Normally I encouraged the other person to talk instead of wanting to let them inside of my own thoughts. But our exchange flowed easily, which led me to yearn to know and share every facet of our lives.

I could listen to the articulations in her voice forever. I didn't want the time with her to end and when it did, all I could think about was finding myself in her company again. My mind became a constant to and fro when I wasn't with her, only to be calmed when in her presence.

This caused my thoughts to rattle with nervous questions. The answers to which I wasn't sure I knew . . . or wanted to know.

They caused deafening screams within my head, which caused the longing to be with her grow stronger by the day. The connection to her was undeniable. The meaning of that connection was confusing.

CHAPTER 12

ONE NIGHT I escaped to the cadaver lab in the Human Sciences Building with the hopes of concentrating on something other than the swirling thoughts of Dr. Sam Lejeune. I hadn't seen much of her in the last two weeks. Due to time restrictions, grand rounds had been divided into two groups with talk of decreasing to once a week.

I found myself fairly separated from both Sam and Grant. Nonetheless this didn't seem to slow my thoughts from betraying me as I sat at the breakfast table in my apartment. I had found the table for two at a local shop advertised as selling antiques yet it seemed to sell mostly old, worn-out furniture instead. The table caught my eye instantly. Its distressed wood was nearly the same coloring of the flooring in Memaw's and my cabin.

Drinking my morning coffee at that table took my thoughts back to the place I missed so badly. Each time I tried to concentrate on the books in front of me, I found my thumb stroking the wood of the table as I wished I could be back at the cabin where everything seemed clearer. The mundane quiet of the walls began to choke the air from me. Ironically, it was the smell of formaldehyde to bring a welcome change to my lungs and the ability to manipulate tissues a needed distraction.

Medical students had access to the lab by way of a key card entry, and it was available any hour of the day for those wishing to brush up on their anatomy. Of course preservation chemicals could keep the structures recognizable for only so long before they became dried and nearly impossible to identity. That was if they survived the destruction that occurred at the hands of inexperienced first-year medical students.

I found a male specimen in the corner of the fairly quiet lab and was virtually alone except for a group of three students huddled over a station in the front of the room.

I had been studying the neurovascular structures surrounding the parotid gland for a case I had the following Monday. I lost myself in the dissection of the facial nerve's delicate opaque, shiny branches as the tiny strands coursed through the parotid gland.

"Hiya. Fancy meeting you here."

I jumped, hit my head on the overhead lamp, and tossed the dissecting instrument over my shoulder.

"Shit, Stormy, watch out where you throw that thing."

Rubbing the back of my head, I turned around to see Sam standing behind me. She was wearing royal blue scrubs splattered with drops of betadine across her belly and thighs.

"You scared the crap out of me," I said.

"Yeah, well . . . you nearly decapitated me." She tucked her scrub shirt loosely into her drawstring pants.

"Oh please, it was a blunt instrument."

She walked around the steel table and peered over the area I had been studying. The V-neck of her scrub dipped away from her body as she bent forward, exposing the top of her bra. I followed the black strap up her chest as it disappeared under the fabric covering her shoulder. My breath quickened and I felt my face blush.

"So . . . whatcha doing?" The childish mocking in her voice was intensified with the brilliance of her eyes reflecting the royal blue material. The shining sapphires were more beautiful than I had seen before in our brief encounters. Her hair was pulled back in a haphazard ponytail. I was amazed at how even when she was a mess, she seemed put together. She reminded me of one of those celebrities who still managed to look like a star even when caught in a candid photo.

I swallowed hard in hopes of squashing the inevitable crack in my voice that happened when I was nervous. "I . . . I was getting nowhere studying pictures in the apartment so I thought I would come look at the real thing. And you?"

"I did some shadowing hours on the OB floor. Got to see a C-section before the attendees took over," she said. "Thought I'd come study the uterus before heading back home but damn if I can find a woman in here that hasn't had a hysterectomy."

"I guess it's true what they say . . . no womb shall hit the tomb."

"Ha! I know, right." She laughed and then stopped abruptly to study me.

The silence between us seemed to last several minutes as I

waited for her to speak again. It unnerved me as she watched me with that particular look—the one that seemed to know everything about me—as if she could read my thoughts like an opened book laid out in front of her, including the ones hidden deep within the chapters of my self-consciousness.

"Wanna get out of here? Or do you need some more time?"

Are you kidding me?

"Sure. Where to?" I said.

"A quaint little place to get a drink. At this time of night everything else will either be closed or packed. You do know it's Friday night, right?"

"Seems like I heard a rumor somewhere that it was."

We walked away from the campus, passing a multitude of corner bars, delis, and coffee shops until we came to a renovated warehouse. The night air had found a chill, causing both of us to hold our arms across our bodies.

"Here we are," Sam said, rubbing her hands briskly over her bare arms. "Thank Gawd, because I am about to freeze my tatas off." She stopped at the keypad outside of the iron-gated door to enter a numeric code. "I'm right up here." She glanced over her shoulder.

Registering we were going to her apartment increased the anxiety in my nerves one thousand fold.

Her apartment was on the upper floor and I realized there were only two doors. The apartments must have been massive if a building this size had divided the square footage evenly between only two apartments. Sam walked toward the door on the right and slipped a key in its lock as she looked over her shoulder to give me another smile. I swear I felt a quiver in my knees.

How does she do that?

"This is me," she said.

The room gave the illusion of being much larger than it was due to the back and right side wall being lined with floor-to-ceiling glass windows, which offered an unobstructed view of Birmingham's skyline. The exposed wooden beam ceiling added to the openness of the room. The only walls in the large room was in the far back left corner. I assumed this was to give privacy to a bedroom. On the opposite side was an open kitchen area composed of copper and stainless steel accents.

She had minimal furniture that included a leather sofa, matching chair with ottoman, sofa table, and coffee table arranged to face the wall of windows. Next to the entrance was a wall composed of sheetrock painted an oyster shell gray and a large wooden built-in bookcase with tightly packed books filling its shelves.

I desperately wanted to walk over to it and read the exposed spines but was frozen paralyzed with nervous fears of being alone with her. I wondered what she saw in me to invite me over. I was never really nervous when it came to meeting new girlfriends. It was never an issue for me. I seemed to be popular enough and went were I was invited to go. Although, I can't say I ever hoped or wished for the invite. But with Sam . . . I couldn't wait to spend time with her. I wondered what it was she saw in me or if she felt the same.

"What'll you have?" she asked, standing behind a long mahogany bar to the center of the room.

"I'll take a beer." I sat on one of four bar stools positioned against the bar.

"Coming right up." She pulled out a nearly full bottle of Petron Tequila and two shot glasses from underneath the bar. "Be right back." She walked to the kitchen and returned with lemon slices and a salt shaker. She filled each of the glasses full and pushed one across the counter toward me. "A beer for the lady."

"Yeah, this is not exactly the beer I'm used to drinking."

"Live a little, Stormy."

"There is a reason they call this stuff Te-Kill-Ya, don't ya know?" I said, studying the clear, harmless-looking liquor as I held the shot glass up to the light.

"Okay, I'll go first." She held the back of her hand up to her mouth and hesitated before she caught my eyes with hers. She slowly ran the tip of her tongue over the skin between her finger and thumb. She shook the salt shaker over the dampened skin that collected the falling granules, licked the area again, picked up the shot glass, and drank it quickly in one swallow. She then squeezed the lemon wedge in between her lips and sucked. I swallowed hard at the small line of lemon juice trickling down her chin.

"Alright, sister, your turn," she said, wiping her chin with the back of her hand.

"You make it look so easy."

"That's because it is, Stormy. Here, give me your hand." Before I could argue, Sam grabbed my hand and brought it to her lips. "Here I'll show you." She ran her tongue slowly over my skin.

I felt my eyes widen as an intense heat flowed through my body nearly knocking me off of the stool. Her expression was unchanged. She was still as calm and poised as I had come to know her to be. I was shaken and confused from the jolt of electricity that had passed through me. Thank goodness she shook the salt out over my dampened skin as my aim would surely have never been able to hit its target with the uneasy tremor I felt in my hands. She released my hand to give me the lemon wedge and shot glass.

"Bottoms up," she said.

I quickly downed the tequila, welcoming the burn it caused in my throat. I hardly wanted the lemon juice to quench its sting as it gave my body some other form of heat to feel.

She gave me a one-sided smile. "You forgot to lick the salt."

"Ooops."

"Guess that means we'll have to do it again." She brought the two glasses back in front of her and poured another shot in each. This time she handed me the salt shaker after she used it and grabbed a lemon wedge. "On three."

I hurriedly ran through the steps she had shown me as she stood waiting with drink poised in her hand.

"One . . . two . . ." Sam slammed the liquor back quickly. "Three," she said through a strained voice.

She watched me for a moment after I followed her action with my shot.

A smile curled up at the edges of her lips. "What is it about you?" She shook her head as she mumbled.

She poured us two more shots followed by another two. The quick succession of tequila reminded me I had little to no food earlier in the evening. And yet another two were poured. My head swam in a dizzying rotation as I tried to continue my balance on the stool.

"Are you okay there, Stormy?" she asked.

"Uh . . . yeah . . . I think so." Another swirl in my head flowed and I grabbed onto the edge of the bar to steady myself.

Sam stepped quickly to my side and put an arm around me as she braced me against her.

Lost somewhere between a fog of drunkenness and a reality

of the arms that held me, my words flowed without conscious thought or filter. "Aw, you smell like eucalyptus mint."

She laughed. "You're not much of a drinker are you?"

"No . . . Not much. A few beers here and there but nothing like this." I steadied the spinning room by leaning into her body. "That and I haven't eaten much today."

"When did you last eat?"

I tried to remember but my brain was foggy. The combination of alcohol and her proximity didn't help with that at all. I had to remind myself of the day and time before I could answer. "I think I had a sandwich for lunch today."

She looked down at the oversized watch on her wrist. "That was probably about twelve hours ago. It's one in the morning."

"Holy crap, really?"

She ticked her head to the side and coiled her lips up into a smile. "Yes, really." She looked aimlessly around the apartment. "Hmmm, I don't think I have much in the way of food to offer you. Come to think of it, I haven't eaten much today either but I have no idea what would be open right now."

"Curly's stays open till three o'clock on the weekends. They make the best artery clogging cheeseburgers you can imagine."

"Sold," she said, looking down at me with that same smile. Her arm was still draped across my shoulders yet my balance hadn't faltered in several minutes. "You think you could make it over to that love seat?" She motioned toward the deep chocolate furniture at right angles of each other. The lights of the city reflected across the inlay glass of the coffee table.

"I think I can but if I'm not there in two hours, send for help."

She laughed and removed her arm from my shoulder. "I'll be sure to do that. Now, let me find that phone number."

A few minutes later, Sam walked back into the room and sat in the over-sized chair next to me. "You're not asleep are you?"

"Nope, just trying to get the room to stop spinning." I raised my head off of the back of the couch and opened my eyes. Sam was using her hand to hide a smile.

"Food's on its way," she said. "You seemed pretty engrossed at the lab. You never said what you were studying."

"I'm assisting on a parotid gland excision on Monday. Or, well, I think I am. It's all a bit fuzzy at the moment."

Sam laughed. "The food should help sober you up. I promise to have you home by Monday morning."

I heard a phone ringing from the back of the apartment.

Sam straightened the drawstring of her pants as she stood up. "I better get that. Hope they aren't lost."

I closed my eyes and let my head drift back onto the back of the couch. *Eucalyptus mint.* My eyes sprang open as a clarity of recognition shone through the alcohol fog like a beacon. *Oh shit! Did I really tell her she smelled like eucalyptus mint?* Sobering up certainly had its downfall.

I heard Sam's muffled voice coming from behind the wall in the back of the room. The conversation continued for several minutes, long enough for me to drift off to sleep.

"Hey you, still with me?" I felt Sam's hand on my shoulder. "Sorry about that. It was my mom." She sat down hard in the chair.

"Everything okay?" I was concerned something had happened back home. If Charlie Grace called me close to two in the morning, something was wrong . . . very wrong.

"Yeah, it's fine. She had come in from a party and figured I'd be up."

The doorbell rang.

"Damn, it's like Grand Central Station around here." Sam stood up.

"Popular girl."

"Apparently so," she called out over her shoulder.

She returned with a large white paper bag in one hand, a bottle of beer under her arm, and a large Styrofoam cup in the other.

She set the bag down on the table and handed me the cup. "Here, I got you a diet coke. I didn't think you would want any more alcohol."

"How did you know I drink diet?"

If I hadn't had a hint of remaining tipsiness, I would have sworn she let her eyes languidly roam over my body. "Lucky guess."

Curly's made their cheeseburgers the way Memaw always did hers. Maybe that was why I liked them so much. The hamburger patty was fried on a large griddle with the cheese melted over it as it cooked. The fries were hand-cut from red potatoes, giving them a sweet little aftertaste to the flavoring.

Sam quickly unwrapped the white, grease-coated paper from

around her burger and took a large bite before I had even gotten mine out of the bag. Apparently she was as hungry as I was.

"Damn. This is freaking amazing." Her eyes rolled slightly back in her head as she took another large bite. I heard the crispness of the lettuce as she bit down a third time.

"I know. They're the best. My memaw makes them like this. I feel the sludge of cholesterol building up in my arteries every time I eat one."

"But worth every damn bite," she said, talking around the nearly full bite of burger.

Three-fourths of the way through her burger, Sam placed the greasy wrapper back in the bag and grabbed a handful of fries. I watched her nibble on them slowly before she stopped to stare out the window. The lights of the city flickered off of the glass beer bottle she held in her hand.

"Penny for 'em," I said.

She looked at me distantly. "I'm sorry?"

"Seems like you're deep in thought. Wanna talk about it?"

Sam tipped the neck of the beer in my direction. "I know I'm drinking a beer but I'm not one to cry in it."

"Ouch, that sounds serious. Do you want me to leave and give you some privacy?" I started to stand but she put her hand on my arm.

"Oh no. Not at all. Please stay. It's late." She took a swallow of her beer. "I mean, why don't you stay the night or what's left of it. Unless you have somewhere you need to be."

The residual buzz of alcohol left me instantly. I supposed to make room for the bundle of nerves that shortly followed. "Ummm . . . no, I don't have anywhere to be."

"Great. Give me one second." She darted back to the corner room and returned a few moments later with a bundle of clothes and a girlish smile. She shook out an Atlanta Falcon t-shirt and matching logo boxer shorts. "Here, you can sleep in these."

"Oh no, no, no. Memaw would tan my hide if she knew I wore those."

Sam arched an eyebrow. "Well, the other alternative would be in your birthday suit but I think you might get cold." She dangled the clothes in front of me. "Your choice of course."

"Alright, but you better not tell a soul." I laughed and grabbed the clothes from her hand. "At least I know what to get you for Christmas."

"Oh yeah? What's that?"

"A New Orleans Saints shirt of course."

"I'll wear it if they ever decide to win a game for a change."

Wow, she even knows football. This may be a friendship for life.

A new toothbrush still in its package, toothpaste, and a wash cloth was on the bathroom counter. She popped her head around the bathroom door just as I opened it and I nearly jumped out of my skin.

"I turned the bed down for you," Sam said, around the toothbrush in her mouth. She must have been brushing for a few minutes as the toothpaste had formed a healthy lather in her mouth. She stepped around me to rinse her mouth out in the sink. "What?"

"What? What?"

Sam laughed. "Your face. What's with the expression?"

"I don't know. You surprised me is all."

"With this?" She shook the toothbrush in the air.

"Uh . . . yeah, I guess so."

Sam laughed again. "You crack me up sometimes, Stormy."

"Speaking of toothbrushes, thanks for the loaner."

"No problem." Sam stepped passed me again and pulled my arm with her toward the room behind the walls.

"So what, you keep a stash of spare toothbrushes lying around?"

Sam looked over her shoulder and smiled. "Don't you?"

My breath caught in my throat as we walked into her bedroom. The same floor-to-ceiling windows formed her back bedroom wall. The bed was positioned as if it rested on clouds floating over the city.

"Oh wow!" I said. "This is gorgeous."

Her eyes lit up in the combination of city lights and moonlight. "Thanks. The view lulls me to sleep some nights."

"I can see why."

Sam leaned against the door frame and watched me walk around the bed to look out the windows. "That cord draws the drapes if you want to knock out the light in the morning. The sun rises on the opposite side of the building so it doesn't get too terribly bright first thing."

"Wait, what?" I turned around.

"I didn't know if you were a light sleeper or not. It's pretty late. I'm sure you will want to sleep pass daybreak."

"Where will you be?"

Sam tilted her head to the side. She let a smile play at her lips. "I'm going to crash on the couch."

"No, Sam, I can't take your bed."

"It's no big deal. I pass out there most nights when I am studying anyway."

Sam walked into the room, turned the lamp on, and then stopped in front of me. "So, I guess this is good night." She looked down into my eyes from her slightly taller frame. "Sweet dreams, Stormy."

Sweat dreams? Would I even be able to sleep?

"Good night, Sam."

Sam flipped the overhead light switch off as she walked out of the room and started to pull the door closed behind her. She peered around the door before it closed completely. "Are you sure Atlanta isn't your team because you look pretty darn cute in their colors?"

I tossed a throw pillow at the door as it clicked closed. Sam's laughter faded with her footsteps.

THE EARLY MORNING sunlight played at my eyelids, teasing them to open. Had it not been but a few short hours of sleep, I would have given into the calling of daybreak. Who was I kidding? My eyes fought the temptation to open as they were quite content to stay nestled in Sam's bed.

I brought the collar of the shirt over the bridge of my nose to inhale deeply its scent. The shirt smelled as if it had been kept in her pajama drawer . . . as if it was used only as a nightshirt. I couldn't describe the smell beyond that. It wasn't a fragrance necessarily. There was a faint hint of eucalyptus mint mixed in with laundry detergent and something else. Something that took me back years ago to when I was a child spending the night at Memaw's. She had kept a couple of white pocket t-shirts in the back of her dresser drawer for me to sleep in. Those shirts smelled just like this one.

I heard Sam's muffled voice from beyond the walls and closed bedroom door. I couldn't make out the words as her voice seemed to be a little louder than a whisper. I cracked open the door to see her pacing along the back of the couch. A cordless phone receiver was held to her ear.

"No, I didn't tell you." Her voice became loud enough for me to make out the words. "Because she called me. That's why. Mom is the only one who does call me. You sure never do. Besides it's not like I would tell you anyway." She ran her free hand through her hair and rubbed the back of her neck. "Why? Because of this. Because of this very conversation. That's why."

She pulled the phone from her ear and tapped the earpiece against her chin before returning it back in place. "It doesn't have to be this way. It doesn't have to be a fight. It's my life . . . not yours," she shouted, startling me.

She turned her back from me but I could see her hand gripping the back of the couch.

"You can't be serious. Why? Why would you do that? Is it your every last wish to ruin my fucking life?" She shifted her weight but kept a tightened grip on the couch. "Fine then. I don't give a good goddamn what you do," she shouted even louder and slammed the phone down hard on the end table. "Son . . . of . . . a . . . bitch!" She drew out each word. "Shit," she muttered and slowly turned around.

I stepped from behind the door and gave a timid wave. I wasn't sure if she had forgotten I was there or if she was realizing how loud the whirlwind of profanity spewing from her a moment earlier had been.

I didn't know if I should retreat to the bedroom, leave as quickly as possible, or try to lighten the mood. *Lighten the mood.*

"I haven't heard that much cussing in a long time and especially not before my first cup of coffee."

She walked to the bar and picked up one of the two to-go cups of coffee. "Oh hell, stick with me. There's plenty more where that came from." She went to the couch and sat on the end of it. She held the cup out to me. "Black coffee."

I lifted the lid off of the cup and breathed in its aroma before taking a sip. "Ummm . . . good coffee. Thank you."

I took another swallow as she sat down hard on the sofa's center cushion.

"So what happened?" I sat down next to her. "Do you wanna talk about it?"

She gave me a half-hearted smile. "Not really."

"Are you sure? I'm a pretty good listener . . . especially when I've been paid with coffee."

"I brought bagels and muffins too."

"You just bought yourself unlimited listener service."

She gave a forced smile. "Did I now?"

"Yes, you sure did."

"I'm not a really good talker about the serious stuff."

I took another swallow of coffee. "Nope, I didn't think you were."

"Oh, and you are?"

I smiled. "Not so much."

"Yeah, that's what I thought." Her smile didn't reach her eyes.

"I'll tell you what . . . if you want to tell me about what all of that was about," I pointed to the telephone receiver, "then I will owe you one of your choosing."

Sam lifted her chin in the air and pinched her bottom lip between her thumb and index finger. "Oh, is that so?"

"Yep, it is."

"Anytime I choose? Any subject?"

"Yep."

She reached out to shake my hand. "You, my dear, have a deal." She stretched her legs out in front of her but turned her face toward the glass wall. "Dear ol' Dad called this morning. He found out I am switching to an OB/Gyn residency."

"Oh, Sam, that's fantastic. Congratulations."

"Says you." She smirked almost apologetically and glanced at me before looking down at her lap. "Thanks, Stormy. I was pretty happy when I got the news that they approved a switch. But renowned Cardiothoracic Surgeon of the South was not pleased. In fact, he was pretty fucking pissed off." She looked back out the window and took in a long breath. She looked so sad—so troubled.

I fought the urge to move closer to her. I wanted to hold her or at least put my arm around her to comfort her. *But what would she think of that? And wasn't that an odd thing to feel?* "What is there to be pissed about?"

"It isn't CT surgery," she said in a defeated voice. "Apparently that's the only residency he'll pay for. He's cutting me off . . . or so he says."

"Would he do that? Would your father really do that?" I was shocked. I mean Charlie Grace and I didn't exactly have an award-winning relationship but I doubt she would ever do something to destroy the life I wanted.

"In a heartbeat." She paused to again fake a smile. "Excuse the pun."

"I can't believe he would do that to his own daughter. He would keep you from becoming a doctor just because it isn't the doctor he wants you to be?"

"I reminded him of that. I'm sure he's already on the phone calling in favors to get me switched over to another residency." She ran both hands through her hair and then rubbed the back of her neck before letting out a deep sigh. "I guess time will tell."

I couldn't fight the craving to touch her any longer. I slid across the couch and placed my hand on her leg. "I'm sure it will be all right, Sam." I squeezed her leg as I ran my thumb across her knee. "Gawd, that sounded lame. I'm sorry. There isn't much I can say because I don't know the man. But surely he would be proud of a daughter that is a doctor even if it isn't in the specialty he wanted."

"Not him. Nothing I can do about it now but wait." Sam covered my hand with her own and lightly patted it.

"That may not be exactly true," I said, remembering back to our orientation days, the days she missed coming late to our program. "Have you met Dr. Breaker yet?"

"No, don't think I have. Why?"

I smiled with the thought I might have a solution to at least one part of all of this. "She is the head of the Women's Health Department. Let's just say she was appropriately named. She seems to be one class A ball breaker. She came on one of our orientation days. I only half paid attention to her because I wasn't planning on doing her residency but Tom thought it would be a good day to show his witty side." I laughed a hardy laugh. "It was *not*. She tore that boy a new one."

"Damn, I hate I missed that but . . . how will that help me?"

"I got the impression her attack on Tom wasn't only because he was stupid enough to interrupt by trying to be funny but a little bit because he was a man too. I don't think she takes kindly to men trying to run over her. I asked around about her after that day and the word on the street is she will not be pushed around by anyone.

Maybe go to her and tell her the situation. Won't help with money but she may not allow you to be traded off if she knows OB/GYN is what *you* want."

Sam locked her eyes onto mine for a long second before smiling. She seemed to be tossing the idea around in her head. "Thanks, Stormy. You may be onto something."

The phone rang and Sam's eyes drifted to the phone on the end table. She looked back at me and smiled. She didn't move to answer it.

I felt a goofy smile cross my face—the one she seemed to cause easily. "You're welcome."

CHAPTER 13

THE FEW CANS of soup I found while rummaging through my cupboard fit the falling temperatures of a late September night. Yet I found them anything but appealing.

Grant and several other general surgery residents were all bidding heavily for vascular cases as competition was pretty fierce within their collective group. Grant had become beyond distracted, trying to be the top force to be reckoned with among them. I couldn't be too judgmental of his ambition as I too had never focused on the present for my vision of the future. The present was merely a stepping stone to my dreams. That was until I met Sam. I found myself wanting to live in the present just for the opportunity to spend time with her.

My new friendship with Sam was starting to change things in me. She had this calming effect on me that I gravitated toward. Of course, she was a gifted student and physician but even in the most stressful of times, she had this calmness about her. I think this allowed her to keep things in perspective. Yet she also had this incredible strength to let her actions be bold and unwavering.

"Hmmmm," I murmured, staring into a refrigerator filled with half-eaten takeout containers of food. "Looks like it's a grocery store run for me."

I decided to walk a few blocks to a new grocery that had just opened. It was one of those big chain type stores boasting a selection of five to ten varieties of any one item a shopper may be searching for. I guess there was a certain attraction to a place such as that but I missed my small local grocery. The city grew more and more buildings of concrete nearly as fast as the crops I was used to seeing back home. I missed the crops. I missed life growing around me. Birmingham was merely a detour in my destination . . . a tollbooth to the road back home.

I walked into the store and saw the large produce section to the right. Shortly thereafter I saw her. Even after getting to know her better, I still caught a nervous hitch in my breath when I saw

Sam unexpectedly. She was looking over a bin of tomatoes while standing next to a nearly empty shopping cart.

"That one isn't ripe enough if you're planning on using it tonight," I said as I came to stand next to her.

She jumped slightly. "Hiya, Stormy." She turned to me. "What, no blunt objects to throw my way tonight?"

"No, not tonight. I promise I'm unarmed. You do seem sort of jumpy though."

"Am I?"

"It appears so. Well . . . unless it's your guilty conscious. I've been told a jumpy person has a guilty conscious."

Sam smiled a mischievous smirk. "Oh, honey, I'm guilty all right but I don't have a conscious about it. Besides I seem to remember you nearly decapitating me from a guilty conscious last time we met."

"Good one."

"Thanks. I try." Sam looked back at the pile of tomatoes. "So what's wrong with this tomato?"

"It isn't ripe enough. Unless you aren't planning on using it tonight and want to set it next to your wall of windows." I reached around her to pick out a different tomato. "Here try this one. It's not great but it'll do."

"What do you mean it's not great?"

"Here, smell." I held the stem of the tomato up to her nose. She inhaled lightly. "What do you smell?"

"Nothing really."

"Exactly." I turned the tomato toward my nose and breathed in its lack of scent. "Smells like wax coating to me. But a fresh tomato? Man, those smell so different."

"I take it you aren't crazy about the selection."

"They're all the same. Big chains ship what they call fresh food all over. I miss back home. I miss the Farmer's Market and the small locally owned groceries. When they say it's fresh . . . it's fresh. Like right out of someone's garden fresh. Slice that puppy up, slap it in between two pieces of mayo-covered bread, and you have a meal."

Sam leaned her hip against the metal lining of the bin and crinkled her nose. "Ummmm . . . sounds delicious."

"Are you crazy? It's the best meal of the summer."

"If you say so." She let a sideways smile slink across her face. "Maybe you can fix me one someday?"

I felt my cheeks warm at how her smile made my heart beat faster.

Her smile widened and I had no doubts my blush didn't pass her by without notice. "So, Stormy. What brings you out shopping tonight?"

"Thought I might make me a salad for dinner. The refrigerator was bare so here I am."

"You said *me* a salad for dinner. Where's Grant? You two aren't having dinner tonight?"

"No. We were s'posed to but he has been wigging out over these vascular cases coming up for grabs so he's with his study group," I said.

"You two don't seem to do that much together. I could be wrong but I see you alone an awful lot." Sam put the tomato I had picked out into her cart.

"No, you're not wrong. We're just both really focused on our school is all."

"If you say so."

"Yeah, it makes us a pretty good pair because we are free to put our time in school and not worry about each other." I reached around her again to try to find another acceptable tomato.

Sam didn't move away from the bin to make my reach any easier. If anything she shifted more in my direction. I sensed her looking down at me. "Do you really feel that way? I mean are you really okay to be alone all of the time?"

"Sure I am." I looked up and smiled at her. "Besides . . . I'm not alone. I'm with you."

She ticked her head to the side and paused. "You sure are." She picked up another tomato and held it under my nose. "How's this one?"

I sniffed and wrinkled my nose. "Ah, it'll do. So what are you doing here?"

"Shopping with a friend for salad fixin's." She winked. I'm pretty sure I blushed again. If she noticed, she didn't comment but rather started pushing her cart down the aisle. "Besides it seems I may need an expert's opinion."

We walked slowly along the produce aisles, filling our carts with similar salad ingredients. Sam suggested a detour through the wine aisle before checking out. I grabbed a six pack of beer while she deliberated over the shelves of reds and whites.

"So . . ." she said, looking over the darkened parking lot, "where are you parked?"

"Oh, I walked," I replied. "My apartment is only a couple of blocks from here."

"Nonsense. It's dark. I'll drop you home." Sam walked across the parking lot to a candy-apple red Mercedes Benz SLK 230.

"This is you?" I asked excitedly.

"Don't be impressed," she said, opening my door and expelling the scent of new car interior into the air.

"I think it's too late for that," I said, sliding onto the leather passenger seat.

As soon as Sam started the engine the raspy voice of Stevie Nicks burst through the speakers. She quickly turned the radio down.

"Oops, sorry," she said. Her childlike smile was highlighted in the brightness of the dashboard lights.

I couldn't help but return a smile. "Don't be. I happen to love Fleetwood Mac."

"Well, all right then." She turned the radio up just loud enough to be heard in the background but low enough for continued conversation. "Good. Me too. I enjoy a little old school every now and then." She relaxed against her seat as she drove us out of the parking lot.

"This is a really nice car," I said, rubbing my hand across the seat. I'm not exactly sure what drew my attention to her legs but I couldn't seem to take my eyes off of watching the contraction of her thigh muscles under the denim of her jeans as she shifted gears.

"Yeah, I suppose so. It was my Christmas present last year."

"Damn, that's some present."

Under the passing street lights, I could see Sam's expression turn sad. "It was parked in the driveway when I got home for winter break. The keys were on top of a card telling me Merry Christmas and sorry they missed me this year."

"What? Are you serious?" I faced her as she pulled the car into the driveway of my duplex.

"Yep. Christmas has never been anything special around my house."

I placed my hand on top of hers. "I'm really sorry, Sam. I'm sorry you were alone on Christmas."

"Really. It's no big deal." She rubbed her thumb along the side of my hand before patting it as if ending the conversation. "So . . . this is you? Nice place."

I looked out the window. I didn't want to allow her to change the subject but I had come to realize this was her style. She would dismiss the things that made her sad as if they meant nothing to her. But I was beginning to read her expressions and knew this was not exactly the case. Yet I was fairly certain I wasn't going to be able to get her to open up any further.

"Yep. It's not too bad. Do you wanna come in? We could make one big salad."

She was quiet for a moment before looking down at the steering wheel.

"You have no idea," she said in a low whisper that highlighted the raspiness of her voice. She ran her hand along the bottom of the wheel and tapped it lightly with her thumb. "But I can't tonight. I have . . . um . . . company coming over. Can I have a rain check?"

"Oh yeah . . . sure. No problem. I was just throwing it out there." I tried to hide my embarrassment but knew I was talking rapidly. It was Saturday night. Of course she had plans.

Sam placed her finger under my chin, urging me to face her. "Rayne . . . I wish I could stay." She looked deeply into my eyes, making her statement all the more believable. "Believe me. I do. Besides it would be nice to have a little chat about some things."

"Oh, okay. A rain check then," I said, hesitantly. *A chat about some things? What does that mean? What things?*

THE TIME GOT away from me since Sam dropped me off. It was after ten o'clock before I finished my salad and sat down on the couch to channel surf the television. Any show would be a welcome distraction from my wandering thoughts about Sam's night and what it was she wanted to talk with me about. Our friendship had just begun but I felt closer to her than any friends I had made before in my life. The thought of something happening to change, or worse, take away her friendship made me feel twisted in knots.

What does she want to talk to me about? It sounded like a serious discussion by her tone. *What is it?*

A gentle knock on the front door startled me from my curled up position against the arm of the sofa. I realized I hadn't actually turned the television on.

"Oh, shit. She came back," I said under my breath as I looked down and remembered I was comfortably dressed in a pair of boxer shorts two sizes too large and a worn-out UAB t-shirt that had seen better days.

I sprinted to the hallway to look in the mirror. Another light knock on the door. My hair was a stylish mess but if I didn't hurry and answer the door, she would surely leave.

"Hi. I wasn't expecting you. I'm glad you're . . ." I said, swinging open the door.

"I know but the study group broke up early. Saw your lights were still on so I stopped by," Grant said as he walked through the doorway and grabbed me up in his arms. "Besides . . . thought we could have a little nightcap." He nuzzled my neck. "If you know what I mean."

I pushed him off of me and turned to walk away. "I know exactly what you mean."

"Rayne, come on. It's been weeks now," he growled.

"You think cancelling our dinner plans and then coming over here saying 'Hey, baby, you wanna get it on' is going to change that?"

"Aw hell. You know I didn't mean it like that."

"I know what you meant." I snatched my salad bowl off of the coffee table and stormed into the kitchen. "Look, it's late and I'm tired. Just go home."

He followed me into the kitchen. "Well, can I at least stay the night?" He opened the refrigerator door and peered inside. He brought the leftover container of Chinese food to his nose. "Hey, is this still good?"

"How should I know? You're the one with his nose stuck in the container."

He leaned against the sink next to me, giving me his best pouty face. "Don't be like that. Don't be mad. I mean I haven't seen much of you lately. I get lonely at night, sugar."

"And that is my fault? You're the one always changing the plans." I grabbed the box from his hands and shoved it into the microwave. The microwave door had to be slammed to get a good catch as it was probably recycled from another tenant. But I most probably would have slammed the door anyway as irritated as he was making me.

"As of late it is definitely not all my fault. I came by here the other night and you weren't here. In fact I came back by the next morning and you still weren't here. I couldn't even get you on the phone. But did I jump your ass?"

"I told you I was at Sam's and my phone had died."

"What's up with you and her anyway?"

I took the heated up food out of the microwave, jammed a fork into the lid, and shoved it back into his hands. *Why in the hell am I waiting on him?* "Nothing. I think she's cool is all."

He dug into the food as if he hadn't eaten in months. "Yeah, but why did you stay the night over there?"

"I told you I had been drinking and we lost track of time talking."

"You lost track of time? Talking? That's not like you, Rayne," he said, around the food in his mouth.

"Yeah, I know. But she's . . . I dunno . . . cool to hang out with."

"Yep, you said that already."

"Look, like I said. I'm tired and I'm going to bed. You can stay the night. But sleep is all you'll get from me in my bed tonight."

"Okay. Then how about the floor?"

"Grant," I yelled.

"Kidding. I'm kidding. I'll be good. Promise. Scout's honor." He held three fingers up in the air.

"You were never a boy scout." I walked out of the kitchen as I was in no mood for his flirting, if that was what he called it.

THE WINDOWS OF the atrium were thick with condensation from the steam of the heated pool. It made looking out of them nearly impossible and my vision didn't extend beyond the glass walls. I was alone in the building as I swam slowly from one end of the pool to the other. The steam seemed to grow thicker over the water's surface, nearly choking me as I struggled to push through it. Fatigue started to take over midway across the Olympic-size lane. I struggled to stay afloat but it kept pulling me under. Once . . . twice . . . my head dipped underwater stealing my breath and causing me to gasp for air when I came up. The weight of the water squeezing across my chest was too strong for me to overcome. My mouth was open to scream—to call for help but no sounds came out before the heaviness of the water took me completely under for a final time. In the distance I heard a man's voice calling me. He screamed my name over and over. "Rayne . . . Rayne."

"Rayne . . . Rayne . . . wake up."

Grant's voice became recognizable as I started awakening from the dream. His arm was lying across my chest. It felt heavy . . . uncomfortably heavy.

"What?" I said, trying to shift under the weight of his arm.

"Wake up," he mumbled. "Your phone is going off."

I looked onto the nightstand to see the light illuminating through the window of the cell phone. I moved his arm off of me and flipped open the phone to see a text message. My heart thudded against my chest. I knew the message was from Sam.

Text Message from Sam, 1:15am: "Salad was great! How about that rain check next week?"
Text Message to Sam, 1:20am: "Sure"

I held the phone against my chest and smiled before placing it back on the nightstand.

"Everything okay?" Grant asked half asleep.

"Yeah. It's fine. Go back to sleep."

Grant reached his arm back over me and pulled me in closer to him. The memory of the crushing weight of the water sprung back into my mind.

CHAPTER 14

"SO WHAT DO you think?" Sam asked as she leaned across the table.

"It's great," I said, looking around the restaurant. "How did you find this place?"

"Figured you may be missing home cooking so I asked around a bit. One of the locum ER docs said this was as close to real Cajun food as you could get here in Alabama."

"It's perfect." I couldn't help but to give free reign to my smile. "It looks just like a place we used to have back home." I pointed at the fishing net hanging from the ceiling. "Although I always suspected Old Man Ike used a real fishing net because it smelled of dead fish. This one seems to be missing that certain characteristic."

"Thank God," Sam said. "It looks pretty cool but I don't think I could stomach the smell and eat at the same time."

She was right. This net was a far cry better than the one Old Ike had in his place. His was filled mainly with discarded Mardi Gras beads and fishing floats. This one was more of a work of art than a simple decoration. Strings of lights and scattered musical instruments were woven in between the netting. The clear lights reflected beautifully off of the brass shapes.

I caught Sam looking up at the saxophone dangling above my head before her eyes shifted to the expanded accordion hanging over hers.

"Do you play?" she asked.

"Ummm . . . no," I said. "I play the CDs. If that's what you mean."

She returned my laugh. "Well not exactly but that works too. Can't say I've ever listened to Cajun music."

"Most people either love it or hate it."

"And which are you?"

"Are you kidding me? I love it," I said, grinning.

"Then you'll have to play it for me one day," she said, studying the menu.

"I could . . . yes. But Zydeco is more of a setting type music to me. It isn't just something you listen to but rather something you experience. Go somewhere to be a part of, you know? The best place to hear it first is a small town street dance or crawfish boil."

Sam peered over her menu. "Is that an invitation?"

"It can be," I said before quickly looking down at my opened menu.

She sat quietly for a moment and then closed her menu. "Okay, Stormy. I have no idea what to order. Pick me out something good." She grabbed a beer from the bucket in the center of the table.

She had ordered the Bucket of Beer as soon as we sat down. The chalkboard easel in the front of the restaurant had proudly displayed a drawing of a metal bucket with six iced down beers as its drink special for the night.

"Speaking of Stormy. Where'd you get a name like that anyway?" She took a long swig from the bottle.

"Marijuana."

Sam choked on her swallow but managed not to let any escape her lips. "I'm sorry. From what?"

"Well, my memaw always told me that my daddy was a," I made air quotation marks, "free spirit. I always imagined he must've been high to name me Rayne Storm."

"What kind of man is he now?"

"I wouldn't know. I haven't seen him since I was eighteen months old."

Sam gave me an apologetic look. "I'm so sorry. I didn't mean to bring anything bad up."

"Oh, no. It's fine. I've been over that for years now." I gently tapped the tip of my beer bottle against hers. "No worries. Really. He was never a part of my life so I guess I don't really miss anything."

"Sometimes I wish mine wasn't a part of my life. He doesn't understand the concept of being a part versus taking over."

"Looks like we are two of a kind."

Sam bit the corner of her lip. "In some ways." She took a long swallow of her beer and winked.

"So the other night you said there was something you wanted us to talk about."

"Yeah, some day but not tonight. I'm in a really good mood. Let's not get into the heavy stuff."

Oh shit! What is it she wants to talk about? She doesn't want to hang out anymore. I just know it. But why bring me to this great place then?

"Okay. I understand. Is it too heavy to continue about you and your dad? What started the rift between ya'll? Or have you always been at odds?"

Sam smiled around the neck of the bottle on her lips. "Oh no, ma'am. I believe I am owed a share from you next. Not the other way around."

"Ah." I couldn't help but to smile back. "Okay, shoot."

"Uh uh. You said my topic, my timing, and I'm not ready yet."

I giggled. "Fair enough."

"Here you go you two. The bowls are hot so be careful," the waitress said as she set down a basket of hush puppies and two bowls of gumbo. I wanted Sam to have the full experience of Cajun food; so I ordered them as an appetizer.

"Thank you," I said to the back of the retreating waitress. I cupped the small bowl to move it closer to me. "Shit, that's hot!" I rubbed my fingers and shook my hand.

I could tell Sam was trying not to laugh. She managed to suppress herself to a small chuckle. "Ummm . . . yeah, she kind of said that when she put them on the table."

"Smartass."

"Takes one to know one." She let her laughter run free as she popped a hush puppy into her mouth.

"So can I at least ask how it's going with your residency and your dad?"

"Yeah, I'll let you have that one." She finished chewing the morsel of fried sweetened corn meal and pulled another from the basket. "Well, Dad seems dead set on not supporting me if I don't go into CT surgery. Mom is working on him from her end. But I did talk to that Dr. Breaker like you suggested."

"And?"

"You were right. She is pretty cool and one tough cookie . . . very dry. I told her everything and at the end she asked what I wanted, which residency did I want. When I told her OB, she slammed her hand down on her desk and said, 'Done then.' She said no one and I quote, 'No one, especially those hard-on cardiac surgeons, will take away or trade off one of my students because Daddy wants his way.'"

"Well, all right then," I said. "I was hoping she could help you out on that end of it."

"Maybe the other too. She had a women from Financial Aid meet me after I left her office. I might be eligible for assistance. We'll see."

I hampered my giggle as Sam reached into the basket for another hush puppy. "Do you think your mom will help in that area? I mean are you close with her?"

"Nope. My only salvation is if I can convince her I will drop out before I go into CT. She would rather have me as an OB doctor than a fry chef. Problem is she probably knows I am too pigheaded to quit because of him and his threats. Are you close with yours?"

"Charlie Grace? Ummmm . . . no. No one is close to Charlie Grace." I pinched off a piece of the last remaining hush puppy. "My mother isn't the type to get close to anyone."

"Are you?"

"What do you mean?"

Sam reached back into the basket and let her fingers roam around its nearly empty contents. She picked up the one I had been pinching off of. "Is this the last one?"

I smiled. "Sorry you didn't like them."

"Whatever." She laughed and handed me half of the one she was holding. "All I am saying is that I don't see you really letting anyone in. Not on their terms anyway. Admit it, you keep people where you want them."

"Two orders of crawfish étouffée," the waitress interrupted as she set the dishes down in front of us.

"Are the plates hot?" Sam asked and then winked at me.

"Yes, ma'am. Quite hot actually so be careful." The waitress placed the empty carrying tray under her arm. "Can I get you ladies anything else?"

"No thank you. We're good," I said.

Sam took the first bite. "Damn that is some good stuff." She let her eyes roll back in her head and then frantically grabbed her beer to take a deep swallow. "And . . . *hot*."

I laughed softly but stirred the spoon around my bowl,

unnerved about her last statement. *I didn't mandate everything be on my own terms, or did I?*

"Don't go getting quiet on me now, Stormy. We were actually talking."

"I'm not," I said . . . quietly.

"Right." She alternated bites of food between swallows of beer. "Sure you're not."

"So what about you? Who do you let get close to you?"

"No one. Maybe that's why I picked it up on you. Like I said, takes one to know one."

"I'm not the one that keeps a stash of new toothbrushes lying around. Repeat company doesn't need a new toothbrush every time."

"Touché." Sam leaned over the table again. "Oh, and by the way, you always do that too. Deflect or turn the question on me when it is something you don't really want to answer yourself."

I felt the blush color my cheeks and was thankful for the dimly lit ambience of the restaurant. "Seems you have me all figured out then."

"Nope, not at all, but it's damn interesting getting there." Sam took the last of the two beers out of the bucket. She wiped the melted ice from the bottom of each bottle before handing one to me. "You mentioned your grandmother. Tell me about her."

I smiled freely. "She's wonderful. If it hadn't been for her, my life would have sucked. I spend every minute possible with her. She's so full of . . . I don't know . . . life, I guess is the word. She is one of those people who takes pleasure in anything they're doing—finding happiness in every tiny detail."

"How often do you get to see her now?"

I sighed as a wave of sadness washed over me. "Not as much as I like to. Only when we have time off." I thought of the last time I had gone home and it was nearly impossible to spend quality time with both Memaw and Mother, not to mention the pull I felt in trying to satisfy Grant's wishes.

"It has been a growing struggle trying to see everyone in the short amount of time we have to go home. As of late Grant has wanted us to spend time with our families together so I have to try to find time with his parents as well."

"You don't like them?"

"No, I like them fine. I just don't want to share what little time I have back home with anyone but Memaw. It's hard finding a balance."

"And Grant doesn't understand that?" she asked.

"He says he does but then comes the disappointment if I don't go with him. After that he'll ask to come with me to see Memaw."

"But you don't want that?"

"Not particularly," I said.

"See," she said, tipping her bottle toward me, "on your terms."

Maybe it was the completion of my third beer that gave me the courage to flip the conversation of relationships to Sam instead of me. "And what about you? Are you dating anyone?"

She smiled. "Define dating."

"You know what I mean."

"Dating as in you and Grant? No. Dating as in I go out have a good time—no strings attached? Yes. And before you ask . . . yes, always on my terms. As I said, takes one to know one." A grin played at her lips.

"Are you close to anyone at all?"

"Can't say that I am."

Her response saddened me. I couldn't wrap my brain around a woman so strikingly beautiful and charismatic not having someone in her life that meant more to her than a casual experience. As much as I knew she was right about me, I also knew I wouldn't be who I was without Meems. I hated Sam didn't have the same foundation in someone like I had. Of course, in the deepest recesses of my mind I knew I should have felt that grounding to happiness in life with Grant but the truth was I didn't. Sure I loved him, but a part of me knew he was the casual experience and she was my center.

"Hey. Wanna go see a movie?" Sam said excitedly.

Wait. What?

"Where'd that come from?"

"I saw a movie theater around the corner when I was scoping out this restaurant. It's close enough that we could walk. But . . . if you're ready for me to take you back home, I could do that too. Up to you?"

"No. A movie sounds good. Haven't seen one in years. Anything good out?" I said, trying to remember any previews I had recently seen advertised. Nothing came to mind.

"Yeah. There is. Saw the previews a while back and it opens tonight."

"Okay, let's do it." I wasn't ready for the evening to end. "Thank you for tonight. It was sweet of you to go to so much trouble to find this place for me. The food was fantastic."

"And *hot*," she said as she drained the last of her beer. "Now . . . let's go get some movie dessert. I'm thinking M&M's."

Sam led us around the corner to a small three movie theater. "Two for *Serendipity*," she said to the teenager behind the glass.

"*Serendipity*?" I asked. "I haven't heard of that one. Is it an action film?"

Sam looked at me with a sly expression. "Not exactly. Looks like a sappy chick flick."

I blinked at her surprised.

"What?" she asked. "You don't think I like sappy romances?"

"The woman who keeps a box of new toothbrushes for her love and leave them dates? Ummmm . . . no, can't say that I did."

"Isn't that why you watch it on the big screen or read it in a book because you don't actually live it?"

"I suppose," I said. "Lead the way, Miss Heart and Flowers."

"I'll heart your flowers." She snickered as she skipped in front of me.

The seats were moderately packed by the time we got into the theater. Sam maneuvered us over folded legs and purses on the floor to two available seats. She opened her boxes of M&M's and Reese's Pieces.

"Gotta get ready," she said. "I can't believe you didn't want anything."

"I couldn't possibly eat another bite. I'm stuffed."

"Yeah, but this is the movie. The best part is chomping down on snacks." She held the open box toward me and gave it a shake as if to use the sound of candy-coated chocolate banging against the box as a temptation. "Go ahead. You know you want some."

How could I refuse her child-like manner? I popped a couple in my mouth, hoping they would find some room in my stomach. *This woman must have a tape worm the size of a football field in hers.*

The movie started and I was fascinated by the expression on her face. She was enjoying every single minute of it . . . even the previews.

"We need to go see that one when it comes out," she leaned over and whispered after the second one.

The heat of her breath against my neck and the butterfly it created caught me by absolute surprise. So much so I had difficulty relaxing in the worn movie seat. I hadn't realized I was squirming until I noticed Sam looking at me. I was frozen in the stare of her blue eyes searching mine. I thought I saw her lips part as if she was about to speak but in that moment the theater went completely dark. She turned back to the screen once the beginning of the film gave us light again.

I watched the reflecting lights off of Sam's face nearly as much as I watched the film itself. I could tell she was into the show. Her face would be one of concern or happiness depending on the scene. I was even lucky enough to catch her eyebrow raise over her left eye a few times. I grinned at the gentle rustle of M&M's against a cardboard box. I may have even giggled at the crunch of the hard candy shell as she chewed.

She held the corner of her bottom lip between her teeth as she watched the last scene with intensity. She was sitting upright in the seat. I looked down to notice the tight grip she had of the seat arm. I swear she beamed when the couple kissed. She looked at me with the warmest heartfelt smile I had ever seen on her . . . on anyone really. It was like she had been teleported into the movie and sat on the cold dampened ice rink next to the couple as they sealed their love with the movie's ultimate kiss. She was beautiful. In that instant I saw everything in her—the choppy layers of her hair with a clump of strands caught on her mascara-covered eyelashes, the small wrinkle that crossed over the tip of her nose, and the point of her chin found below two equally plump lips covered in a light pink lipstick.

The lights came on fully and I feared I would not be able to take my eyes from her. I was entranced. She didn't look away. The beat of my heart was so strong I felt its pulse in my throat. Sam closed her eyes. I watched the lids covered in a coating of brown eye shadow tense before she opened them again. She swept away the cluster of bangs that had fallen on her lashes.

"See," she whispered, "it never happens like that."

"What doesn't?" I managed to squeak out after I swallowed hard.

"Love."

The beat of my heart pounded in my ears. "No, I suppose not."

Sam stood up, flattened the empty candy boxes, and slurped the last swallow of her coke. "You ready?"

Not really.

CHAPTER 15

"HEY," SAM SAID as I opened the door.

She was wearing capri sweatpants and an over-sized sweatshirt with her hair pulled back into a ponytail.

Damn. How does she do that? How can she make sweatpants look good.

"Hi, yourself," I said. "You ready for a night of cramming."

"Yep." She pulled a six pack of Mountain Dew from behind her back. "I even brought reinforcements."

I crinkled my nose. "Eeeew. Mountain Dew?"

"Hells yeah, Mountain Dew. It's the Mac Daddy of caffeinated sodas."

"I'll stick to coffee but thanks."

"Figured you'd say that." She smiled and pulled her other arm from behind her back. She was holding a large cup with Bettye Jean written across it. "Glasses, huh?"

"Uh, yeah." I felt my eyes widen. *Damn forgot I was wearing those.* I pushed the wire frames higher up on my nose. "Forgot I was wearing them. Sorry. My contacts make my eyes tired after I study for a while."

Sam brushed past me, handing the cup of coffee to me as she walked inside. She let her hand linger on the cup before releasing it completely to me.

"They're cute, Stormy," she said, tapping her finger on the side of the cup. "Really cute."

And here came the blushing cheeks again.

Grant came a few minutes later with a box of pizza and bag of chips. We snacked and studied for what must have been several hours before I dozed off, curled up against the arm of the couch. I'm not sure how long I had been dozing before I noticed the silence of the room. No longer did I hear the rustling of pages, tapping of pens, or reading with low murmured voices. Instead I heard heavy deep breathing close to my ear. I opened my eyes to see Grant sound asleep against my shoulder.

Wait . . . where's Sam? I glanced around the room to see if she had left. She hadn't. She sat in a chair directly across from me. She had her leg bent in the seat of it with her arm hugging her knee close to her chest. She was watching me—watching us.

I couldn't blink. I couldn't look away. Her stare was intense.

Her eyes narrowed as she chewed on the end of her pen cap. *Is she studying? Looking off to try to get the facts to burn into her memory? What?* She gave me a half smirk before looking back down at her paper. I watched her for several minutes, hoping she would look up again so I could attempt to read her thoughts. She didn't.

TEXT MESSAGE TO Sam, 1:40pm: "Hey. What you been up to?"

Text message from Sam, 2:30pm: "not much"

Text message to Sam, 2:33pm: "Are you ok?"

Text message from Sam, 2:50pm: "yeah"

Text message to Sam, 2:52pm: "Ok."

Text message to Sam, 3:55pm: "I'm sorry for whatever I did to upset you."

Text message to Sam, 4:10pm: "I wish you would talk to me."

The phone vibrated in my hand as I was setting it back onto the table. My heart skipped when I saw Sam's name flashing across the screen.

"Hey," I said, answering on the second ring.

"Hey, yourself."

"Look. I'm sorry for whatever I did to upset you."

She sighed. "You didn't do anything wrong, Stormy, and I'm not upset with you."

"Well, then what is it? You've hardly responded to any text. I must have left you at least three voice mails over the last several days. I've hardly spoken to you since you came over that night to study."

"I've been busy. That's all. Got behind with school stuff and had to crank it out to catch up." Her voice was flat—nearly monotone. "How's Grant?"

Grant? She never asks about Grant. Not like this anyway.

"Fine. He's fine."

"That's good." Her tone remained the same.

I was suddenly very uncomfortable as if there was some tension between us. Yet I had no idea what it was nor did it seem I was going to find out.

Silence.

I took in a deep breath. "Well, okay then. Guess I better let you go. Have a good day, Sam." I didn't know what else to say. She was obviously too busy to talk or she didn't want to talk. The latter would have been too hurtful to find out.

"Yeah . . . you too, Stormy."

I pulled the phone away from my ear.

"Hey, Stormy . . . wait a sec."

"Uh huh?"

"I'm sorry. Really I am. Got stuff on my mind that's all but I shouldn't have been short with you."

"It's okay, Sam."

"No, really it isn't, but thanks. I'll talk to you later."

I miss you. Could I have told her that? Was it appropriate for friends to express a longing to spend time together? What did I know? I hadn't experienced this with girl friends before.

NEARLY TWO WEEKS passed before I talked with Sam again. We ran into each other at the Corner Café. We were both preoccupied with studying; so, we barely said more than a greeting. Shortly after, Sam text me, inviting Grant and I out to dinner. She had a friend visiting from Atlanta and wanted us to join them for a night out. Grant happily accepted, deciding we all needed a break from school. Although, I would have happily accepted an invitation for a root canal if it meant spending time with Sam. I was hoping this would give us a chance to talk and maybe . . . just maybe I could find out what had been bothering her.

Earlier in the week, I snuck away to shop for my evening's outfit. I wanted to look nice when I met Sam's date. The black pants accented my waist and hips before expanding to a free flowing material down my legs. The accompanying top was of the same material and fit me snugly with its plunging neckline and cropped sleeves. The night air of early November occasionally brought with it a slight chill. So I truly had no choice but to buy the white waist-length jacket that matched.

"Whoa, Rayne. You look freaking amazing," Grant said as I opened the door. "What say we call it a night and stay in?" He waggled his eyebrows as he motioned toward the bedroom. "I suddenly lost my appetite." He jokingly pulled my hand along with him as he walked to the bedroom. "For food anyway." Judging by Grant's reaction, I had done well with my outfit selection.

"I don't think that would be proper etiquette of southern hospitality, do you?" I said in my best southern accent, trying to deflate the situation. "Besides I can already taste the sushi," I pretended to whimper.

"No, don't suppose we should be rude. But give a guy some warning before he shows up to find this at the door," he said as he waved his hand up and down my body. "Damn, if you don't look good girl." He opened the door for us to leave.

Sex had never been something I would say I enjoyed. It was merely part of being in a relationship—a chore that must be done to keep the other happy. But tonight for some reason his flirtations made a wave of nausea pass over me. I couldn't be honest and say that my thoughts hadn't become acutely aware of Sam's image slipping more frequently into them. Especially at times when I saw her less frequently like over the last few weeks. Honesty being what it was, I couldn't really admit that spending time with her hadn't caused distance between Grant and me. Not that he would notice as his attentions were solely focused on his residency. I rationalized this as a major reason for our distance.

We had chosen to meet at Sapphire, a chic sushi bar found in the heart of Four Points. Four Points was a collection of restaurants, pubs, coffee shops, and eclectic boutiques at the center of where four main streets intersected. It had become one of our favorite locations for decompression after long periods of studying. Sapphire was known for their cocktail menu and happy hour. The combination of the two made for a rather loud environment some nights. This seemed an appropriate atmosphere for the anticipated awkward silence in meeting Sam's visitor. Silently I hoped Grant and Sam's date would become fast friends; therefore, leaving Sam and I to a sound sampling of cocktails and uninterrupted conversation.

Text Message to Sam, 7:10pm: "U r late. Got a table. Far right corner."
Text Message from Sam, 7:12pm: "shit dude who picks a restaurant with no freaking parking"
Text Message from Sam, 7:14pm: "Found a spot b right in"

Sam strode up to the host's podium. I stood at our table to show her where we were sitting and became awestruck when she came into full view. I was stunned by her striking beauty. She wore a brown singlet underneath a matching sheer shirt. The silk material hugged closely to her tall slender frame. Her legs seemed to stretch even longer in the knee high boots and short leather skirt. Waves of blonde hair danced around her face as she spun in my direction.

I sensed an equivalent admiration in her expression as our eyes met. Her pace was hurried as she maneuvered through the crowd to our table. My excitement faltered when I noticed a hand firmly clasped within hers as she made her way closer to us. Not just a hand, it was a woman's hand. Not just a woman's hand, it was an exquisitely beautiful woman's hand. She stood an inch taller than Sam with black hair cropped short and stylishly wild without structure. She was dressed in gray slacks with a silk white shirt that exposed an olive-skinned chest. They owned the stares of each table as they passed by them.

Sam's face glowed with excitement as she reached our table. "Rayne . . . Grant . . . this is Claire. She's visiting me from Atlanta. You two look fantastic." She stepped toward me for a light hug. She smelled gloriously.

"Hello, Claire. It's very nice to meet you. We're both so happy you invited us to join you tonight," Grant said.

Thank goodness he was my date for the evening as I would have looked like an idiot had I been the one responsible for carrying on the conversation. I seemed to be absent of speech, lost somewhere in between smells of eucalyptus and the sight of a woman's hand held tenderly within Sam's. Was I shocked or surprised of this visual revelation? Was I completely clueless or had I ever subconsciously entertained some fleeting notion Sam might be gay or at the least bisexual? More importantly had I hoped she would be? And if I did, what did this mean toward me?

A tender tug at my arm pulled me from my inward deliberations.

"Hey, you okay?" Sam asked softly in my ear.

I felt warmth on my forearm and looked down to see her hand gently gripping it, burning my skin beneath.

"Yes, I'm fine," I replied in a whisper only she could hear. "Maybe shocked a bit . . . but fine."

"Looks like it may be a while before someone gets to our table with this crowd. I'm going to go up and grab us some drinks," Sam said, pulling the chair out for Claire to sit down. She looked at me. "You wanna walk up there with me, Rayne?"

"Sure."

"Let's start with a round of Mojitos," Grant called to us as we made our way through the crowd.

When initially discussing the dinner plans, we had designed a plan in which each of the four of us would chose a drink selection for the round. Considering the last time I drank around Sam, I had no expectations of making it past the second round—not lucidly anyway. Nonetheless, I had told myself to put my big girl panties on and do the best I could to keep up. A small part of me was terrified of the looseness of my lips that seemed to follow intoxication.

I followed Sam up to the bar. She walked to the end of it before squeezing in to find a spot and placing our order.

"Hey you," she said, nudging her shoulder against me.

"Hi." I think I was starting to feel a twinge of anger. Who was I kidding? I was pissed. She couldn't have told me this when we were alone. I had to find out by seeing her caressing some gorgeous woman.

"Stormy, look." She sighed and looked at our table. "I'm sorry I've been so distant."

I looked back at our table. Grant and Claire were apparently hitting it off and already in a fluid conversation. "Is she the reason why?" I heard the acid in my voice.

Sam seemed to be surprised by my tone because she flinched and blinked a few times before answering. "No. Well . . . yes. Sort of . . . I guess."

"Kinda going to need a coherent sentence to understand what you're trying to say." My tone was unchanged.

"Are you angry at me? Are you angry because I'm here with

a woman?"

"Give me a break, Sam."

"Well, then what is it? Because you're pissed."

"I'm not pissed." I sighed, trying to change the ice in my tone.

"No, don't do that." Sam grabbed both of my bare upper arms. "Don't change how you feel just because I said something. You do that too much. Feel what you feel but explain to me why you feel that way."

"I thought we were friends."

"Friends."

"Yes, friends. Probably the best friend I have ever had and you didn't trust or like me enough to tell me this."

"It wasn't like that."

A gentleman trying to get up to the bar stepped behind me which pushed me closer to Sam. "Then what was it?"

She looked down at me tenderly. "I wanted to tell you but the time never seemed right. Remember I told you I wanted to talk to you about something. Guess a part of me feared it would change us."

"Why should it change us?"

She arched her eyebrow. "I don't know. Should it?"

I felt the pressure of the man's back move away from me. I started to take a step back away from Sam but she caught my arm and held me close to her.

"I don't want it to change us," she said.

I felt her breath on my face and my voice caught in my throat, making it difficult to speak loud enough to be heard over the crowd. "And the distance?"

"I needed to step back and look at the whole picture again instead of focusing on a piece of it. Had to get some things straight in my head. You know, remember reality."

"And did you?"

She smiled and bit the corner of her lip. "I sure as hell hope so."

"So . . ." I looked back over my shoulder at Claire who was now looking directly at us. "Your date. Does this mean you're bisexual? Gay?"

Sam turned to me with a wily grin. Our faces were inches from each other. Her blue eyes stared deeply into mine, causing a fiercely flapping butterfly to develop in my stomach.

"Oh, honey, I'm one hundred percent lesbian."

"Oh." Yep . . . that's all I said. *Oh.*

"CLAIRE, HOW'S IT over at Emory?" Grant asked.

"Dreadful without this woman beside me." Claire's eyes flowed up from her and Sam's intertwined hands to Sam's eyes. "I still can't believe she's gone." Her voice was smooth and articulate.

What was it? What was that look in her eyes as they met Sam's? It was an expression that had so far in my life been quite unknown to me, until I met Sam that was. Suddenly it became clear. Sam was passion. That persona about her that I had not yet called to name was passion. She exuded it as a visible aura for all to capture. Those that absorbed it had no real hopes of escaping it. It seemed the list of those infected was growing: Tom, Kylie, Claire, and I was beginning to fear . . . *me.* All of a sudden tonight seemed a very good night to venture past round two.

"Your turn, Rayne," Grant cued as the waitress returned. "Knowing your history, we better put in a food order if we're going to make it past this next drink."

"Yeah, I could do with a little alcohol deterrent," I said. "Let's have a round of Brazilian Daiquiris next."

Grant looked at me in surprise. He had most likely expected me to order my usual beer which I normally would have but tonight I wanted to act like I had some sort of knowledge when it came my turn to order. I had suspected Grant would order Mojitos since he was the one who introduced them to me awhile back; so, I had researched different drinks that would go well with those. I hoped the mixed rum, vanilla, and pineapple of a Brazilian Daiquiri would go better with the Mojitos than beer. Silently I feared a very painful morning of a headache and extreme nausea.

"And then I think we will start with . . . hmmmm . . ." I studied over the menu. "How about the shrimp and vegetable tempura? We probably should order our sushi too. It may take a while in this crowd."

Everyone nodded in agreement.

"Okay then, we'll take the chef's sushi boat for four." With big parties, the chef's sushi boat was the most popular item and rarely the same collection twice as the chef chose what he wished to mix together for the night.

"I predict a taxi service in our very near future," Sam said to Claire. "We can come back to get your car in the morning."

Morning.

"So how did you two meet?" I asked.

"Honey, can I take this one?" Claire touched Sam on the arm and left her hand to linger there. "It was last year during my first year as an attending. This little bugger came bee-bopping into the ER one day as if she owned it. She announced that she wanted to shadow a doctor . . ." Sam chuckled under her breath, catching Claire's attention midsentence. She lightly ran her hand along Sam's arm. "I thought she was the cutest thing ever, so I offered my services. In appreciation . . . she offered hers."

"Claire," Sam exclaimed.

"What?" Claire looked at her in surprise. "You did? In fact that night—"

"So," I felt mildly protective of Sam's discomfort and extremely uninterested in hearing the rest of her sentence, "Claire, so you're an attendee. I'm sure Grant would love to pick your brain about that."

"Hmmmm?" Claire murmured as she redirected her attention to us. "Oh. Yeah, sure. Ask away?"

This opened a floodgate of questions from Grant. I sat quietly, watching the interaction of the three of them—well, the two of them. Sam sat nearly as quiet as me.

Claire continually found means to touch Sam. Tiny reminders of togetherness—a squeeze of the shoulder, a tracing up the arm, a tucking of her hair behind her ear, a rub of her hand across Sam's back. Her affections were simple enough toward Sam but they sparked a rare emotion in me. I was growing quite jealous of Claire's attentions toward Sam. She was so blatant with her displays. Almost as if she found a benefit in keeping them right before my eyes. Honestly, I had never thought of engaging in such interaction on a date. That was until now and I had most surely never felt jealousy before.

"Bite Me Beer," Sam said with emphasis on the "Bite Me."

Apparently the waitress had once again approached our table while I was occupied with my thoughts. She brought with her a wooden boat-shaped platter full of every kind of sushi roll and sashimi imaginable. Thankfully my buzzing intoxication did not prevent successful use of the accompanying chopsticks.

Halfway into the Bite Me Beer and sinking boat of sushi, I could no longer deny the urge to excuse myself. My head swam as I rose to my feet. The degree of my intoxication quite obvious as I tried to focus my vision on the length of the distance between my table and the rest room. The path of which seemed to stretch endlessly. One foot fell somewhere in front of the other, guiding me along the way. The room itself seemed to spin about me.

I found the way to the lavatory sink and splashed cold water on my face and neck, which proved to be a failed attempt at adding focus to the two Rayne reflections in the mirror.

A familiar silhouette approached me from behind and joined me in a reflected image. My visions were a clouded victim to the evening's alcohol. My thoughts were a blur. What was real? What was not? Through the haze of uncertainty, my body felt her chest firmly pressed against my back. Her arms reached around me and her hands slid down along each of my own into the running stream of water. Our fingers pirouetted together in the flowing coldness.

"God, Rayne." Her breath was warm against my ear. A wave of sensation jolted down my spine. "You look so gorgeous tonight." Her breath was a deep inhale and slow exhale against my ear. "You don't know what torture you bring me, do you? How I can't stop thinking of you . . . wanting you."

She moved her face away from my ear to nuzzle my hair with her nose and mouth. I felt her deep inhalations against me with each turn of her head. Her body pushed stronger into me, tightening the squeeze of my fingers locked within hers. My mind was a continuous fog, swirling between the heat of her body and the heat of her breath passing across my ear. She stopped the steady rhythm of our gliding fingers to trace a wet trail up my arms. My eyes were unable to open as I felt her grip on my shoulders turning me toward her. Fearing this was only a figment of my imagination's desire, I kept them tightly closed . . . holding onto every second of the sensations causing my heart to pound wildly.

With the sense of damp fingertips at the base of my neck, I heard her voice say, "This cross? You wear it constantly." Her fingers held its shape. Water dripped from their tips down my chest. "As if I need something to draw my attention to your neck." Her voice trailed into a whisper as the familiar breath found its way to awaken the skin underneath the chain she had been holding.

Giggles. Laughter. Incomprehensible speech patterns burst through the bathroom doorway, jarring the body once held captivated in her arms. And then there was nothing. I opened my eyes to realize I was standing alone, leaning against the bathroom counter and letting it support my unstable equilibrium. The uninterrupted water was running in the sink. A single much clearer reflection of myself was shining back in the mirror in front of me.

"It was a dream. A damn drunken dream," I uttered under my breath. As was my belief until I felt droplets of water drift from my neck trailing further down my chest.

The incessant giggling of the female customers now occupying the bathroom with me forced me to go back to my table. Sam's back was to me as I approached—she had already returned to her seat next to Claire. I could nearly feel the soft fibers of her hair tickling my neck again as I noticed the light reflecting off of her blond strands. The drying drop of water upon my chest still stirred evidence of the hands recently found there. A wave of jealousy coursed through me at Claire's hand resting on Sam's thigh as I crossed the table to my seat.

Sam met my eyes briefly before both of us looked away.

"So . . . I guess it's my choice then?" Claire asked when the waitress returned. "As if any of us need to have one further ounce of alcohol. But we need to finish this night off right, let's have a Barbados Punch. That'll give a little sweetness for our dessert."

I looked away from Claire as she spoke with the waitress to find Sam gently rolling her thumb around the tips of her index and middle finger. The same two fingers that recently held a delicate piece of gold. She looked up and her eyes were filled with desire—taking me wholly in her stare. *Butterflies.* It was as if she was searching my expression for a reaction to our interlude. I wondered if she could sense the voices in my head damning those that had interrupted her body against mine.

"Sam, what do you have going on for the Thanksgiving break?" Grant blurted, startling both of us.

"Oh . . . uh . . ." Sam stuttered as if collecting her thoughts as she focused her attention from me to him, "I'm sorry, what?"

"What are you doing over the Thanksgiving break?" he repeated.

"Nothing much. Why? You got big plans?"

"Lord willing I do," he said. "Dr. Coy, Chief of Vascular is taking call and his attendee is off for the break. I'm hoping to score a few cases with him."

"Yeah. Heard he was pretty pissed when Chase told him he was taking off," she replied.

"You don't go home for the holidays, Sam?" I asked.

"Home to what? A catered dinner and people I don't know filling the table." She sighed. "No, I don't waste my break for that."

"You should totally go with Rayne then. You can keep her company on the drive," Grant interjected. "I hate it when she drives home alone."

"Geez, Grant. It's eight hours. I think I can handle it," I replied in an aggravated tone. "Besides I subject no one to Charlie Grace, especially when she is on high holiday alert. The woman is insane this time of year."

"I would love to go," Sam said.

Grant and I looked at her in surprise.

Planning the road trip occupied the majority of the remaining conversation while we sipped our last drink and paid out the tab. As we left the restaurant, we said our good-byes. No one seemed to notice the awkwardness of the good-bye hug that Sam and I shared.

"Should I apologize?" she said quietly in my ear.

I pulled away to meet her eyes and managed to whisper, "No."

CHAPTER 16

THE NIGHT WITH Sam at Sapphire remained a lasting vision in my head. So many questions sprung to life that night—questions about her sexuality . . . questions about my own. I couldn't ignore the effect the sensation of her skin against me caused. Nor could I ignore the lingering smells of eucalyptus mint that continued to fill my daydreamed senses. I realized all too well how much I longed to again know the feeling of her body against me. There was so much more to know about Sam LeJeune but I was beginning to know or in the very least understand some of the things that had drawn me to her.

The impending road trip of over eight hours in the car with her filled me with excitement. Maybe the time together would allow me to get to know her better. Sam had a talent of only showing me glimpses of feelings or thoughts she wished to keep hidden. I dare say she was better at it than me. There were questions I couldn't allow to enter my thoughts much less spend any time giving them true consideration. After the night at Sapphire, I had no doubt I was attracted to Sam and I knew this attraction went beyond a friendly one. But what I was prepared to do about that was altogether different. Was I ready for events to occur in my life that would change it forever? Was I prepared to change my life in just a short amount of time? I would have to know the answers to those question before I let myself venture down the path leading me into Sam's arms.

"Hello."

"Hiya, Memaw?" I said.

"Sis! What ya know?"

"Is Mother planning a big family dinner for Thanksgiving this year?"

"Is a witch's tit cold?"

"I was afraid of that." I sighed.

"What's up, baby girl? I thought you were a looking forward to Thanksgiving? You sounded excited last week when we talked."

"I am, Memaw. I can't wait to see you," I reassured her. "It's just . . . well . . . y'know Grant isn't coming, right?"

"Yeah, you told me as much already. He's staying to suck up to some fancy smancy doctor. But I wasn't thinking you were upset 'bout that."

"Yep, that's the reason all right. Well . . . we went to dinner with some . . . er . . . friends . . . and well . . ."

"Spit it out, girlie. You're a spending all my minutes with your stuttering around." Memaw had done well to accept the many booms of technology throughout her life. She did rather well with her cell phone except for remembering that she was on an unlimited plan. I swear she watched her clock the moment she answered the phone. Truth be told, there was probably a small notebook with a running tally of the minutes of her calls lying on her end table.

"I'm bringing a friend from school with me. But, Gawd, you've got to help me keep Charlie Grace off of her. I don't want a thousand questions thrown at her the first fifteen minutes we're there."

"You might as well be asking me to keep Lester's hound dog from howling all night. But I can sho' try," she said. "You must like this new friend?"

"I do, Memaw. She isn't like anyone I've ever met before."

"Then I can't wait to meet her."

"I was hoping maybe we could come stay at the cabin Saturday?"

"Sure, Sis. I'd love to have you girls out there. Don't stay at the old place much without you." Her voice broke a little as the next words fell. "Makes me miss you more." We were quiet except for the crackles of static in the air between us. "Now let me get off this thing and get to work. Love you, baby girl."

"I miss and love you too, Memaw, so very much. See ya in a few days."

CHAPTER 17

NOVEMBER PROVIDED A perfect atmosphere for a drive home. The crispness of the air blew into the Jeep from our partially cracked windows, providing a natural coolness that made it a comfortable drive home and a means of keeping a quieted conversation.

We had not yet spoken about the night at Sapphire. To me the unspoken words thickened the air between us but Sam carried herself with an unchanged demeanor as if nothing had happened. She seemed relaxed in the fact that we had not spoken of anything beyond idle conversation since that night. I fear this intensified my inner struggles. My foundation was so shaken that I had nearly let my thoughts convince me everything had been an alcohol-induced dream—a betrayal of the desires I had unknowingly held within myself. It seemed as I was beginning to let my thoughts roam freely beyond those generally thought of toward a friend, she began to pull back. Yet wasn't this who she was? She never pretended to be anyone other than the person who entertained different bed partners.

I watched Sam study the landscape as we drove south to Louisiana. I had veered off of the interstate as soon as I was able. Taking the two-lane highway running parallel to the congested interstate allowed us not only to lengthen our driving time by slowing our speed but also let us pass through the small towns scattered along the road. I watched her from the corner of my eye. I couldn't help but smile with her as she saw a couple of children playing in the front yard with their four-legged companion. She had a child-like stare of envy as she watched them.

"I miss those days," I said. "Days when all I had to do was ride my bike and play with my dog."

She looked at me with sadness behind her eyes. "I never had days like those."

"Are you serious? Not ever."

"Nope." She looked back out the window and traced her

knuckle along the glass. "We didn't play much in the LeJeune household."

"Have you heard from your dad?"

"Not one peep. He's doing the mature talking through Mom thing right now. Seems he thinks I'm not coming home for Thanksgiving because I'm pissed at him."

"And are you?" I asked.

"Well, hells yeah I am. I'm screwed, blue, and tattooed if he doesn't change his mind about paying for my residency. I found out I can't get a dime of government assistance because the son-of-a-bitch makes too much money. I am waiting to hear back from my loan applications. Keep your fingers crossed. I'll be damn if I go into CT surgery just to please him." She looked at me. "But that isn't the reason I didn't go home."

"Then why didn't you?"

"To spend time with you."

I felt the heat of my blush rise up from my neck and I was sure I had some goofy smile on my face. Judging by her reaction, I must have been right because she chuckled a little before looking back out the window.

"So, I guess we should talk about the other night before we get to your family's house, huh?" she said several minutes later.

"Talk? About what?" I said, gripping the steering wheel tighter and dreading the fact I had actually wanted this conversation to happen.

A part of me feared her telling me it was a drunken mistake, yet another part was terrified she wouldn't. I was so conflicted on what I wished she would say that I almost didn't comprehend the words when she did begin to speak.

"Well, I do believe you drunkenly made a pass at me the other night."

I nearly ran the Jeep off the road with the tightened grip and my swift head snap in her direction. "Me? I did *not*."

She laughed hardily. "Simmer down, sista, before you run us off the road." She turned in her seat to face me fully.

I had never been so thankful I was driving. I couldn't imagine how nervous I would have been sitting right next to her without anything to lure my attention from her eyes.

"I was really afraid you were going to take back your offer for me to come with you. Guess that's why I've dodged the whole conversation up until now. I wanted us to be too far away for you to turn around before I brought it up," she said, her voice more serious. "I'm truly sorry if I made you uncomfortable."

"You didn't make me uncomfortable."

"The hell you say." She sighed.

"You didn't, Sam." I turned briefly away from the road to look at her. "I'm serious. You didn't."

"Well, I'm sorry. I should've never done that to you. No matter how drunk I was."

"So, it was because you were drunk?"

"No," she replied quickly. "No, not that at all."

"Then why do you say you shouldn't have done it?"

She looked at me puzzled. "For one you're straight and practically engaged to a man."

"I am *not!*"

In a sideways glance, I could see the arch of her eyebrow and the smirk across her face. "Not what? Not straight? Not engaged?"

"You know what I meant." The heat of my blush returned to my cheeks.

"I can't deny I'm attracted to you, Stormy. I have been since the first time I saw you at UAB. I remember thinking how fun I thought you would be in bed."

I tried to swallow down the knot in my throat. I felt my eyes darting back and forth and a ripple run across my stomach. I couldn't speak.

She shifted in her seat to where she was now looking out of the front windshield and no longer at me. "You pretty much keep me twisted in knots when I'm around you. It's just . . . I don't know . . . you're different."

"How?" I said quietly, fearing the answer.

Did I really want to know why she was apologetic for trying to kiss me and obviously no longer wishing me to get into her bed? The vision of being in Sam's bed again with her lying next to me forced my eyes closed for longer than a normal blink.

She continued to stare out the window. I had started to believe she wasn't going to answer until she whispered, "Because . . . because that wouldn't be all I wanted. For the first time in . . . well . . . forever, I would care what happened the morning after.

I would care what it did to us. I've never had a friend before, Stormy." She looked down at her lap and rubbed her hand across her thigh as if she was wiping something away. "Now that I have found you, I don't want to lose you."

I reached across the console and clasped the top of her hand. "You won't, Sam. You won't."

"I don't know. We've reached this impasse now, especially after I was stupid enough to act that way in the bathroom. So stupid." She slapped her hand down hard against her thigh.

Stupid. This time I felt another lump in my throat but it wasn't embarrassment or nervousness . . . it was sadness. I withdrew my hand from the top of hers.

"Why do you have to say it like that?" I knew my voice was nothing more than a hushed mumble.

Sam reached over and took my hand back in hers. "Because it has already changed us. Look at the tension between us now . . . on this drive. We never had that before. Well, we did, it was just one-sided. I swallowed my attraction and tried not to let you see it. Now it is out in the open. So what do we do with that? Do I watch everything I say or do because you may fear I am coming on to you? Or do we go on as we had before. If that is even possible now."

"Of course, it's possible. I've never had a friend like you either. I'm always wishing for more time with you. I always want you around and I can tell you I've never brought a friend home with me before." I squeezed her hand. "You mean a lot to me."

She squeezed back. "Back at ya, sista."

"HEY, I SAW a sign back there for a farmer's market. It should be coming up in a few miles," Sam said excitedly. "Do you think we could stop? I want to bring something with me as a thanks for letting me crash the holiday."

"Oh Gawd . . . no. Please don't do that," I said.

"What? Why shouldn't I?"

"Because Charlie Grace would never leave me alone about it. She would go on and on about how well-mannered you were. Then it would spin on me because I am the heathen daughter she failed to train right. Please don't give her anything to start hounding me about."

Sam put her hands up in defense. "Okay . . . Okay, I won't. Is she really that bad?"

"Yes, she's really that bad."

"Yeah, I remember you telling me you two weren't that close," she said with questioning in her voice as if encouraging me to elaborate.

"No, we aren't in any way. About the only thing I can count on Charlie Grace for is criticism. Criticism as to how I didn't turn out to be the girl she wanted . . . how I'm not married yet . . . how she doesn't have any grandkids yet . . . how I want a career . . . you name it, she can complain about it."

"Sounds like we need to take our mothers away for a weekend trip and well . . . *leave them*," she said, laughing.

"You've got that right."

"So do you want kids?"

"I don't know. Do you?"

Sam laughed. "Oh boy. There you go again dodging questions."

I rolled my eyes and sighed. "I don't honestly know if I do or not. Right now and for as long as I can remember I've been focused on finishing school. It's all my dreams have been, not marriage or children. Maybe after I've done it and started my practice then maybe my head will be clear enough to think of having kids."

"And marriage?"

"Suppose that would have to come with it."

"Hmmmm."

I turned briefly to look at Sam. "And you? Do you want kiddos?"

"Yes, definitely."

I shook my head. "You never stop surprising me."

"What because I want kids?"

"Well, yeah. I mean . . . the woman who keeps a toothbrush stash wants kids."

"My toothbrush stash really threw you for a loop, didn't it?"

"Just wasn't expecting you to say you wanted the pitter patter of little feet when you don't keep someone around long enough to use a toothbrush twice."

Sam tapped me on the shoulder. "You're still around."

I laughed. "Yes, but we aren't having kids together."

"We'd be a damn medical anomaly if we did. Oh wait. Slow

down . . . here it is. Can we stop anyway? Bet they have some good ice tea." She snickered as she looked at me. "Extra sweet."

I pulled into the small country stand a few feet off of the road. Its parking lot was made of gravel and old railroad beams. Sun-dried corn stalks tied around the posts of the small porch stood as remnants of the October corn maze. The orange of a few leftover pumpkins were speckled out across the area delegated as The Pumpkin Patch. Their bright color was shining from underneath the dark green leaves. Sam sprinted past the opened door of distressed wood and paned glass.

I walked in to see her gazing over the jars of jellies, jams, and preserves.

"I love places like these," she said. "Are you sure I can't take some of this stuff to your mom?"

"Oh, I'm very sure," I said.

"Oh, my God. They have fried apple pies. I haven't had those in forever," she said as she read the menu hanging over the counter.

"Have you ever gotten a fasting glucose level on yourself."

"Oh, whatever." She pranced along the length of the back wall. Above her was one long chalkboard with the menu written across it in a variety of colors. Some lines even had cute little drawings next to them. Sam ordered two fried apple pies and two large sweet teas.

I opened the door leading onto the back porch and motioned to the empty picnic table at the edge of the grown Christmas trees.

"My grandmother used to bring me to a place like this every Christmas," I said.

"Oh, yeah?"

I smiled as I thought fondly of the memories of Memaw and me picking out our Christmas tree. "Yeah, we would come out every year the Friday after Thanksgiving to tag our tree. We would walk down each of the rows until we found the right one. Then we would tie a bandana around its trunk and sit underneath it, drinking the hot apple cider Memaw would bring in her thermos."

"You don't go anymore?" Sam asked.

"No, we haven't been in several years. The family shut it down when Old Man Amos got sick. Memaw couldn't bring herself to go anywhere else. I don't blame her. It wouldn't have been the same for me either."

"I can't wait to meet her, Stormy. Your face lights up every time you mention anything about her. She must be quite a woman."

"Oh, she is that. Honestly, I think of her more as my mother than Charlie Grace," I said. "Memaw feels the same way about me. She told me once that she had to remind herself I wasn't her daughter. I always felt gypped in that way . . . like I'd been robbed a real mother."

"Honey, she can't be any worse than mine."

"I wouldn't bet on it."

She covered my hand with hers and her thumb lightly brushed across my knuckles. "It seems we have a lot in common. It'll be fine. Trust me. I'm used to moms like her."

Her caress was meant for friendly reassurance. It was nothing more than a simple touch yet the response in me was anything but simple. I felt a slow deep breath escape my lips as the skin under her hand tingled. Her eyes danced across my face until they rested on my lips.

"Sam?"

"Mm-hmm?"

"You said you used to think it would be fun to get me into bed . . . past tense."

She gave me a half-way smile. "I wouldn't say entirely past tense but what would happen then? Where would we be the morning after? I'm not saying I've never slept with straight women who had boyfriends, married women even. But they went home to their men the next morning and I couldn't have cared less. Not sure I could watch you cuddle with Grant on the couch if I had felt you in my arms the night before. Hell, that study night at your place was hard enough without ever having kissed you."

Kissed me.

"Besides what I really said was I thought you would be fun in bed." She tapped the end of my nose. "And that thought, my dear, has not changed."

CHAPTER 18

SAM SAT QUIETLY in fascination through the remaining miles of our journey until we reached our destination. She sat straighter in the seat, craning her neck as I turned in between the large gate posts. A pasture of no longer harvested pecan trees bordered the road before us. The cast of the setting sun was shadowed above the canopy of oak tree branches that lined the main drive leading to the house. Minutes passed before the road swung into an opening, giving first sight to the plantation home facing us.

Its architectural style was that of Greek revival with Louisiana French accents. A majestic home since its origin in the year eighteen hundred and thirty-eight. The white columns and balcony railings, both upper and lower, sat in contrast designed against the home's rich golden paint. The roof was adorned with four brick chimneys. French doors of gorgeous pecan wood gave entrance into the home. Through the open doors we could see the foyer's brilliantly lit hanging crystal chandelier. I had forgotten to appreciate its beauty until I saw it again in Sam's reaction.

"Holy shit, Stormy! *Holy . . . shit.* This is your house?" Sam said, looking around as we pulled to the front of the circle drive and parked by the large Fleur de Lis fountain. "What? Are you guys like the fucking Kennedys of Mayberry or something?"

I couldn't help but laugh. "Nothing quite that exciting I assure you."

"Oh, you have much to spill over this little visit, Dr. Storm. Much . . . to . . . spill." She glanced at me as she emphasized the words. Her eyes focused on me as she leaned against the fender of the Jeep. "You know, I had every intention of talking to you about us before we left school but I was afraid you would run from me. Now I'm thinking," she paused as she studied the two floors of the home, "you have more room to hide here than on campus."

"My baby girl is home!" Mother burst through the doorway in full actress flair. Her arms wide spread in formation to accept her rightful hug . . . rightful yet notwithstanding brief hug as her attention turned to the stranger beside me. "And you brought a friend from school with you."

"Yes, Mommy, I brought Sam home from school with me to play and then spend the night. Her momma said it was okay."

"Don't be crass with me, young lady. This is a time of Thanksgiving for the blessing of our loved ones. Not the time to remember the peace we have while they are away. Hmmmmm?"

That was the condescending tone I did not include in the list for those things I was thankful for this season. "Yes, ma'am. Mother, this is Sam. Sam, meet the infamous Mrs. Charlie Grace Doucet."

"Sam? Would that be short for Samantha?"

"Actually, yes it is, Mrs. Doucet. Although I do like to be called Sam."

"Yes, well, I prefer Charlie Grace. Mrs. Doucet makes me sound incredibly old, dear. Let's see who gets called their preference first, shall we?" With that delightful retort, she turned on her heel and beckoned us to follow her. "Honey, leave your luggage. Jacques' friend Glenn is here with his family. Let those boys get your bags later. Lord knows they need something to do with their time besides play those God forsaken games all night long."

As we followed Charlie Grace inside, I began to explain the Thanksgiving ritual to Sam. Glenn, his wife, and their three children would come up from the gulf nearly each fall. Jacques and he traded hospitalities dependent on the sporting season. We had a more ample place to deer or duck hunt while Glenn had a large saltwater fishing boat off the coast. Charlie Grace would play hostess to her guests which usually allowed me time to slip away. I assured Sam we would have plenty of time to escape the house during our stay.

Sam and I stepped inside. I stopped midsentence as I smelled the scent of cooking basil, oregano, and thyme. Sam seemed engrossed in looking at the home's accents of rich browns, oranges, and reds as the rooms were fashionably decorated for the season.

"Dinner will not be ready for another hour or so. Let's go into the parlor with the other guests for coffee," Mother said.

The night before Thanksgiving, Mother always prepared some type of pasta dish. She left our tastes craving for the turkey and trimmings until the final hour at hand. Tonight she had prepared crawfish and shrimp stuffed pasta shells. The smell of sautéed garlic, green peppers, and onions permeated nicely through the halls.

"Coffee? Isn't it a little late for coffee?" Sam whispered in my ear.

I chuckled at her unfamiliarity to our family traditions. "Not this coffee."

As if on cue, Mother handed us each a large fluted mug topped with whipped cream. I sipped mine slowly, savoring the sting of the Irish whiskey as it trickled down my throat.

Sam followed suit. Her eyes widened as the first taste touched her lips. She took another small sip. "Mmmmmm." She gave a satisfied smile. "Now *that* is coffee."

Dinner ran late into the evening as we all enjoyed the conversations mixed among the Irish coffees. Sam possessed a natural talent of seeming at ease in her surroundings. She joined in the discussions without hesitation. I was at ease in watching her. Her laughter turned into giggles as the whiskey took effect. Her steps were slightly staggered down the hallway to our rooms. Charlie Grace had her bags delivered to the room next door to mine. A shared bathroom adjoined the two rooms.

"This is you," I said, opening the door to her room. "I'm right next door and through the bathroom if you need anything."

"Oh, I need something al—" She snapped her mouth shut. "A shower . . . I need to grab one before I go to bed? I feel icky."

"Icky?"

"It's a highly technical term. I'm not surprised you don't use it." Sam gave a tipsy giggle and followed me into the bathroom. She let her hip rest against the counter as I pointed out the linens and toiletries for her to use.

"That should do it. I'll see you in the morning," I said.

"Hey, Stormy," she said, now leaning her head against the door. Her stare focused on me with intent. "I've had a great day." She smiled shyly. "Good night."

"Me too. Good night." I smiled broadly as I turned into my room.

My eyes were closed to the sights above my bed. Yet my ears were fully open to the sounds behind the closed door. I heard the unobstructed stream of water flowing freely from the shower and hitting the tiled wall. The sound of denim falling to the floor followed. I envisioned the sight of her legs being stripped of the jeans as they crumpled to the floor. I heard a soft click of the shower door closing before I noted the changing sound of the shower's flow.

Waves of visions flooded my thoughts as I pictured the nudeness of the body impeding its flow. I pictured the stream of water flowing from her hair down the small of her back carrying the soapy lather with it as it trailed down her legs. Attempting to muffle the torment of the sounds, I buried my head deep in the pillows. *It's final. I've got a serious crush on Dr. Sam LeJeune.*

And then there was silence but for a single tapping against the door—soft . . . quiet . . . shy.

"Good night, Stormy. Sweet dreams," Sam whispered through the door.

Dreams I was now quite sure would happen—dreams of kissing the lips of the whispered voice. *Sweet or tortuous, it could go either way.*

CHAPTER 19

AFTER A RESTLESS night, I opened my eyes to see the bathroom door remained shut. How I had wished for the bravery through the quiet of the night to change that closed door. I wished for the strength to climb into bed next to her as the sun peeked through the eastern windows. How I longed to lie next to her, smelling the scent of morning on her skin. Yet Sam's words of not wishing to lose our friendship echoed through my mind as I suppressed those desires. Hadn't she said she didn't wish for us to cross that impasse for the morning it would bring? Denying my body's longing was in essence granting Sam's wishes. Being honest with myself I knew I wasn't prepared for the meaning of my desires. I tabled those thoughts yet again as I went downstairs in search of coffee.

The kitchen had been remodeled with a modern style. Charlie Grace specially ordered the restaurant quality appliances. A large ten-foot island centered the space between the kitchen and breakfast nook. Along the back of it was an elevation to the countertop which allowed for bar seating with a sink and prep area in the center.

Cora and Flossie were diligently working around the gas stove. Flossie stood tall and slender with the top of her head almost touching the copper vent hood hanging from the ceiling. The shorter more roundish Cora stood next to her and was doing most of the talking. Her mouth was moving nearly as fast as her arm briskly whisked the contents of the bowl in front of her.

I walked into the kitchen and heard their musings as they puttered about the kitchen. Charlie Grace had met Cora and Flossie during one of her Ladies' League outings to Magnolia Assisted Living. She realized soon after meeting them that they had no family to spend the holidays with. In her ever present unselfish actions, she started bringing them to our house for Thanksgiving week. Of course, they were free help with the decorating, shopping, and cooking of the feast. Yet somehow Charlie Grace managed to make it seem she was a humanitarian, offering the elderly ladies a place to go when they had nowhere else to be.

I listened to their chatter for a few minutes. "Good morning, Miss Flossie . . . Miss Cora."

They turned in unison toward me.

"Shit fire and save the matches if'n Charlie Grace's daughter hadn't come home!" Flossie was at least five foot eight. I imagined she must have been close to five foot ten before her elder years began to shrink her.

"I see you're already up working away this morning," I said. "Is the general still getting her beauty rest?"

"Good Lawd, child, if you ain't the spitting image of Addie when she was young and sass like you." Cora laughed as she hugged me tightly.

My nose was tickled with the crispness of her recently styled hair held firmly in place with a healthy dose of hair spray. Each time I saw her, the color of her hair varied somewhere between blue and gray. Cora was the epitome of pleasantly plump. She was at least fifty pounds overweight with half of that carried in her chest. A hug from her squeezed the very air from my lungs.

"Adelaide's old ass may be as wrinkled as ours, Cora, but she's still full of piss and vinegar." Flossie pushed up the sleeves of her oversized button-down shirt as she raised her arms to hug me.

"Now you try to be nice to yo' momma this year. She's worried herself into a tizzy, trying to make everything perfect for you and yo' little friend," Cora said, defending Charlie Grace as always. She shook her finger at me as she spoke, which caused the brightly colored one piece dress hanging from her chest like a tent to shake as well. She once told me Thanksgiving was her favorite time of the year because she got to spend the entire week with my family. "You take a seat while I get you some coffee. You can tell us all about your schooling while we finish up this here dinner."

Footsteps rounding the corner caught Cora's attention as she turned toward the coffee pot.

Mother walked into the kitchen with Sam shadowing close behind. "Good morning. You ladies plop down there next to Rayne. I'll gets you some coffee."

Sam looked more beautiful today than I had ever seen her. She wore a purple-striped button-down pajama set. Her hair was loosely tied in a ponytail with waves of light, blond curls falling about her face. She turned to me to catch my eyes with hers. I swayed within the blue waves of their color. The sounds of the kitchen faded from my consciousness as I lost myself to her. *Oh yeah, it's a definite crush.*

Memaw ungraciously slung open the kitchen door as she wrestled with a rectangular box in her arms, jarring me out of my enchantment.

"You lost all your manners up there with the Yankees, Sis? Making a poor old lady struggle!" Memaw wore an ear-to-ear smile.

"Memaw. I do believe Alabama is still considered the South." I rushed to her aid, took the box from her, and put it on the table. I returned to her arms for a hug and breathed into my soul the scent of brown sugar and honey. The number of hugs I had already received since arriving well out numbered ten, yet this rivaled them all. It wasn't a hug as much as it was being held. She *held* me to her.

"Damn, Sis, you're a sight for sore eyes." Her eyes glistened with the collection of a single escaping tear.

I sighed deeply. "You too, Meems. You too." I held her briefly in my stare before looking at Sam. "I want you to meet a friend of mine, Sam Lejeune. Sam, this is Addie Cormier, my Memaw."

"It's a pleasure to meet you, Mrs. Cormier," Sam said.

"They call me Memaw around here, Sam." Unlike the others, Memaw didn't make the gesture of offering a hug. The apple not falling far from the tree, we hugged those we knew and wished to share our space . . . not ones we just met.

Memaw walked to the table with the box of delicious fried pastries. "I knew these two old hens wouldn't be a feeding you this morning, so I stopped at Sugar Bakers on my way over. Crazy heifer says this was one of her busiest mornings of the year. Got us some beignets to go with that coffee I'm a smelling."

"Don't you come in here with your catty insults, Addie," Cora said. "I don't need yo' lip a flapping at me on this beautiful morning."

"Why, Cora. Y'know that flapping is all saggy tits over there can do. Flap, flap, flap," Flossie said as she gestured with her hands over her breasts. The raspy changes to her voice from years of smoking added to the effect of her sarcasm. I hadn't honestly ever seen a cigarette held in between her fingers but she had the voice of a woman who had smoked for years.

"Oh good Lord, you three. Must I remind you that we have a guest in our home?" Charlie Grace interrupted in true scolding school teacher fashion. "Samantha, please accept my apologies on behalf of these three women who have forgotten the manners taught them."

"I was rather enjoying the entertainment, *Mrs. Doucet*," Sam said.

Damn I like this woman!

Fine granules of powdered sugar escaped into the air as Memaw opened the box of heavenly goodies. The coffee pot brewed another carafe as we all sat around the breakfast table. Cora and Flossie stopped their cooking to join us. They all four fired off questions to Sam and me about the school's program before turning their attentions solely on Sam's aspirations and future endeavors.

I sipped my coffee and felt Sam's knee rest against mine. I nearly choked with the surprise of the touch of our fabric-covered skin. The warmth it elicited in me was as if we were touching skin against skin. I panicked and wondered if the whole table could see the blush I felt rising to my cheeks. Never before had I encountered the same worries when a part of Grant's body rested against mine. Many times at our meals our arms laid side by side, skin upon skin yet not with the same response in me.

"So, Samantha, tell us more about you. Why is it that you aren't with your family this holiday?" Charlie Grace asked.

"Jesus, Mother. Subtle much?" I yelled, astounded at the audacity of her question.

"Do *not* use the Lord's name in that manner in this house, Rayne Amber Storm. I'll not have that here."

"No, it's okay, Stormy," Sam said. "*Mrs. Doucet*, my father is away at a medical conference. My mother invited me to go with her to our beach house. But how could I have gone there and resisted Rayne's invitation to spend Thanksgiving with her lovely family?" A bit of syrup seemed to fall from her lips as her tone was entirely too sweet.

Damn, I really like this woman!

"Is your father a physician, dear?" Charlie Grace asked, ignoring to respond to Sam's comment. I believe she probably sensed the sarcasm as well.

"Yes, ma'am. He's a cardiothoracic surgeon at Emory in Atlanta."

"Oh, my Lord alive. You do *not* mean to tell me your father is Dr. Edward LeJeune, the physician who developed that new heart device thing, do you?" Her voice escalated in her excitement.

We all looked at her in surprise.

"Yes, ma'am. That's him. You've heard of him?"

"I knew your last name sounded familiar." Charlie Grace gave me a solid slap across my shoulder. "Your father spoke at a Woman's Health Conference I orchestrated a few years ago. He's a brilliant, charming man. How dare you not tell me this, Rayne."

"I didn't realize this was information you needed to know, Mother. Sam is here as a guest . . . not her father."

"Don't be coy with me. I'm so very pleased you have met such a wonderful young lady to be friends with. That's all I'm saying."

"Uh huh, Mother. I hear ya."

"So, Sam. Do you have a special man waiting for you back at school like our Grant?" Cora asked, coming to Mother's rescue as I was sure she sensed an impending argument.

"No, ma'am. There is but one Grant at school and Rayne has staked her claim to him."

"Don't encourage them, Sam, or they'll have you in a bridesmaid dress faster than you can imagine, especially now that you'll be bringing a world-renowned surgeon to the guest list," I said. "Mother is nearly salivating over there as it is already. She won't be happy until I'm married, barefoot, and pregnant."

"Well, ladies, the boys will be in from the deer stands soon. We best get back to our cooking," Cora said as she pulled Flossie to her feet.

"Yep, back to it. Thanks for the sweets, sour puss. Now get your flabby ass up and go fry that bird." Flossie ran her slender fingers through her short-cropped silver hair.

Unlike Cora, Flossie didn't seem to spend much time on her appearance. She reminded me of a true farm girl. She dressed as if she could be found in the fields at any given moment. Truth be known, she probably wished she were back there half the time.

"We should all be getting dressed as well." Charlie Grace stood from the table. "Samantha, I look forward to getting better acquainted after the hustle and bustle has died down. I've booked us a reservation at the club Saturday night."

Warning Sam of my impeding lie, I clasped her hand under the table. "I'm sorry, Mother. We'll be leaving early Saturday morning."

"What? Why?" Charlie Grace said, setting her empty coffee cup down with a thud on the table.

My attention was drawn to the feeling of Sam's thumb tracing over the skin of my hand she now firmly held. "We need to stop off to see some of Sam's friends on the way back to school."

Her hand felt proper within mine as if it was designed to fit. Grant's had always felt overpowering to me. Friends had described a feeling of comfort when holding a man's hand. I did not—nor had I ever described it that way, not to them and not to myself. Bulky, that was how I described it. His large hand always squeezed mine, spreading apart my fingers in an uncomfortable fashion. Sam's molded into mine.

"Funny thing . . . I don't remember any friends I need to visit," Sam said, looking over her shoulder as we walked up the stairs to our rooms. "Do you mind telling me where we're going?"

"We're going to my happy place." I couldn't resist smiling. "Come to think of it, you'll be the first person I have taken there. In fact you'll be only one of three to know it even exists."

Sam stopped and looked back at me. She rested her back against the long curved stair railing. "No one knows? Not your Mother?"

"Nope."

"Not Grant?"

"Nope. No one."

Sam turned back and resumed walking up the stairs. "Mmmm . . . hmmm. Interesting."

WE WALKED TOGETHER in silence in the autumn air. The quiet was broken up by the crackle of fallen leaves beneath our feet and the rustling of leaves left on the branches above us as the breeze gently blew. Our steps were slow and rhythmic as we walked under the brilliant shades of reds, yellows, and oranges.

The sky's backdrop was filled with a bright blue and clear of any clouds. Our bodies were side by side nearly sharing the warmth between us. Sam's scent was carried in the current of the wind. It had become an intoxicating smell to me. I drank upon it the desire it stirred within me.

The trail dividing the pecan orchard from the thickened forest of hardwood and pine trees was my favorite to walk on the plantation. What remained of an old home was at the end of the dirt path. The grayed wooden logs of the structure were worn and warped with age. Its four walls were covered with a rusted tin roof.

"I used to come here when I was a kid," I said as Sam walked up the stone step and ran her hand along the frame as she entered the doorway. "I would sit for hours, imagining what it must have been like to live here back in the day it was built."

"I can see why," she said. "This place is amazing. To live in a time like this. The peace, the comfort of a life made by your own hands."

I walked to the stone fireplace built into the far back wall. It was deep and wide. "Can you picture cooking your meals right here?"

She walked to the fireplace and stood a foot away from me. "No, honestly I can't. Up until recently, I wouldn't necessarily call life peaceful." She leaned against the wall. "Thank you for bringing me here."

"You're welcome. I . . . I'm glad you're here, Sam."

"Me too," she said as she slid her fingers over the palm of my hand.

I felt the strength of her hand pulling me closer to her. I couldn't speak. I couldn't do anything—anything other than take the step closer as she pulled me to her. She pushed herself off of the wall and stood inches from me. Her eyes darted back and forth as she looked at me. She pulled me tightly into her arms and held me there. I rested my head against her shoulder as we swayed together in the quiet. I didn't know what it meant to her to be pulled into her like this. At that moment I didn't care. I breathed in the innocence of our caress and let it fill me with a peace I had never known.

She released me from her embrace to walk through the doorway and sit on the upper wooden step leading off of the porch. The current of a small creek with its water flowing over moss-covered rocks would normally have been a soothing backdrop. Not today. Not at the moment anyway. I didn't know what to say—where to take this conversation or if I could even take it anywhere beyond the stuttering of a nervous woman.

Thankfully she was the first to speak when I sat down next to her. "I have to force myself to remember, you know? Remember reality. A reality of a guy that your family and friends practically have you marrying. It's just . . ." She stopped and looked at the creek.

"Just what?" I asked.

Sam turned and looked me deep in the eyes. "Just those. Those gorgeous green eyes of yours. Sometimes when you look at me, they tell me you want me as much as I want you. Sometimes I swear they hold me as if I can almost feel you reaching for me. It's times like those that make me forget. When reminders slap me in the face I have to refocus on reality."

"Is that why you disappear or pull away from me?"

Sam smirked. "Yeah, pretty much."

Angry at myself, I was still lost for words. *What do I say? How much do I reveal?*

"Stormy, can I ask you something?"

"Anything."

"That night at Sapphire." She hesitated. "Did you want me to kiss you?"

I opened my mouth to answer but she put her finger across my lips.

"Wait . . . don't answer that." She shook her head. "I don't think I want to know. Not sure I could handle yes or no at this point. Either answer may change this trip, and I'm having too good of a time to do that. Fuck, I don't know why I keep coming back to this damn topic anyway." She looked at me with pleading eyes. "Can we forget I said anything?"

Anything. I'd give you anything to not see the look in those eyes again.

CHAPTER 20

"WHAT IN TARNATION are you doing, you crazy damn heifer?" Memaw's voice carried high through the well-manicured path that took us back to the house.

Sam and I broke into a sprint toward the voices. We found them at the clearing behind the house. The three women stood around a metal pot resting over a large gas burner. Memaw and Flossie were flailing their arms while Cora stood in between them turning her head from side to side as each of them spoke.

"I'm a fixin yo' damn mistake. That's what I'm a doing!" Flossie yelled back.

The seam of her faded blue jeans stopped a couple of inches above her bare ankles. She stomped her white Keds tennis shoes in the grass to emphasize her point.

"The only thing you fixin' is my temper," Memaw said. "Look at my grease popping out everywhere."

"You gotta have hot grease to fry this damn bird, you stubborn ole' mule!"

Hot grease was popping in every direction around the pot. Cora squealed, rubbed her face, and jumped to the side of the spewing pot. The grass underneath the flame had already deepened in color from the heat.

"Ladies . . . ladies," I stepped in between them, "please let's calm down a bit."

Sam walked up to stand behind Cora. She was obviously fearful of the hot grease as it continued to spit out over the rim of the boiling pot.

"This ain't her bird, baby girl," Memaw said. "Frying this turkey is what I do for dinner. She needs to take her meddling hands back to the kitchen where she be belongin'."

"It ain't a gonna be much of a Thanksgiving without a bird fittin' to eat," Flossie said.

I looked through the plume of smoke to see Sam giggling. *Smoke? Is that smoke?* I quickly realized the origin was the side of Cora's head. The thickened white line of smoke stretched from her hair into the sky above.

"Hey! What is that gosh awful smell?" Flossie said, looking around.

"Cora!" I grabbed the dish towel from Memaw's hands and patted the side of Cora's head. A baseball-sized clump of hair fell to the ground as the remaining burnt strands curled toward her scalp.

"Aaaaaahhhh!" Cora screamed. "My hair! You done burnt up my hair!" The tears flowed and formed a heavy mask of mascara around her eyes.

Sam turned quickly away, hiding her laughter and leaving me to face Cora without showing my own desires to join her. I turned Cora's head to the side to make sure she didn't have any burns to her skin. Nope, nothing there except for the residual matted hair and stench from burning. I put my arm around the sobbing Cora to comfort her.

"Oh hell, Cora. We'll run and get you another one of your wigs before dinner," Memaw said.

"This ain't no damn wig, you mangy-no-good-for-nothing cow," Cora said. "This my real hair."

Memaw looked at Cora with surprise. "How come it's so stiff then?"

Flossie could hold her laughter no longer. "Maybe we should a coated yo' turkey in Cora's hair spray, Addie. That a given it a nice, crispy crust."

Memaw and Flossie doubled over laughing as Cora ran off cursing them both for the heathens they were. By the time Sam faced us, she had fresh tears running down her cheeks and her laughter broke free. I had no more strength to fight my own laughter at that point.

IN THE EVENING we dined on Thanksgiving trimmings. Charlie Grace reserved a banquet hall table for all of us to sit around. The centerpiece and settings were gorgeous under the sun porch. The colors of fall decorations were along the linens and draperies. Candlesticks had small sprigs of wheat tied together with a string of rope twine. All together we must have had thirty people dining with us.

Sam and I sat at the far end of the table lost in our own conversations. Occasionally Cora and Flossie would break our concentration as they flitted around the table and made sure each guest had plenty of food on their plates and wine in their glasses. Cora tried to hide the bare spot in her hair by picking the hair around it. Unfortunately the hair spray kept returning the hairs right back to where they originally were. Occasionally they returned to their chairs beside Memaw to enjoy their own meals. All three of the women pecked at their food like little birds. Flossie and Memaw were an odd pair to describe. Apparently, I wasn't the only one who noticed.

"Look at those two," Sam said.

Flossie and Memaw's heads were thrown back in laughter. Memaw gripped Flossie's shoulder to not fall backward out of the chair. We couldn't hear what they were saying. Undoubtedly it was over the burning of Cora's hair because their eyes kept resting on Cora's head. Cora apparently sensed this as well and slapped both of them in the back of the head as she walked behind their chairs.

I lost myself in watching their laughter. I felt an overpowering love for Memaw as I took in the joy in her face. I was amazed by how just watching people laughing from across the room and not hearing the words that brought them to their happiness could cause the same feelings of happiness in me.

"Well, now, look at you." Sam's smile was brilliant as she looked at me. "Do you know how much you light up when you're around her? You're a beautiful woman, but the smile on your face, the way you look at her, the peace you show this very moment . . . mmmm . . . makes you quite breathtaking." She took a long sip of wine as her eyes held me over the rim of the glass.

I felt a blush rise to my cheeks. Fearful it was a glowing beacon for all to see, I looked around the table to ensure the attention of everyone hadn't focused on me—on us.

"And now the blush . . . adorable. Don't worry. No one is paying attention to us."

I hated I looked around to see if anyone was watching or listening to us. Not that I was ashamed of Sam at all. It was more my own fears of someone being able to read my eyes when I looked at her. I feared I wasn't keeping my feelings hidden very well.

"I can't wait to spend more time with your grandmother. So I can see more of this side of you."

"You'll love her, Sam," I said. "She's an amazing woman."

"If she's anything like the woman sitting next to me, I know I will."

Memaw wiped the joyful tears from her eyes as her and Flossie's laughter died down. Memaw noticed we were looking at her and she winked at us.

I FOUND SAM sitting in one of the rocking chairs on the upstairs balcony that spanned the back of the house. She had excused herself early from the after dinner conversation to call and wish her parents a Happy Thanksgiving. She rocked methodically in the chair as she stared out across the grounds. The landscape was sparsely visible under the moonlit sky.

"I thought you might could use one of these," I said, holding up a six pack of cold beer.

"Or all of them," she said with a half-hearted smile.

"That bad, huh?"

"Not really. I got Dad's voice mail but I did talk to Mom. Her speech was surprisingly coherent . . . slurred, but . . . coherent. She says she's going to pay for my residency because," she made quotation marks in the air, "no daughter of hers was going to sling burgers for a living."

"Yikes." I sat down in the rocking chair next to hers and pulled it closer to hand her a beer. "Looks like I may be stealing more beer before the night is over."

"Nah, I'm okay. It's nothing new. Besides now I get my school paid for. That is if I want it."

"What do you mean if you want it?"

"I don't know, Stormy. You've changed me where that's concerned." She looked at me and popped open the beer. "Well . . . where a few things are concerned."

"Oh yeah? How so?"

"After the way they've acted, I think I may want to do this on my own. Dr. Breaker took care of the residency part and I heard back from the Financial Aid office. Turns out there are some student loans with pretty good interest rates I qualify for. I'll owe

out the ass by the time I'm done but it may be worth it to be free
of them."

"Free of them? Do you really want that?" I asked.

"I don't know. Maybe for a while I do. At least for right now.
I don't have to take the loans every year if I change my mind."

"No, you don't. You can take it day by day," I said, taking a
long swallow from the can. "You said I changed you in a few
ways. What other ways?"

Sam stared out into the darkness over the balcony while the
crickets played their violins to the night. She turned to me and
cocked her head. Her lips twitched as if they were either struggling
to keep the words back or trying to form the exact ones to use.
Instead of speaking they formed the most incredible smile.

"What?" I said. "What are you thinking?"

"I'm thinking I might need to keep those to myself," she said.
"At least for the time being."

"Come on. You can't do that to me."

"I can and I am." She smiled again. "So . . . Flossie and Cora
are together, huh?"

I spit the mouthful of beer out across the porch. "What?"

"You know. They're lezes."

I laughed too loudly for a house full of sleeping guests.
"They're what?"

"Aw, come on. Like you haven't noticed it or at least thought
it. I mean look at them."

"They are *so* not lesbians. I've known those two since I was a
teenager. They're little sweet old ladies that are very good friends
and that's all."

"Uh huh . . . sure they are," she said in a sarcastic tone. "You
don't think they get busy over there at the home? If the bed's
a'rockin . . ."

I couldn't help but to laugh at her accusations. "Ummm . . . no.
Seriously Sam, they're not. They are both widows. Neither one of
them had any children before their husbands passed away."

"How did it happen?"

"Cora's husband had a heart attack in his early fifties. I think
they had tried to have children but never did. Now Flossie's . . .
Flossie's was different. She and her husband had a big farm they
worked. One day he thought something bit him but never saw

a snake or anything so he kept working. Apparently his leg got infected but he wouldn't go see a doctor. By the time Flossie got one to come look at her husband, the leg had turned gangrenous and he was septic. He wouldn't let them amputate. She never left his bedside. Even after he passed, Memaw said she had to drag Flossie away."

"Wow. That's tough," Sam said. "So neither of them ever married again?"

"No," I said, "they didn't back then. You married once and that was that. Memaw's the same. She never even looked at another man after Papaw passed."

"Ha. Hell, I think my mother would bring a date to Dad's funeral."

"You don't mean that. Do you?"

"Afraid I do. They're only married because it would cost too much for them to get a divorce. I've always wondered if they had some type of spoken arrangement. They're only together when appearances force them to be. Dad has an apartment in downtown Atlanta. He's hardly ever home anymore."

"Sam, I'm so sorry. That must hurt. No wonder you didn't want to go home."

She looked at me briefly before gazing back out into the night sky. The night was eerily quiet except for the crickets. Usually there were other random animal sounds but not tonight. "Do you remember me telling you why I was kicked out of Emory?"

"Yes."

"Do you wanna know the whole story?"

"If you want to tell me I do," I said and I believe I meant it.

My mind had invented many different scenarios of the supply closet rendezvous. Of course the sex of Sam's partner changed after the night I met Claire. Although, I believe it was easier for me to imagine a male than a female as the latter made me all the more jealous.

"I do and I don't." She sighed heavily. "She was one of the brightest, sexiest CT attendees Emory had seen in years. She soared through medical school and her residency. During her fellowship is when her career really took off. Administration and the higher-ups were nearly salivating to make her a part of the department permanently."

"I can see why you were interested in her."

Sam positioned herself in the chair to face me. "Yes, I was pretty taken with her. I think it was the first time in a long time someone had my attention like that. She was special, different than most of his residents."

"Oh, she was one of his students."

"In more ways than one."

"I don't understand."

"Dear ol' Dad had other lessons he aimed to teach her. He had her marked as his next conquest the minute he realized I was dating her. It was disgusting to me the way he so blatantly flirted with her. He was twice her age and married to my mother for Christ's sake. I thought he was making a fool of himself the way he swooned over her. The way he opened all of the doors for her at Emory. That is until I realized I was the fool. I'm not sure when the affair started but at some point it did." Sam looked down at the pillow next to her. She tugged at a loose string dangling from its corner and then clutched the pillow tightly to her chest. "One day I surprised him at his apartment and there she was dressed in nothing but his shirt. I was sick, Rayne. Literally sick to my stomach. I was sick of him and everything about him."

I rested my hand on her shoulder, hoping to relax the squeeze she had on the pillow. "You don't have to tell me anymore if you don't want to."

The lights shining over the porch kept Sam's face from being completely shadowed by the night. I could see her eyes searching mine. "No . . . I want to. Strange as it is to me . . . I want you to know me. The real me. Sometimes that scares me because it's new for me and well . . ." She looked over my shoulder out into the lawn. "I'm scared you'll run off."

I lightly squeezed her arm. "I'm not going anywhere."

She covered my hand with hers and brought it down to rest under hers on top of the pillow she now had laying across her lap. "Where was I?"

"You were telling me about finding her at your dad's apartment but was this after you were caught with her at the hospital?"

"Before," she said flatly.

"Okay, so I think I'm confused. When did the hospital come in?"

"She started calling me the minute she left his apartment that day, trying to convince me she had only had the affair because she was afraid she would lose her residency spot. She swore it was over. Swore she would never do anything like that again."

"Did you believe her?"

"Not for one second. At that point though, I couldn't have cared less for her. All I thought about was getting back at him. I wanted to embarrass him . . . to bring shame to the LeJeune name at that hospital. And I didn't care who got hurt in the process. I pretended everything was okay between us. Pretended I forgave her. I took her into that closet, knowing damn good and well we would be caught. I would have left Emory had they not asked me to leave. I was . . . so . . . disgusted with myself. I didn't want any chance to see her or him again. It was when I resigned that dad stepped in to have me transferred. I guess the embarrassment of me screwing his little slut wasn't as big as me dropping out of school." She squeezed my hand. "So there you have it. The real dirt."

I didn't know what to say. I was still trying to absorb what she said when I heard her shift in the chair.

She moved her hand from the top of mine. "It's who I am. It's what I am."

"Why do you say that?" I asked.

"Because I used that girl. I didn't care for her at that point. I had sex with her in a supply closet, knowing what it would do . . . hoping for what it would do to both of them really. Doesn't very well make me a good person now, does it?"

"Doesn't make you a bad person either," I said. "It makes you a woman hurt by her father and a woman she cared about. Yes, your actions can not be excluded or made right but you were hurt by betrayal. I believe we learn from our mistakes."

We sat in silence for several minutes, the night noises of the crickets rising up around us. "Sam?"

"Hmmmm?"

"Would you do it again?"

Sam's chest rose deeply and fell before she pinched the bridge of her nose. "No, I wouldn't. Not like that."

"Not like that?"

"I wouldn't use someone like that again but I can't say I think of sex any differently."

"So is that why you don't date anyone seriously?" I asked. "Is it because you got hurt by them?"

"I can't honestly say that. Would be a good excuse I guess but I've always been somewhat of a pig when it comes to sex. Sex is sex. Never really more than that."

"Shouldn't it be?"

"Is it for you?"

Now I was the one looking out into the night sky.

CHAPTER 21

TO APPEASE CHARLIE Grace after I cancelled Saturday's dinner reservations, I subjected Sam to a day of Black Friday shopping downtown. The city's largest population of shoppers would focus on the chain stores. They were notorious for putting on ridiculous sales in order to attract customers. But there were a select few that found their way to the quaint downtown area. Generally it was the same crowd every year so it was as much of a social gathering as a shopping event. Which was why I knew Charlie Grace would settle for this instead of dinner at the club.

Honestly, there had to be some means for her to show off her daughter's new friend—you know, the daughter of a famous heart surgeon. Sam was a pro at the formality of introductions and appeared to be experienced in the spectacle in which airs were put on. She gave a respectful smile and polite responses to each she met. But I was the one gifted with the brightest of her smiles.

I was surprised by Sam's girlish humor. On the exterior she was this composed, confident woman I had come to know back in Alabama. I suppose we both let Louisiana show a different side to ourselves as here her humor began to flourish, allowing me to see its goofiness. She would contort her expressions into funny faces when we were pulled away from each other by Charlie Grace. On several occasions, it was damn near impossible not to burst out laughing. This side made her all the more appealing to me. It was one of the first days in forever with Charlie Grace where I found myself not wanting the day to end.

We stopped in at Sugar Bakers for a small break of dessert and coffee. Sam's eyes widened in excitement at the warmed peach cobbler served with a topping of pralines and cream ice cream.

"Oh, I have *got* to have that," she said.

"Honey child, you ain't eva gonna be the same once you taste it!" Mrs. Bell exclaimed in her usual fashion.

Charlie Grace reached her hand out for Sam to come stand next to her. "Samantha, I want you to meet Mrs. Imogene Bell.

She owns this little bakery and is one of my dearest friends in the Ladies League." She turned to Mrs. Bell and squeezed her shoulder. Mother stood a whopping five foot tall so she was generally three to four inches shorter than most. The phrase "dynamite comes in small packages" was definitely coined with her in mind. "Imogene, this is Samantha LeJeune. She came with Rayne to celebrate Thanksgiving with us."

Mrs. Bell's smile spread wide across her face. "Aaaawww, Samantha. It's so good to meet you. We love our little Rayne Amber. Any friend of hers is a friend of mine. The peach cobbler is on me!"

"You don't have to do that Mrs. Bell and she likes to be called Sam," I said.

"Nonsense! It's my pleasure! That is if Sam thinks she can hold another bite? I know the spread Charlie Grace lays out for Thanksgiving. I 'magine a tiny little thing like yourself is pretty full from those fixin's."

Sam raised her eyebrows fully. "Oh, I can handle *that*." She looked over the counter at the peach cobbler.

"Mrs. Bell, I have learned Sam can always make room for sweets." I stood next to Sam at the counter and pointed to the peach cobbler. "Although I'm thinking I could handle a piece of that too."

Charlie Grace locked her arm around Mrs. Bell's as they walked over to the counter. "Samantha's father is Edward LeJeune. Do you remember him, Imogene? You remember the cardiothoracic surgeon who came down from Atlanta to do our talk on heart disease?"

Mrs. Bell looked back over her shoulder at Sam. "Oh! I sure do! He was an excellent speaker. And oh my, was he ever easy on the eyes!"

"Thank you, Mrs. Bell. I'll be sure to tell him," Sam said.

"Be sure that you do and after you taste this cobbler I suspect you'll want to bring him back with you so he can have some. Only dear," Mrs. Bell paused from working behind the counter to look up at Sam, "give an old lady some warning before you walk in here with him. I'm afraid my heart couldn't take a surprise like that."

Sam laughed.

I could tell it was a forced laugh but I don't think the other two noticed over their own cackling.

"I sure will," she said.

"Looks like those beautiful blue eyes of his were heredity." Mrs. Bell winked at Sam.

Sam blushed. She actually blushed. *Adorable.*

"Thank you, ma'am," she said.

Mrs. Bell brought four servings to the table, and promptly sat down with her own helping to join us. She slid a plate over to Sam. "Let your taste buds rejoice, my dear!"

Sam dipped her spoon into the cobbler first and then ran it along the top of the ice cream. The pralines slid from the melting ice cream and dripped freely off of her spoon. Her lips curled into a smile as she brought the spoon to her mouth. I was transfixed on her every movement. She put the entire spoonful in her mouth.

"Oh, dear God." Her eyes rolled back in her head and she gripped the edge of the table with her free hand. "That's incredible."

Mrs. Bell's face lit up with pride. Her smile was beaming. "That, my dear, would be an old family recipe! I put up the peaches myself every year."

Sam devoured the dessert–her words replaced with a few groans of pleasure.

"I tell you. I don't know what that girl's gonna do with herself!" Mrs. Bell began talking to Charlie Grace about her granddaughter, Gentry—named after Mrs. Bell's maiden name.

Gentry had always been artistically talented. To be truthful, she was a natural. When she was sixteen she was accepted into a gifted arts program in Savannah, Georgia. The school recruited high school students starting their junior year into their accelerated program. Their education completed the basic requirements for a high school diploma yet they added hours into the student's coursework to include a multitude of art courses. This plucked young teenagers from their homes of parental guidance to live on a college campus with very little supervision. Gentry basked in her newfound freedom, taking full advantage of it and vowing never to return to our little town.

"Lawd, that child done colored her hair blue!" Mrs. Bell continued. "Blue! What girl wants blue hair? I told her, the paint go on the paper, child, not on yo' hair! I do declare if I was the

kinda woman to color my hair, I would have to on the account a
she making my gray hair turn plum-near white!"

Charlie Grace and I shared a glance, both of us knowing Mrs.
Bell kept a standing appointment with Myrtle at Hair Addictions
every Friday afternoon. A few times I was unlucky enough to
catch Mrs. Bell leaving the salon after her hair had been freshly
colored. She spent at least ten minutes telling me how she didn't
have the heart to tell Myrtle something must be wrong with her
shampoo as the color of her hair seemed different every time after
her shampoo and set. She would later tell me that if she wasn't
such a fine Christian woman she would have asked Myrtle not to
use it anymore. I was never quite sure what being a Christian and
hair dye had in common but I didn't dare argue as I would have
surely been kept another ten minutes.

"I was always partial to purple," Sam said.

We all three looked at her. I nearly spit my bite of cobbler out.
She had a healthy dollop of ice cream dead center on the tip of
her nose.

"Honey, you s'posed to eat it, not wear it!" Mrs. Bell laughed.

Sam looked at me and winked. "Maybe I was saving that bite
for later, Mrs. Bell."

After dessert we walked next door to find Charlie Grace a hat
to wear to her next charity brunch. Of course, she dragged me to
the back of the store so I could give my opinion as to which one
looked the best on her. Charlie Grace became distracted, talking
to the sales lady, and I wandered back toward the front of the store
to look for Sam.

"Howdy, ma'am," a dusky voice whispered low in my ear, "I'd
sure like to butter your muffin."

"Excuse me." I snapped my head around but instead of cussing
the offender I broke out into a belly laugh. There in front of me
and grinning ear to ear was Sam dressed in Dickie brand blue jean
overalls and a plaid long sleeve western shirt. She had left one of
the overall gold metal clasps undone so the material on that side
folded down across her chest.

"So is that a yes?" she said, arching her eyebrow as she tipped
the brim of her straw hat.

"That's a yes to you're crazy," I said.

She laughed and turned back to walk into the dressing room.

"Oh and Sam," I called to her.

"Yeah?"

"Memaw has that exact outfit."

"You're shitting me." She laughed.

"I shit you not."

AFTER LEAVING THE store, I walked Sam down the sidewalk to the main focus of Charlie Grace's renovation project. The entire downtown had been renovated with a few different courtyards scattered throughout the area. The one I was directing Sam to was the largest one of them all and it just so happened to be in front of Lagniappe. In the center was a big water fountain surrounded by a landscaped bed of annual flowers.

Sam sat on the stone ledge and patted the spot next to her. "This place is really quite nice for a small downtown area."

I sat next to her. "You are looking at Charlie Grace's downtown beautification project."

"Well, it's fabulous. I really like how they left the trees and built the sidewalk area around them. What's that place over there?" she said, pointing toward the restaurant. "I love those patio tables around that large tree."

"That's our restaurant Lagniappe."

"Your restaurant?"

"No, I actually should have said Charlie Grace's," I said sarcastically. "Mother was hell bent on being independent when my dad left. So after she married Jacques, she went back to school to earn a business degree. She had an eye for business that's for sure. Wasn't long until she was on the city council and starting this little project. I often wondered if anyone other than me noticed the majority of all of this work centered around her restaurant."

"I can see why people are impressed with her. She did a great job."

"I always suspected she did all of this to prove she was worthy of Jacques. Of course she would deny it. Jacques is from old money. When she met him, she was the talk of the town gossip after Dad's affairs. Jacques was the answer to end all of that. The Doucets are one of the most influential families we have here. His family's wealth goes generations back. But Charlie Grace wasn't going to feel like charity or be dependent on anyone. So she set out to make herself more than she was."

"She sounds like she has always been one tough cookie," Sam said.

"You have no idea. Spent more time worrying about being more than being a mom." I felt the sadness trickle in.

"So . . . Amber, eh?"

"Hmmm?" I looked down to notice I had been rubbing the soil of the landscaping bed between my fingers. "I'm sorry, what did you say?"

"Mrs. Bell called you Rayne Amber."

"Caught that did you?"

"Mmm . . . hmmm," she said. "Is it your real name or what she calls you?"

"Afraid it's real," I said.

"No, I like it."

"Uh huh, sure you do."

"No, actually I do." Sam pulled a petal from a flower. "In fact, it's what I said I would name my daughter if I ever had kids."

I gave her a surprised look. "Really?"

She half smirked, half smiled. "Yes, really."

"I still find it hard to believe you want kids." The sun warmed the bridge of my nose quite uncomfortably but I didn't dare stop the flow of conversation. I loved it when Sam opened up to me. If I was to be totally honest with myself, I would say I loved being at ease enough to open up to her as well.

"And I find it hard to believe you are shocked by my wanting kids." Sam chuckled.

"I don't mean anything by it. You just seem so driven like me. Wouldn't have thought you had time to think about kids."

"Oh, I do. But then again, sometimes I fear I will most likely fuck them up like my parents have done to me," she said, throwing the flower petal onto the ground. "But then again, maybe that's exactly why I want kids. I want the chance to give them a better childhood than I had. Show myself there is one, you know?"

"Makes complete sense."

"And what about Grant? Does he want kids?"

"Can we not talk about him right now?" *Why did I just ask that?* I stopped and stared at her wide-eyed, waiting for a response.

She tilted her head and studied me. "Okay, then . . . new topic. What was your favorite movie when you were little?"

A few movie clips flashed through my thoughts but I couldn't really say any of them stuck out as a favorite. "Can't say I have one. Didn't really get into TV or movies."

"What? Really?" Sam exclaimed.

"Afraid so. I spent most of my time outside."

Sam slid a sneer across her face. "Ooooh. A tomboy. Now that's hot."

CHAPTER 22

SATURDAY MORNING, SAM and I packed our bags and left for the cabin. Charlie Grace walked us to the Jeep, reiterating to Sam that she was welcome anytime to return for a visit. Of course, her gracious hospitality was extended for Sam's father to join her as well. She insinuated there may be a special occasion to celebrate in the future—one she hoped Sam and her father would be able to attend. I wondered if Charlie Grace truly believed she was as subtle as she pretended to be.

Sam asked few questions about Charlie Grace on the drive to the cabin. She already had a pretty good handle on who Charlie Grace was and how to deal with her. Inwardly I hoped Sam was a good match for her, particularly if there was any sort of challenge between them. I had seen the wrath of Charlie Grace's anger a few times in my life. A few being all that was needed to leave a lasting impression. It was an experience I never wanted directed toward me or anyone I cared for.

"So you two really have never been too close, have you?" Sam asked.

"No, not really. Y'know, I've spent some time thinking about that. I've thought back to my childhood, trying to pick one moment when I was close to her. I never could come up with anything. If I wasn't with Memaw, I was alone. Even sitting right next to Mother . . . I was alone. I honestly don't know who she is most of the time."

"I know you don't see her love for you, Stormy. You have to look through the ice. Melt some of it away and then you'll see the love she has for you."

"Are you high?"

"Ha, no. Not in years," she said with a giggle. "She does love you. More than you think."

"She sure has a funny way of showing it."

"Oh, I'll give you that one all right but it's there."

Sam let the windows down. "Do you mind? I want to feel the breeze now that we've slowed down."

"No, not at all." I looked out at the fallen leaves covering the worn two-lane country road. "What are your plans after school? Will you move away or do you plan on staying in the south?"

"Oh, hell no. I'm not staying here." Sam rested her elbow over the open window frame. "I've got to get out of the south. I plan on moving up north somewhere. I want to live where I can have some culture—go out where you have to wear something other than jeans. You know like theater productions, fine dining restaurants. I want to shop in real boutiques."

I looked down at my jean-covered legs and tried to think what was in my closet that didn't involve the same material.

"And anonymity. I want anonymity," Sam continued. "I want to be able to walk down a street and no one, absolutely no one, knows anything about me." She maneuvered in her seat to face me. "So where do you want to live?"

The complete opposite from you. "This." I pointed out in front of me. "I want all of this. I want to smell the honeysuckle through an open window. I want to have a garden where I grow my own vegetables. I want fruit trees across an open lawn. I want a practice where I celebrate my patients' birthdays and mourn their losses. I want all of it. Boring, huh?"

Sam tucked my hair behind my ear. "Actually," she said as her finger traced along my skin, "it's beautiful."

Butterflies.

The roads to the cabin hadn't changed much. The same homes peppered the pastures along our drive. Nurturing had transformed our little cabin into a home away from home. Grass now covered the lawn that was once mostly dirt and dust. Memaw had landscaped a bed of shrubs and flowers along the sidewalk leading to the front porch. A single Hibiscus shrub grew in the center of the largest bed.

"Memaw!" I called from the Jeep window as I pulled into the drive. She was slowly rocking under the screen porch.

She jumped to her feet and sprinted through the door to greet us. "Lawd, I thought you girls was never gonna git here!"

"Good morning, *Memaw*. How are you this morning?" Sam said as she walked around the front of the Jeep.

"Well, I be finer than a frog hair split now that you two are here." Her smile was as wide as her face could possibly stand.

She wore her usual attire—blue jean overalls and a white t-shirt. Sam looked at me and winked.

Memaw grabbed me up in a tight hug before turning to Sam. "Come on in, Sam. I'll show you 'round the place." She wrapped her arm around Sam's and led her up the steps. "Sis, grab those bags while I show our guest the living quarters."

"Yes, madame. Shall I pour us a spot of tea after I finish?" I said in a most horrible attempt at a British accent.

"Tsk, tsk," Memaw whispered to Sam. "Where does she get that sass of hers from?"

"I wonder," Sam replied in a joking undertone as they entered the house.

I paused on the porch to giggle at the cat pissed furniture. Memaw had added brightly colored pillows on the love seat and chairs. A small table sat next to the rocking chair where Memaw had been sitting. On its center was a mason jar filled with iced tea. The condensation in the humid air dripped down the glass to form a ring on the glass-top table.

A feeling of peace washed over me as I entered the house a few steps behind Memaw and Sam. The home was exactly as I remembered it . . . as I had hoped it would be. Of course, Memaw could have done anything at all to the place. Yet, she chose to leave it just as we had shared before I went off to school. A small stack of firewood rested beside the wood-burning stove in the center of the large room. Refurnished furniture was placed around the focal point. Yes, everything was exactly the way I remembered it.

Oh Shit. Everything is exactly the same. I rushed to the back corner bedroom and found Sam sitting on the edge of the queen-size iron-framed bed.

Her devilish grin broadened as she ran her hand across its duvet. "Seems like this will be a sleepover." She gave the bed a little bounce up and down. The old metal springs squeaked in contempt.

Oh Shit. "Sam, I'm so sorry. I completely forgot about there only being one bed."

"No worries, Stormy. I *have* slept with a woman before, you know." She raised an eyebrow. "Should be fun."

"Oh shit." I do believe that one may have been said out loud. Sam let out a laugh.

Memaw collected us to take the boat out onto the water. Since my last visit, she had bought a small john boat. The aluminum hull was empty all but for a few fishing rods and cane poles. Three bench-like seats were molded into its frame. She sat in the back, steering with the hand control of the twenty-five horsepower Mercury motor.

The motor's power gave the boat enough speed atop the water to whip the wind through our hair. The breeze carried the scent of eucalyptus mint from Sam's blond tassels. It awakened and heightened my senses as it flowed passed.

I was taken back to times gone by on these waters with Memaw. I looked back to see her white hair blowing freely behind her head. She had a tight-lipped smile until she slowed the boat down to enter a cove of thickened vines and branches. Her smile relaxed once the threat of inhaling a flying critter diminished with the slowing of the boat. We motored gently along the water through the bare branches of the cove. The leaves had fallen in the cooling temperatures of night. I pointed Sam's attention to turtles sunning in the warmth of a cloudless sky as they sat on logs breaking the water's surface. They slipped silently one by one into the water as we passed.

Memaw dropped the trolling motor into the water and turned to us. "Ya'll wanna throw at some fish?"

"Sure, Memaw. I haven't fished in what feels like ages," I said.

"Yes, well," Sam looked blankly at the both of us, "I've never fished."

"Oh Lawd, Sis, this should be fun." Memaw laughed as she handed Sam an ultralight fishing pole. "I figure this one's a gonna be best fer you." Although she herself still used the long cane poles that could reach into the farthest areas of the bank.

"Yeah, this one should be good." Sam held the foreign object, presenting no knowledge of what to do with it. She turned it over end to end as she studied it.

"Alright then here you go," Memaw said, handing Sam a white cup with green lettering. On the top of it was a lid with a few punctured holes in it.

"What's this?" she asked.

"Sis, you a gonna have to work with this one. I got fish to catch." Memaw laughed while she pulled a fat red worm that wiggled in her fingers from her cup. She tightened her grip on it and set the hook.

"Oh God!" Sam exclaimed.

Memaw chuckled as she aimed her line toward a marshy area close to the bank. The baited hook made a plop as it hit the water. An orange cork sank and then rose quickly back to the surface to float like a ball.

Sam opened the cup in her hand. She peered into the soil mixture. "Mine is empty except for this dirt."

"Here," I said as I sat next to her. "I'll help you." I placed my hand on top of hers. Her grip on the cup tightened beneath mine.

"Please," she said in a low tone as she looked into my eyes.

I gently shook my hand to stir the contents of the cup, causing the worms to appear at the surface. Yet I was unable to take my eyes from hers as she held my stare. I wondered if she could hear the questions screaming from within me. I marveled at the dilation of her pupils as she focused on my face . . . on my lips. Their reaction even in the brightest of daylight gave away the feelings she surely felt as well.

"*Aaaaaaaah*!" Sam tossed the cup over her head into the hull of the boat.

I looked down to see a worm slithering across the web space of her hand. It must have escaped the cup while we were preoccupied with each other.

"Get it off. Get it off," she screamed.

I was frozen to assist her because I couldn't stop laughing. I could hear the same response from Memaw behind me. I looked back to see her bent over her lap. Her shoulders and chest were vibrating as she snickered.

"It's not *fucking* funny, Rayne. Get the little bastard off of me." Sam stopped quickly to look up at Memaw. "Oh *shit*, Memaw. I'm sorry."

Memaw rose to wipe the tears from her eyes. She started to speak but instead raised her hand and waved off the futile apology.

"Here I got it," I said, still laughing at the composure or lack thereof of my cool companion. I took the worm from her hand. "I think you earned a pardon there little buddy." I placed it on the branch of the cypress tree we had floated under and collected the remaining worms back into the cup. "How about I bait your hook for you?"

Sam rolled her eyes at me before tossing the pole at my feet. Trying not to laugh at the memory of her screams, I instructed her on the positioning of the line, the bobble of the cork, and the proper setting of a hook once a fish nibbled on the bait. I showed her the forceful flick of the wrist needed to set the hook. I watched her from the corner of my eye as she fixated on the dipping of the cork in response to the current. Swiftly it was taken under water and then bobbed back up. Again it was taken under—a little deeper this time before popping back up.

"There. That's one. Get it," I said.

Sam jerked the rod so hard with the grip of her two hands that the line came flying out of the water. Attached on its end was a tiny fish now soaring straight for her.

It hit Sam dead center of her cheek with a loud *smack* before falling to the floor of the boat. The small fish still attached to the hook flopped around at her feet.

"Holy hell," Sam yelled and wiped the bayou water from her face.

Memaw and I were joined in our laughter until Memaw finally caught her breath. "Sis, dis the best damn fishing day I've ever done had."

"Laugh it up you two. I'm done." Sam handed her fishing pole to me and leaned back against the boat, crossing her arms over her chest.

"All right, Memaw. S'pose we better get to catching or there'll be no dinner tonight."

Memaw guided us along the bank to fish around the cypress trees. The three of us became lost in our conversation. Memaw asked of school and our lives in Birmingham. Not once did she interrogate Sam as Charlie Grace had done. She never questioned her about her boyfriends nor anything of a personal nature. She merely went with the flow of the conversation, taking it where Sam led it. After catching the last of our fish for the day, Memaw motored us slowly back to the dock.

"You girls better get to a cleaning these here fish while I get the batter ready," she said as she tied off the boat.

"All right, Memaw," I said. "We'll meet you back up at the house when we're done."

"You've lost your mind if you think I'm touching those slimy fish. In fact, the next time I do handle one it will be fried and going into my mouth. Think I'll help in the kitchen."

"All right, then I s'pose I'll meet the two of you up at the house." I laughed as I watched them walk up the hill.

Both of their mouths were moving ninety miles an hour. I had no doubts they were talking of me. Earlier I had figured Sam would do her best to get Memaw to herself as I felt she was anxious to hear the embarrassing childhood stories all family members seemed to share.

It took me a good hour and a half to clean and wash the fish. By the time I made it up to the cabin, Memaw and Sam were sitting on the front porch drinking beer. Apparently they had finished their contributions to dinner much quicker than I had. Their conversation was still as active as when they had left me at the dock.

"What kind of beer is this anyway?" Sam asked in full sincerity.

"Sis, what you mean not giving this city folk our state beer? Honey, dis Pabst Blue Ribbon. The only beer fit'n to drink. All that other stuff is high-priced skunk piss."

"My bad, Memaw. Lord knows Sam is learning some new things today," I said.

"Too bad she hadn't done learnt to duck when a fish a flyin' at her face."

Memaw and I roared with laughter. This time Sam joined in.

"You two are hilarious." Sam's face was highlighted by the glow of the lights from inside the house as the sun set behind us. "I'm enjoying seeing this side of Rayne. I've only gotten glimpses before."

"Oh no, I'm a bettin' you haven't. You prolly only know that serious, always in control prude she puts on."

"Hey. I'm not a prude, woman. I may be serious and controlled but I'm *not* a prude."

"Prove it," Sam mouthed slowly so I could read her lips.

My heart jumped up into my throat and my cheeks burned with blush at the connotation of her words. I had hoped the setting sun was enough to dampen the glow of my cheeks from Memaw.

We placed some lawn chairs around the gas fryer Memaw had set up outside the porch. The oil swirled and crackled once it was hot enough for her to fry our dinner of fish, fresh cut red potato fries, and hush puppies. We sat under the stars, having our fill of food and conversation.

"Gawd, this is the best fish I've ever eaten, Memaw," Sam said as she took a bite of her fourth piece of fish.

"Nothing like catching 'em fresh from the water," Memaw said. "Tell me, Sam. What type of doc you aiming to be? I'm a sure hoping you ain't wanting to fix tits and ass like Rayne over here."

"*I'm* going to *fix* your old ass if you don't lay off," I retorted as I launched my last bite of hush puppy in her direction.

"No, ma'am. I am going for some specialty in Obstetrics/ Gynecology, maybe Gyn/Onc or Infertility."

"Good Lawd. You're going into another form of ass like Sis. Can't you girls treat the high blood or sugar instead of something to do with tits or ass?"

"You do what you know, Memaw." Sam shrugged.

Memaw didn't hesitate or even show a flicker of change. "I s'pose'n you right about that." She laughed.

After finishing the last swallow of her beer, Memaw excused herself to bed. "This been one helluva day, girls," she said over her shoulder as she opened the screen door to go back into the house. "One helluva day."

NEITHER SAM NOR I were ready for bed after we cleaned up the dinner mess outside. The night was too serene to spend it indoors. Its sky beckoned us to return to the dock. The surface of the water was as smooth as glass reflecting a mirrored image of the moonlight above. Its beam stretched across the water to shine its light on our bare toes as they dangled from the edge of the wooden pier. The stream of light across the water was occasionally broken with the gentle splashing of fish breaking the surface. Its current changed enough to cause a rippling against the posts of the pier. A bayou awakened played a midnight's symphony to our quieted conversation. The deep throaty croaks of bullfrogs gave the serenade its base while chirping crickets provided the woodwind section. The soprano of a whip-poor-will's call sounded in the distance.

"I never knew it was so loud," Sam said.

"Yes, it is. The bayou is alive at night. It's my favorite time of the day. I used to sit for hours out here after Memaw had gone to bed." I kicked my toe against the water, splashing drops out away from the deck. "I sure miss this place."

"You really are a different person out here, Stormy. You know that?"

"I s'pose."

"And I'm really the only one you've ever brought out here? Shown this to?"

I hesitated before answering, knowing this meant something beyond simply bringing a visitor. Bringing Sam here when I had never considered telling anyone of its existence much less actually bringing them with me, meant far more than the act itself. I knew that. Now with her questioning, I knew she did as well.

"Yep, only you. No one but you even knows this place is here. That it's ours."

"Not even Grant?"

"No, not even him."

She turned her body toward me. She placed her finger under my chin, urging me to look at her just as I was trying to turn away. "Rayne, do you question why that is? Why it's me that you brought out here?"

I broke away from the pull of her finger and stared into the night sky. Not a cloud covered the stars above. They burned brilliantly over us. I caught myself wishing I could soar to their altitude. I wished I could rise high enough to see all around me and use their sparkle to ignite my soul. Maybe then I would have some comprehension as to the questions that twisted and tormented me.

"Rayne, have you thought of it?" she asked again. "Have you questioned this at all? Questioned anything?"

"Yes." I sighed in desperation of acceptance. "Yes, I've thought of it." *Especially lately.*

"And what were the answers you came up with?"

"I don't know, Sam. I just don't know."

"ARE YOU ASLEEP, Stormy?" Sam's voice was but a whisper yet it boomed in the quiet of the room.

We were side by side in the small queen-size bed. I could feel the warmth of her closeness under the shared duvet. No, I wasn't asleep. In fact, I hadn't closed my eyes longer than a blink. I had lain there listening to her slow, steady breaths since the moment we had gone to bed.

"No, I'm not," I said.

"Now is the time."

"Time? Time for what?"

Sam turned on her side to face me and bent her arm to prop her head up as she looked at me. The brightness of the moon shining into the window made her face as clear to me as if there was a bedside lamp.

"You owe me a conversation remember?" she said. "Any subject . . . any time?"

"And you want to do that now?" I whispered.

"Any time . . . any place. Those were your rules not mine."

"Okay." I pulled my hands out from under the cover and rested them across my chest. "Shoot."

"I'm sorry. I can't stop thinking about this place . . . about you. I'm so touched you brought me here. It means a lot to me."

"I'm glad. I wanted you to see how beautiful it is here."

"I do, but why me?" she said. "Why was I the one you brought?"

"I don't know. I . . . I guess because I'm closer to you than any other friend I've ever had."

"And Grant? He's your boyfriend. Why not him?"

I sighed heavily. "Why do you always bring him up?"

"Why do you not?" she said, sounding frustrated.

"I don't understand what you're getting at."

"You hardly ever talk about him. Your family hears wedding bells but you don't seem to hear anything at all. I mean . . . have you even talked to him during this trip? I haven't seen you on the phone at all."

"Do you want me talking to him?"

Sam raised her free hand from her side and shook it. "No, I'm not saying that. I'm . . . I'm trying to figure it all out is all. Remember perspectives?"

"There's nothing to figure out. Grant and I got together the summer before med school started. It's easy being with him. We are both focused on school right now. As for wedding bells, you're right I don't hear a thing. I don't even think about it. I'm going to be done and practicing before I even let those thoughts cross my mind. I have too much I want to do before then. Being with Grant lets me do those things without the drama of a needy boyfriend."

"Are you happy?"

"Happy enough," I said without needing much thought before I answered.

"You should want more."

"Are you happy?"

Sam rolled back onto her back and stared at the ceiling. She blinked several times. "Yes . . . but unfortunately only when I'm with a woman who has a boyfriend."

CHAPTER 23

"HI. MERRY CHRISTMAS." I answered the phone as soon as I saw Sam's name flash across the caller ID screen.

"How in the hell did you do this?"

"It's Christmas. I couldn't let it go by without sending you a present."

"Rayne, no one has ever surprised me like this. I can't believe you did this." She sounded so happy, which was a far cry better than our earlier phone calls. I hated she felt forced to go home for the holidays. Her dad pulled one of his ultimatum stunts and then promptly left her at home alone with her mom.

"So did you like it?"

"Oh, I haven't opened it yet."

"What?" I laughed loudly. "Then what the heck are you thanking me for?"

"For sending me a present. It's right here in my lap but I thought I should wait until the morning to open it."

"Sam, it's Christmas Eve. You can open it tonight if you want."

"I was hoping you would say that."

I heard frantic tearing of wrapping paper and then silence. Nothing. "Sam? You still there?"

Silence.

"Sam? If you don't like it you can take it back for another DVD. I won't be upset."

"No, it's perfect." Her voice cracked.

"I . . . uh . . . I bought me a copy too. I thought if you weren't busy later tonight maybe we could watch it together again."

"I don't know what to say." I heard her swallow hard. "It's very sweet and well . . . sort of . . . romantic."

I smiled like a damn fool. *Yes, yes it was.* "Great. I'll call you back in about two hours. Will that give you enough time to get ready?"

"You, my dear, have a date."

Two hours to the minute I called Sam back. She answered on

the first ring. "Hello. I'm all set." I heard the sound of hard candy shells hitting against a cardboard box.

"Ah, I see you've got the M&M's ready to go."

"Yep, and the popcorn you sent too. Do you know how hard it has been not to dig into them over the last two hours?"

"You are a rock."

"That I am."

I heard loud shuffling. "What are you doing?"

"Getting under the covers. Why?"

Oh damn. She's in bed. "I heard the shuffling. You watching it in bed?"

"Well, yeah, where are you?"

"In a chair."

"Oh hell, Stormy, you might as well get in the bed. It'll sure be the safest you'll ever be in bed with me." She snickered.

"I seem to remember being pretty safe last time."

"Wanna go for round two?" She giggled. "Now, let's start the movie before this conversation starts to head in an all new direction."

"*Serendipity* take two. Hit play on three," I said.

"One . . . two . . . three."

"HAPPY NEW YEAR!" I heard Sam yelling when I flipped the phone open. Her voice was barely audible over the background noise of loud music.

I quickly ducked out of one of the open patio doors to try to hear her better as the crowd around me was nearly as loud. I put my finger in my other ear. "Happy New Year to you! But you're early."

"Not where I am. We struck midnight right as you answered."

"That's right. You're in eastern time."

"Yep."

I think I detected a slur to her speech. "Where are you?"

"I'm at a party with Claire." I could tell Sam was still yelling over the crowd. "At ten minutes till I came outside to call you but fuck it's just as loud out here as in there."

"Wait a minute. Where is Claire?"

"She's inside."

"You weren't with her at the stroke of midnight?"

"Nope."

"Oh shit, you're gonna be in trouble."

Sam laughed. "I'm a big girl. I can handle it. Besides isn't there some kind of saying that at the stroke of midnight you're to be with the person you want to spend the new year with?"

"Think I've heard of something like that before."

"Well, I was with you."

I bit my bottom lip and smiled into the phone.

"Hey. Are you blushing?"

"Good Lord . . . probably."

"Adorable." I heard her muffled chuckle. "Happy New Year, Stormy."

"Happy New Year, Sam."

Forty-five minutes later I found my way back to the patio and snuck into an opening in the bushes lining the pavers. I rubbing my finger over Sam's name as it flashed on the screen when I dialed her number.

"Hiya." The music and voices were much louder than before.

"Happy New Year," I screamed into the phone. I didn't care who heard me or looked in my direction.

"Déjà vu. Is it midnight there?"

"Just turned."

"We are something else, aren't we?"

"You can say that again."

"I wouldn't have it any other way." I heard Claire's voice calling Sam's name. "Hey, Stormy?"

"Uh huh?"

"I miss you like crazy!"

"Me too. Happy New Year, Sam."

"Have a good night."

I clicked the phone shut and walked back into the party to find Grant.

CHAPTER 24

"HEY, WHAT YOU doing?" Grant said when I answered the phone.

I closed the anatomy book I had been staring at aimlessly for the last several minutes. "Not much. Trying to study a bit."

"How's that going?"

"Not great. How about you? What's up?"

"I was calling to see if you wanted to go shopping with me."

"What are we shopping for?" I asked already stacking the books I had spread out across my kitchen table.

"Golf clothes," he said. "I got asked to play in the UAB charity tournament this next weekend."

"But that's Memorial weekend. I thought we were going home?"

"Baby, I can't pass up this opportunity. The chair of the vascular department asked me to be on his team. Someone told him my handicap. This will be a chance for me to have some serious schmoozing time."

I sighed. "Geez, how much schmoozing do you have to do? You didn't go home for Thanksgiving because you were too busy trying to suck up to the department heads. We said we were going home."

"I went home for Christmas, Rayne."

"Technically you did. I mean you were there in body but you spent the majority of the time either talking about school to anyone that would listen or on the phone trying to line up extra operating hours. You can't really call it going home when you don't spend time with anyone."

"I don't want to fight. Can't we just go shopping? You can still go home. Why don't you take Sam with you? Ya'll had fun during Thanksgiving didn't you? Besides how long has it been since you two have done anything together?"

I sighed. "A while."

"Exactly. So why don't you ask her to go?"

It amused me how he masked his selfishness with unselfishness. Truth was I didn't need him going home with me. I much rathered the drive alone than have to hear his ramblings. He had been nothing but distracted since we were sent to other hospitals in Alabama to do rotations. He was sent to Montgomery and apparently met a surgeon who offered him a vascular residency at Baptist if he wasn't accepted at UAB. I was sent to the nearby Gadsden but Sam had been shipped south to Dothan. We had hardly seen each other since returning back to UAB after the holiday break. As fabulous as his idea sounded, I was not going to let on to him I was happy about the possible change in plans.

"Do what you want. Look . . . I need to get back to studying. I'll talk to you later."

"Wait, Rayne . . ."

"Good-bye, Grant." I hung up the call and reopened my books.

"GET OUT OF that Jeep this instance, Dr. Storm." Sam came running out of the front door of her apartment building.

I jumped out of the Jeep and ran around to the front of the vehicle scared something was wrong. "What? What's wrong?"

Sam swooped me up in a hug that nearly lifted my feet completely off of the ground. "Damn, I've missed you girl!"

"You scared the shit outta me," I said into her shoulder but remained in her embrace.

She squeezed me tightly, rocking me back and forth before releasing me. "Now let's get this party started." She threw her bags in the back and hopped in the front seat. "So no one knows we're coming?"

I turned the key to start the Jeep and then grinned at her devilishly. "No one but us and Memaw."

The Memorial holiday had given us an extended weekend, which was enough time to have a short three-day pass home. Sam didn't hesitate when I asked her to come with me.

"You seem rather giddy there, Stormy," Sam said.

I felt my grin creep into a full-blown smile. "I do believe I am, Dr. LeJeune."

"Seems like this weekend may be some serious fun." She looked out the window and tapped her knuckle lightly against the glass. "I wonder. Are the sleeping arrangements still the same at the old camp?"

I didn't look at her. Instead I watched the blur of white-and-pink dogwood blooms lining the road. "I do believe they are." I tried, in vain, to curb the flirtation in my tone.

From the corner of my eye I could see Sam's head snap up and turn to me.

"Oh, yeah," she said, smiling broadly, "this could be one helluva weekend."

"DAMN, THAT FELT great," Sam said as she stepped out onto the porch where I was sitting.

"The run or the soak in the bath after?" I asked, looking up at her with all intentions of sharing a smile.

Occasionally I had been struck speechless or near motionless when my eyes first cast directly on her. Today was no different. She had her hair pulled back in a loose ponytail. The Louisiana humidity gave her blonde waves a springy curl that danced around her face. That within itself was enough. Although today there was something different drawing my attention to her—something navy blue with bright green lettering across the front. It was the first time I had seen her wearing this shirt. It looked worn as if it was a longtime favorite of hers. The collar and sleeves were frayed with a few small holes scattered about. The "Just Do It" saying across the front taunted me . . . daring me to reach out to feel the softness of it and the skin beneath it. Let's not forget those damn jeans. *How could I overlook those?* I wondered if she knew she had brought my favorite pair—the ones with holes over both of the knees. They were the stumble that tossed me head first over the proverbial cliff.

"Both," she said, grinning foolishly. She looked out into the yard. "Where's Memaw?"

"She left a note saying she was going into town." I took a sip of the freshly brewed coffee I now held too tightly within my grip. "She should be back before too long."

Sam sat down hard on the love seat next to me. The hole in her jeans opened wider, exposing her knee. It took a conscious effort not to stroke my thumb across her bare skin.

Sam peered into my cup. "What you drinking there?" She

placed her hand over mine and lifted the cup to her lips to take a swallow. "Yuck." She pretended to spit and sputter. "Needs sugar."

I was frozen. The proximity of her had my every nerve on high alert. Truth be known, they had been since the night before. I had found little sleep. Lying next to her, listening to her breaths proved too much to allow my thoughts to quiet. When I did manage to close my eyes, visions of her body lying next to me filled my head. I pictured the location of her hands—one was elevated and tucked under her head while the other rested across her belly. In the filtered moonlight I watched the slow, steady rise of her chest. Nope . . . I wouldn't dare say I got much sleep.

Sam looked me in the eyes and her expression changed from one of light banter to something more serious. I had no idea what she found on my face but if it was any indication as to the feelings I was having after her hair brushed against my arm, I could understand the change in her.

I watched her study me.

"What are you thinking about right now?" she whispered.

"You," I replied softly. The word came out without thought . . . without hesitation.

Her eyes drifted closed for a moment before she cupped my hand with hers once more. Without taking my eyes from hers, I followed the encouragement of her fingers and opened my hands to let her take the cup from me. I felt myself drown in her intoxicating scent as she leaned over me to put the cup on the table next to me. She stopped inches from me, giving me closer vision of the blue sapphires vibrantly dancing across my face.

"Stormy." Sam's voice was throaty, hoarse, and barely audible above a murmur. "What you do to me with those eyes of yours." The pit of my stomach filled with a wave of tingles at the touch of her thumb faintly tracing my bottom lip. "God help me, I'm going to kiss you unless you tell me not to."

I said nothing.

Involuntarily my eyes closed as her lips came nearer to mine. I could sense the warmth in her lips even before they touched mine. The crunch of tires rolling across gravel was like a deafening screech between my ears. *No! No, not now!* Feeling the sun warm my skin from the loss of Sam's shadow, I opened my eyes to realize she was now walking out of the screened porch.

"Shit," I muttered.

"Aaaaaaa EEE eeeee," Memaw yelled, getting out of the truck. "We gone have us a good time tonight."

"What do you have in there?" Sam asked, walking around to the open tailgate of the truck.

"Shit fire and save the matches, Sam. We's about to show you an ol' fashion Louisiana good time," Flossie said, springing from the truck's passenger door.

"Flossie?" I said in surprise.

Memaw hadn't mentioned she was bringing her out this weekend. Heck, I didn't even know Memaw had told anyone about this place.

"Hey, Sis, hoping you don't mind me crashing this here party," Flossie said.

"Of course not," I said, shaking my head for emphasis. I reached my arm around Memaw and gave her a side hug. "And just what are you two up to?"

"Sounds like we're having a party," Sam said. She was grinning ear to ear.

"Damn skippy to that," Memaw said. "We wanted to surprise ya'll with a crawfish boil. Sis here tells me you ain't ever had you a mudbug, Sam. We gone fix that up right today."

"Hot damn!" I yelled out. I turned to Flossie. "But what about Cora. Ya'll didn't bring her."

"Hell no," Flossie said. "You a meanin' Mouth of the South Cora? We'd a had the whole damn town out here if'n we'd a done that."

I chuckled shamelessly. "You're probably right about that one."

Sam and I unloaded the truck and took everything to the back of the camp where Memaw had set up a gas cooker and table.

"I don't get this," Sam said, kicking at the child's plastic wading pool. "Surely we aren't getting in this."

"Of course," I said, laughing. "What? You didn't bring your bikini? Meems brought hers."

"Don't you go scaring this poor girl back to the city, Sis," Memaw said as she poured a fresh bag of ice over the beer cooler. "Ain't nobody wanting to see this in a bikini." She looked at Sam. "This here what we gone purge them there crawfish in."

"Purge? What does that mean?" Sam asked.

"Well." I paused, trying to find the best explanation. "It's a way of cleaning them I guess."

"Baby girl. Why don't you take Sam over there and shuck that corn. Flossie and I got dis." She caught my arm and gently pulled me closer to her and whispered, "Hope you don't mind I brought Flossie? She a been going crazy in that assisted livin' place. I try to get her out as much as I can."

"Of course not, Meems," I said, patting her arm. "Anytime."

"ALRIGHT, GIRLS . . . come and get 'em," Memaw yelled over her shoulder.

Steam rose off of the pile of deep red crustaceans as Memaw dumped the overfilled strainer out onto the table. The moisture and heat from the red potatoes and cobs of corn left a wet trail as they rolled out across the newspaper. Long ago, Memaw had discovered this to be the best tablecloth when eating the messy mudbugs. Their stain left a forever reminder in any linen cloth. Flossie slapped down a loaf of soft bread and a roll of paper towels on the table before pulling out ice cold beers for each of us.

Sam stared aimlessly at the pile of food. "This I know how to eat." She bit off a corn on the cob. "I'm a bit lost on the rest. Don't we need plates?"

"No plates, city girl." Flossie tore off a piece of the red potato lying closest to her and popped it into her mouth.

"It's a eat as you go sort of meal," I said, leaning my shoulder into Sam as a playful nudge. "Pick out what you want to take a nibble of and have at it."

Sam looked at me and raised her left eye brow high in an arch. "Is that right?"

I swallowed hard on the images in my head.

"Pinch the tail and suck the head," Flossie said. "That's how you do it."

"I'm sorry?" Sam stared at her with wide eyes.

Memaw tried to stifle her giggle. "Sis, I'm a thinking you gonna have to show this city girl how to eat these here mudbugs."

"Sorry," I said to Sam. "Here lemme show you."

I picked up a plumper crawfish off the top of the pile. I peeled away its shell. "And you peel them like this. Here taste it."

Sam bent forward and took the bite into her mouth. Butterflies returned to the pit of my stomach as her lips closed over my fingertips.

"Hey," she said as she chewed the crawfish tail. "That's pretty damn good." She looked at Flossie. "What's she doing?"

Flossie had the head of the crawfish in her mouth and sucked hard on the shell as any true Cajun would do. I, however, had that habit curbed in high school biology class.

"She's sucking the head," I answered.

"Hell yeah, I am," Flossie said. "City girl that be where all the flavor is. Rayne here throws away the best part."

"Ya'll go right ahead," I said to both Memaw and Flossie as they continued to hold the crawfish in their mouths. "I know what is in that part of the body. So eat up, ladies."

Sam took the crawfish's head from my hand and placed it between her lips. She sucked in hard. Within seconds her eyes watered. She spit the hard shell from her mouth and guzzled nearly half of her beer.

"Fuck. That's hot," she yelled.

Memaw and Flossie looked at each other. "City girl!"

If it had been a race, the elderly women would have surely beat Sam and me. They tore the first two rings off of the hard shell, freeing the rest of the meat by pinching the bottom of the tail and pulling with their teeth. Possibly driven to overcome the city girl nickname, Sam peeled her remaining crawfish without any help from me.

Flossie popped the tops off of four more beers and served up yet another round. "Sam, Rayne been telling us you got that who ha rotation you wuz wantin'."

Sam chuckled hard, accidently spitting out a corn kernel from her mouth. "A what?"

"She means your Gyn rotation," I said.

"Who ha, huh?" Sam said.

"Well, what the hell you girls calls it? One of them there virginias." Flossie pulled a piece of claw meat between her teeth.

I looked at Sam and Memaw and we burst out laughing.

"It's a vagina, Flossie," I said.

"Well, ain't that what I said?"

"Something like that," Sam said. "And yes, I did get the rotation I was hoping for."

"Rayne was right proud for you, Sam," Memaw said. "She pert near called me the minute she found out."

Sam leaned into me, worsening the blush I felt escalating in my cheeks. "Did she now?" I was praying the rose in my cheeks was hidden in the dusk of the day. *Why did she always do this to me?*

Memaw folded the corners of the newspaper and wrapped the shells and leftover food in between the sheets before sweeping it off into the trash. "Sis, why don't you pull the truck around and give us some tunes while Flossie lights that there fire to keep the skeeters away?"

I settled into a lawn chair next to the fire a few minutes later and let my body relax into the beer's buzz and the crackling fire. We sat for several long minutes.

"This has been the best day I've had in a really long time." Sam held her bottle up in the air. "Here's to the best ladies I have ever had in my life. I hope to share many more days like this."

"I'll drink to that," Memaw said, raising her bottle for the toast.

"What she said." Flossie had never been much for words that exposed her feelings.

I tapped the neck of Sam's bottle with my own. "Infinitely more."

Hank William's voice began to sing from the truck's speakers. With only a few chords any true Louisianian would recognize "Jambalaya (On the Bayou)."

Flossie and Memaw stood and grabbed each other's arm as they sang the lyrics loudly. The fire's smoke circled them as they danced. Flossie turned and pirouetted Memaw around in the glowing light.

"Son of a gun," I sang and sprang up out of my chair and grabbed Sam's hand. I followed Flossie's steps and twirled Sam around me as I sang carefree into the night.

Flossie finished the dance by tossing her empty bottle into the trash can. "Whew, girls . . . I'm a drunker than Cooter Brown. I gotta leave ya to it." She stumbled over the leg of Memaw's lawn chair.

"Aw, hell. I better help her old drunk ass into the house," Memaw said. "You girls go catch the moonlight over the bayou. She's a pretty one tonight."

We watched them sideways walk and stagger until they disappeared behind a closed door.

"She's right you know," I said. "We really should go down to the dock."

Sam pulled the last two beers from the cooler of melted ice. "I'm all yours."

Damn.

"REMEMBER THE LAST time we were out here alone?" Sam asked, maneuvering the levee's downslope better than I had expected given our alcohol consumption.

"I do. Seems like that was years ago."

"Nope, just a few months."

"Why do you think it seems so long ago?" I said, quickly trying to recover my footing after tripping over an exposed root.

Sam reached the end of the dock before me and patted the wooden plank next to her. "I dunno. Maybe because our residencies are kicking our asses?"

"Ha! Maybe so," I said, sitting down next to her.

"Or . . . maybe it's because we've grown closer?"

"Maybe."

In the stillness of our words, I heard the cicadas' crescendo chorus surrounding us. The vibrating noise was so overpowering it nearly drowned the sound of an owl's rhythmic questioning to the night.

"What is that?" Sam looked around as if trying to find the location of the noise.

Smiling, I looked out across the still water. "Cicadas or locusts as Memaw calls them."

"Wow, I didn't realize they were so loud."

"They are this year."

"Come again?"

"The ones you are hearing are called Magicicada. There is no telling just how many males you are listening to right now. It's said that each female can lay up to six hundred eggs." My memories replayed a younger version of myself sitting with Memaw as she told me the story of the locusts. "They are cyclic—coming out around late April or early May."

"What do you mean coming out?"

"Well, these cicadas were hatched thirteen years ago. Once they're hatched they drop to the ground, burrow in, and wait."

"For what?" Sam asked with enthusiasm.

I couldn't suppress a snicker, remembering how interested I was the first time I heard of their cycle. "To grow up. Takes thirteen years and then they all come out at once. That's why it's so loud. Imagine six hundred eggs per each female rising up at once. But it doesn't last long. Usually by mid-July they'll all have disappeared."

"Disappear . . . disappear?"

"Yep. They live only a few weeks."

"Damn, that sucks. They stay buried for thirteen years and only live above ground for a few weeks," Sam said. "You said it was the males making the noise."

"I did. They're singing to the females. It's a mating call."

"Oh!" In the moonlight, I could see a smile spread across Sam's face. "So their only purpose to come out of the ground is . . ."

"Sex." I knew my voice was a drawn out whisper.

Sam turned her head away from me and stared at the bayou.

"Sam?"

Silence.

Nervously, I shifted on the wooden planks, trying to see her face.

"Rayne," she finally said in a soft voice as she turned her head back to me. "Butterflies . . . why did I get a swarm of butterflies when you said that word?"

"Welcome to my world."

"What do you mean?"

"I have had nothing but butterflies since the moment I met you."

I felt her inch closer to me until her thigh rested against mine. A thousand nerve endings fired at once with the touch of her fingers tracing along my wrist up my arm and then back again. My body's tension betrayed me under her touch.

"And why do you flinch every time I touch you?" she said.

"I don't know."

I felt my breath hitch as her hand caressed my face. She traced her thumb down my jawline and over my lips.

"God, Stormy, you don't know how badly I want to kiss you."

She sighed deeply and dropped her hand onto the top of mine and squeezed it as she exhaled.

I wanted to reach for her. I wanted to pull her against me and feel her lips against mine. I wanted to scream, "Then why don't you?" I wanted. I wanted to do so much more than sit there speechless, breathing heavily within her touch.

She lowered her head to stare into the darkened water, "But if I do . . . if I were to kiss you . . . I know I wouldn't want to stop?"

"Why would you have to?" I heard my voice in the air yet it sounded foreign to me. *Had I really spoken?*

Sam looked up at me in surprise. I felt the warmth of her fingertip under my chin urging me to let my eyes meet hers. Her thumb gently traced my chin. "Stormy . . . I've never wanted anything more than to end the aching I have to feel your lips against mine."

A hard swallow nearly smothered the breath from me.

"Please." The warmth of her breath tickled my lips.

"Kiss me," I whispered against her lips. "Please. Kiss me."

The words briefly hung in the air between us before I consumed her butterflies deep in the pit of my stomach. No words described her lips upon mine. Soft? *Yes.* Warm as she took my upper lip between hers? *Yes.* Dizzying with the touch of her tongue against mine? *Yes. Oh God, Yes!* I had never felt anything like this before. I could feel her every thought—her every desire for me in her kiss. She longed for me as much as I had for her. I could feel it in her touch, taste it upon her lips.

My labored breath fought to regain a controlled rhythm. The darkness behind my closed eyelids grew blacker as I struggled to keep my body upright. I melted hopelessly into her when I felt her hand on the back of my neck pulling me in closer to her.

A DOCK'S KISS seared through my mind as I lay at the edge of an increasingly shrinking bed. Nervously I awaited the woman who possessed the lips I still tasted upon my own. Desperately I tried to force sleep to overcome me. I feared what would happen if I stayed awake. I feared what I wanted to happen.

I felt a depression in the mattress before hearing the squeaks of the springs groaning to its weight. The room was silent all but for a breath inhaling . . . exhaling—repeating with each cycle coming faster than the one before. Rustling movement of the body behind me caused the old springs to squeak once more.

My heart pounded as I envisioned her positioning. Had she turned toward me? Had she turned away from me? Fingers tracing across my shoulder gave the answer to my unspoken questions. My already racing heart quickened its beat. I felt a single fingertip trail down the center of my back, around my hip, and back up to my waist. My breath caught steadfast in my throat as I felt the bare skin of her hand slide underneath the material of my shirt. She rested it flat against the tightened muscles of my stomach, gently pushing the weight of it to encourage me to roll over onto my back.

"Please turn over," Sam murmured in a raspy, warm breath.

Her silhouette before me was radiant in the lamp light. Her hair was slack and falling about her face. Her eyes were fixated and unwavering in their attention to my lips. A quivering thumb traced the edge of my bottom lip before it tucked the fallen hair behind my ear.

"Rayne," she whispered inches from my face. "I'm dying to kiss you again." Her finger traced skin over my collarbone. "But I won't if you don't want me to."

The tightness in my throat choked the words from me. I watched her eyes searching mine, waiting for me to give an answer. A small twitch of her bottom lip caught my sight. The release of her breath was hot against my thumb as I traced the pattern of the twitch.

A feathery wisp of sensation fell across my lips with her kiss. She let them linger in repetition before taking my lip between hers. She pulled away from me and searched my eyes as if pleading their permission. She bit the corner of her lower lip, betraying her confidence and showing me a sign of her shyness . . . of her hesitation.

I returned my response in gesture alone, cupping my hand along the back of her neck and letting the silkiness of her hair don my fingers like a glove before bringing her lips back to mine. Her tongue traced my lips between successions of delicate kisses. The dizziness felt on the dock returned a thousand fold with the deepening of her kiss and the weight of her chest against mine. I felt the warmth of her labored breath against my neck as she let her kisses travel away from my mouth.

An unfamiliar urge to moan built within me as the pressure of her hand passed over my cloth-covered breast. Heat streamed through my body and fogged my brain of voluntary control. The moan escaped my lips as a dulled whimper with the cupping force of her hand upon my breast. My body writhed under her touch, lifting closer to her, wanting to be one with her. I felt myself lost in everything about Sam LeJeune. The softness of her hands roaming my body . . . the mouth that possessed my lips. I began to hear my inner screams. Deep in her kiss I felt it for the first time. I wanted her. Wanted all of her. My body was hers and I wished for no one else to know its curves. In the moment of her kiss, her tongue soft, warm against mine I knew I could deny it no longer. *I love this woman! I'm so in love with this woman!*

As soon as I heard my voice confessing my love for her another voice screamed just as loudly. *Sex is sex.* It was Sam's voice. What was I doing? How could I lose myself to her? How could I ever recover, return to a friendship after making love to someone for the first time. This wasn't sex for me. I loved her. My eyes sprang open when I felt her fingertip slide along the inside of my waistband.

Sex is sex.

I jerked away from her kiss. "Wait!" I panicked. "Stop!" I realized the words were more than inner screams when she quickly pulled away.

"What?"

"Please stop." Tears rapidly followed my words. Their flow was relentless to my attempts of control.

Sam sat up and faced me. "God, Rayne. I'm so sorry. What did I do? Did I hurt you?"

"No."

"Then what? I thought you wanted this?" she said. "Out on the dock . . . here in the bed, I thought . . . I thought you . . . I thought you wanted this too."

"I did." I couldn't comprehend the magnitude of emotion crashing down on me in that moment. Thoughts I had never uttered aloud to myself were suddenly being screamed into my consciousness. "I did want you to kiss me. I do want you to kiss me. I . . . I met you and all of these questions started to surface." My tears choked the words as I tried to reason with both myself and Sam. "For as long as I can remember, I was terrified that I might be different—might be gay. I mean there had to be a reason, didn't there?"

"A reason for what?"

"As a child Mother always warned me that it would feel so good. That sex and being with a boy would feel so good that I wouldn't want it to stop. But I always did. I *always* wanted it to stop . . . to never start. Even with Grant. Even tho' I love him. It could always stop." My tears continued as strong as they had started. My body ached with the sadness and confusion that overwhelmed me. "Then I meet you. This amazing woman I was instantly attracted to. God, mesmerized by you. So the fears start to come back. And then you kiss me. Oh God. When you kiss me. I've never felt like this . . . never felt what your touches do to me. Never felt out of control."

She tucked my hair behind my ear. "Isn't that a good thing?"

"No," I said louder than I wanted. "No."

"Okay."

"You yourself said it. What would happen next? Where would we go from here? How do I go back to being your friend after feeling this for the first time in my life?"

"Shhhhhh, Rayne. Quiet now." Sam held me tightly in her arms. "Breathe, sweetie . . . Shhhh . . . Just relax and take slow breaths." She rocked me in her arms and held me to ease the weeping. "We don't have to figure this all out tonight."

"We do if this goes any further."

"You're right. I'm sorry. I moved too fast that's all. I just moved too fast. This is my fault. Not yours." Sam laid back on her side next to me. She slid her arm under my neck and rested her other arm across my belly. "Shhhh . . . I'm so sorry."

Sam held me like that until I gave into the fatigue and fell asleep in the arms of the woman who was the first to take my breath with a kiss.

CHAPTER 25

I WAS CAPTIVE to the night's sleep until I was released to the day. Sunlight burst into the room through the sheer curtains to awaken me. Its light burned my eyes which were swollen from the forceful tears wept the night before. Emotions I had hidden even from myself had broken free—free to feel, free to show . . . but not free to accept nor express. The task of it all left me fatigued in her arms as I lay against her cotton shirt that absorbed each tear.

I awakened in the bed alone with sunlight my only companion. The sheets were left ruffled from where her body had lain. On the pillow next to me was a note telling me she had gone for a run.

I walked into the kitchen and found a single empty coffee cup next to the percolator on the stove. Its base was kept warm on the iron. I accepted this as Memaw's silent invitation to join her on the porch. She rocked in her chair silently staring out at the crop-barren field.

"Good morning, Meems," I said.

"Why, good morning," she said, turning to me and appearing startled by the sight before her. "Why, Sis, you look like hell."

"I love you too," I responded in a dry tone, unable to muster enough cheerfulness in my voice to play off the emotions that brimmed at the surface.

Memaw motioned for me to sit next to her on the love seat. "Come now, Sis. Tell me what's eating at ya to bring that face 'bout this morning."

I exhaled a deep sigh as I fell into the seat next to her. "I don't know. I just don't know anything anymore. I thought . . . I thought for a split second I did but it isn't real." The tears built in my eyes again.

"What you talking 'bout, baby girl?"

"I'm scared. I'm just so scared."

"Of what?"

"Of what I am . . . of *who* I am. I'm scared to be who I know I want to be and I'm just as scared not to." I leaned my head on her shoulder, powerless to hold it up another second longer. "Why, Meems? Why do I have to be so screwed up?"

"What in tarnation are you talkin' 'bout? How you screwed up?"

"I just am. I've always been. And now I know I'll always be."

"Why? Cuz'n you don't fit in a mold folks try to put you in? Sis, you da most beautiful being I've known in dis world. You not put here to be anything but that. You can't be stuffed in a mold someone else done picked for you."

"Then why don't I know how to be who I am? Why don't I know where I belong? Shouldn't I have it figured out by now?"

"You belong to you, Sis. You belong where you take y'self. What you trying to figure out? You find what you a searching for. And you findin' it for you. Ain't nobody's business but yours."

Silence filled the air between us as Memaw stroked her fingers soothingly across my arm. I became lulled in watching the steam rise from the untouched cup of coffee. I was scared to put a voice to the truth of my concerns. I was afraid to put words to something I was only now beginning to understand yet unable to explain to anyone . . . even myself. I was more terrified with the knowing of my deepest beliefs of where my truest desires laid.

"Sis?" Memaw said, breaking the silence. She continued to run her fingers along my arm. "I really like your friend, Sam. She all right in my book."

"Thanks, Memaw. I do too." I tried to position my face to hide the tears that again blurred my vision.

"She'll be a big part of your life, Sis." She looked out into the yard a few seconds. "Love got no definition, baby girl. It don't need no reason to be. It just be. Your heart be open for love. That love gonna take you away from this day. When you find it, you hold on with both hands. You hear me, girl? Both hands. Don't you ever let go. And don't you let anyone bring doubt to your choices. You'll find your butterflies."

I've found them. Did she understand easily what I was struggling to face? How could she have so much knowledge behind those blue eyes? Her words spoke volumes to me, leaving me speechless to continue. Our exchange ended with those last few words.

CHAPTER 26

SHORTLY AFTER BREAKFAST, Sam and I packed the Jeep up to travel back to Alabama. Memaw had made cat-head biscuits and country gravy for us before we left. Her homemade biscuits were so large that the tops of them were as big as a cat's head, thus the name we called them. Her white country gravy with chunks of sausage poured over the top was my favorite way of eating them. I had thought Sam would have enjoyed them too but she merely picked at the plate of food in front of her. Her conversation with Memaw and me at breakfast gave no indications to the last few hours we spent together. She gave no hint that anything had happened.

"Ya'll come back this way real soon," Memaw said to Sam as she hugged her good-bye. "It done my heart some good to be around such a wonderful friend of my Rayne's."

Sam gave her a shy smile. "I enjoyed it too, Memaw. Thank you for making me feel so welcome."

"Anytime," she said with a wink. Her good-bye to me came with tears building in the corner of her eyes. "This part never easy, baby girl. You be careful on your drive, you hear?"

"Yes, ma'am," I said, joining her in the falling of our tears. "I love you."

She held me tightly in her arms. "Aw, Sis, I love you too."
Brown sugar and honey.

THE DRIVE WAS quiet—solemn. Each of us faced the windows holding the passing of trees without a word spoken between us. Even the wind was still without a rustle of a breeze evident among the branches. Minutes became hours as the miles crept along in the silence.

"Sam?" I said, finally breaking the hush between us as we passed into Birmingham's city limits.

"Hmmm," she replied.

"I don't want our trip to end this way. I don't want to drop you off back home with this distance between us."

"I know. Me either." She paused and shifted in her seat to face me. "But I don't know what to say to make it not feel like this."

"Say it won't stay this way."

"It won't. We just need some time to process what happened or," she said as she looked out the window, "what nearly happened. We both need to think through some things."

"I s'pose you're right," I said. Although I had no idea where those thoughts would take me.

I questioned myself a hundred times over on the drive back to Alabama. I regretted stopping Sam's advances every mile I drove. The only sense of it all was that I reacted out of sheer panic and fear for what would happen the day after—what distance or change would happen between us if we had followed our desires. Yet here we were experiencing such intense change and distance that we hardly spoke a word to each other. Would it not have been better to have a night, my first night, of passion in someone's arms—Sam's arms if the end result was to be the same? "But you were different last night before I fell asleep."

"I know."

"You acted as if you understood . . . as if it was going to be okay."

"I do understand how you feel. I guess I'm having trouble understanding how I feel. But yeah . . . we'll be okay."

I reached the corner parking area outside her apartment before I realized we had gotten that close to her home. Time was lost in my thoughts—in my questions. She got out of the Jeep and reached into the backseat to get her bag within seconds of me parking. She stood with one hand remaining on the frame of the door but didn't walk to my side to tell me good-bye.

"I'll talk to you later. Okay, Rayne?" she said flatly.

"Okay." It stung to hear her call me Rayne. I missed the sound of Stormy floating from her lips.

She gave her head a slight tilt before turning on her heels and walking toward the apartment building.

I couldn't stop myself from calling out to her. "Sam!" I heard desperation in my voice. She stopped but didn't turn around. "I don't want it like this. What can I do?"

Her shoulders rose and fell as she took in a breath. She didn't turn around. Her silence spoke more than any words she could've said out loud. I watched her walk into the renovated warehouse before putting the Jeep in drive and slowly removing my foot off of the brake.

WITH THE CONTINUED distance between Sam and I along with so many questions I kept asking myself, I let school once again become my deterrent to self-exploration. It was the life I would accept. The life I knew how to accept—the life I understood. I tried to force my mind to forget the crossed boundaries Sam and I had shared.

Grant remained a constant through it all. Our relationship was untarnished in his eyes. He was excited to tell me about his hours in the operating room and hardly took notice to my demeanor. If he had, he gave no clue to it. He also didn't seem to mind us not having sex since my return. It had been over three weeks and not a word from him about the lack of bedroom activity. Eventually I knew it would have to change but I was certainly not going to push it if he didn't, especially not as long as I wished for the touch of Sam's hands instead of his.

Inwardly I feared I wouldn't be able to go through the motions as I had done so many times before. As for now we seemed to be a comfort . . . a support for each other during the hectic schedules of residency. Our focus was on the bigger picture versus the stagnancy of our relationship. I couldn't pretend I didn't think of Sam. In the quiet of my apartment, my thoughts automatically drifted to her. I missed her terribly since we returned. I told myself I was giving her space by not calling but I knew something deeper brewed under the surface of our distance. Those were the thoughts keeping me up at night.

One mid-morning Sunday, Grant coerced me into going to the Corner Café for brunch. He was craving a short stack of pancakes and nothing else would do but for us to walk down the block to the café.

"Hey look," he said, pointing over to a booth along the far wall, "it's Sam."

I looked over to see Sam staring at us. She looked down at the table as Grant pulled me toward where she sat. Across from her was the back of a brunette's head.

"Hey, Sam. Fancy meeting you here," Grant said once we reached the booth.

"Hi, Grant," she said, darting her eyes over to me. "Rayne." She motioned toward the woman sitting across from her. "This is Kim. Kim, this is Grant and Rayne. We go to school together."

"Hi," the woman said, smiling as she nodded in our direction.

My stomach lunged at the way she described us. *We go to school together.* It hurt to hear her emotionless expression of what I was to her. Not that I expected her to say, "The best friend I lost after she kicked me out of her bed."

"It's pretty packed here this morning. Would you mind if we joined you so we don't have to wait for a table?" Grant asked.

"Uh . . . no, that's fine," Sam said. She slid herself and her cup of coffee closer to the wall.

"We just got here and haven't even ordered yet." Kim got up quickly to join Sam on her side of the booth.

Grant motioned for me to slide into the empty seat. "Thanks, girls. I'm starving. I didn't think Rayne would ever get out of bed this morning."

Sam's head snapped up to look at me with a hardened expression. No doubt she must have immediately thought we had spent the night together, which we had but it wasn't as what I pictured her imagining. Yet, I was quite sure I couldn't say the same for her. Sam looked as if she herself had climbed out of bed minutes earlier. Her hair was pulled back in a lazy ponytail with sprigs of it tucked behind her ears. She had on a well-worn Def Leppard t-shirt that hugged her chest in the most tantalizing way. A small line of pink gloss covered her lips. Kim seemed a little overdressed for the crowd around us. She had on a black snug fitting dress that stopped an inch above her knees. A line of crumbled wrinkles were spread across her torso.

The waitress brought over four fresh cups of coffee after she took our order. The conversation up until then had been fairly quiet as we all studied over the menus. Sam took a long sip of her coffee, keeping the cup held inches from her face while she rested her elbows on the table. She took another deep sip.

"Long night?" I asked with more callus in my voice than I intended.

All three of them snapped their eyes at me. Grant's eyebrows were formed in a frown as if questioning the nature of my tone.

Sam held her eyes locked into mine, not wavering to my stare. "You could say that."

Kim blushed and gave Sam a shy smile. A wave of nausea hit my stomach.

"So, Sam, whatcha been up to?" Grant asked. "I haven't seen you much since Memorial weekend. How's things with your dad? Rayne told me he cut you off and you are living off of student loans."

"For the most part. I still don't talk to him. Mom says the money will be in my account if I ever want it. I've left it there because she keeps insisting I try to switch specialties as soon as I can."

"And are you?" he said, reaching under the table to hold my hand.

Sam followed his hand with her eyes. "When hell freezes over."

"Grant, will you let me out?" I asked, nudging his leg. "I need to go to the rest room."

I slid out of the booth and quickly sprinted to the bathroom. I had to get a grip on the anger—on the jealousy I was feeling before I made a spectacle of myself. I stared at my reflection in the mirror. *What the hell is wrong with you?*

"What the fuck was that about?" Sam said, bursting through the bathroom door.

The black shirt hiked up above the waist of her faded blue jeans as she raised her hands in expression. A linear hole was stretched across the thigh of her jeans just below the left pocket. I was left speechless, watching her walk in.

"I'm serious, Rayne. What the fuck was all of that about out there?"

"What was what?" I said, letting the acid build back up in my voice. "I'm not the one dragging in here looking like I just fell out of bed."

"Oh, but apparently your man couldn't get you out from under the sheets long enough to come get breakfast."

"It isn't like that. And even if it was at least he isn't wearing the same clothes he had on last night when I picked him up at the bar."

"He doesn't have to," she spat. "He has his own drawer at your apartment."

"It isn't like that and you know it."

"Then what is it like, Rayne? Tell me. Huh? What exactly is it like?"

"You know what it's like, Sam." I felt the tears welling up in my eyes and quickly turned to hide them from her.

"Whatever," she shouted as she stormed out of the bathroom.

It took several minutes before I could compose myself enough to go back out into the restaurant. I had no idea how I was going to manage sitting across from Sam and Kim while trying to pretend nothing was wrong. I walked out and saw Grant alone at the booth. Two plates of pancakes sat on the table, one in front of him and another across the table in front of the newly empty seat.

"Sam left. She seemed pretty pissed and obviously she isn't the only one," he said to me as I sat down. "What's going on between you two? I haven't seen her around since y'all got back. Did something happen?"

"No. Nothing happened," I said, twirling my fork in the puddle of syrup at the bottom of the pancake stack.

"Are you sure?"

"Yes. And please . . . I don't want to talk about it anymore. Okay?"

He studied me for a moment before pursing his lips. "Okay. If you say so."

I ABSENTLY REACHED into the back of my scrubs pocket to answer the vibrating phone as I walked out of the back entrance of the hospital toward the employee parking lot. I was exhausted after finishing a sixteen-hour shift, the last eight of which was spent on call in the emergency room. All I wanted to do at this point was to go home, plop down on the couch, prop my feet up, and drink a cold beer. If I had the energy to walk back into the kitchen, I may even have another beer after that one. Although the way I felt now, I would most likely pass out asleep after the first one was emptied. The last thing I wanted interfering with those plans was the vibrating phone.

"Hello," I answered exasperated.

"Did I catch you at a bad time?" Sam's voice was tentative and shy.

Caught in surprise at the sound of her voice, I stopped to sit on the park bench under an old oak tree. The setting sun of the spring sky cast a shadow over the landscaped sitting area.

"No, not at all. I was just leaving the hospital." I nervously sat erect not yet resting against the back of the bench. It had been almost a month since the morning in the café. We had run into each other a few times but we never said more than a few cordial pleasantries. "Are you okay?"

"Yeah." She sighed heavily. "No . . . I'm not okay."

"What's wrong? What happened?"

"I miss you, Stormy."

I relaxed against the wooden seat. I felt a smile form across my face and my heart. "I miss you too, Sam. I've missed you so much."

"What are you doing now? Can you meet me for coffee or something?"

"I had my mouth set for a beer. Could I interest you in that?"

"Hell's yeah you could."

We met at a replica of an Irish Pub in Four Points. They had over thirty beers on tap at the local favorite happy hour spot. It was crowded enough to be able to speak freely without fear of being overheard but not so much that we would have difficulty carrying on a conversation. We sat at a small patio table next to the iron gate separating the pub from the sidewalk. A breeze carried the scent of eucalyptus mint in the air, causing me to smile.

"What is it?" Sam asked, arching her eyebrow at the change in my expression.

My smile broadened. "Nothing. Happy to be here with you is all."

Her eyes brightened in the light. "I'll drink to that." She lifted up her glass of dark, lager beer in a toast. An orange slice floated on top of the brew. "To friendship."

I clinked my glass against hers. "To us."

"To us." Her gaze was soft as she looked into my eyes. "Damn I've missed you." She took a long sip of her beer. "I'm sorry about that morning at the Corner Café."

"I am too. I truly am. I don't know what came over me." *I was jealous as hell, that's what came over me.* I looked down at the beer glass resting between my cupped hands. "I'm sorry about a lot of things."

Sam sucked in a deep breath and then took another large swallow of her beer. "I don't guess it would be possible to table all of that for a while, would it?"

"I'm sure game if you are."

Sam clinked her glass against mine. "Done. So tell me everything. What has been going on in your life? How is your residency? And Memaw? How's she?"

I chuckled at the mention of Memaw. "Funny you should ask about her. She called me the other day to tell me about some guys she caught sneaking onto the property out at the cabin. They were climbing over the fence along the tree line. Who knows why they were. Memaw said they were going to scare away all of the good fish so she decided to put a hot wire along the fence. She was watching with binoculars when the man got caught straddling the fence. Good Lord . . . she was laughing so hard that I could hardly understand a word she was saying. Apparently he got the shock of a lifetime."

Sam choked on her swallow of beer. "That woman is something else."

We sat outside on the patio lost in each other's conversation well into the night. In fact we were on our third round and appetizers before we noticed how late it had gotten. I hadn't even remembered how exhausted I was. Sam was loving every minute of her Ob/GYN residency. She was happy she had stood her ground with her father, knowing deep down she never would have been happy in cardiothoracic surgery. Her father was starting to become resigned to the fact that she wasn't going to join him in his practice.

Outside on the sidewalk, Sam pulled me into her for a good-bye hug. She held me in her arms tightly, swaying slightly as I stood collected in her embrace. I didn't want her to let me go—to ever let me go. I had missed the closeness we shared—the ease of our connection. I had missed being held. I had missed *her*.

"I needed this," she whispered. "I need . . . you."

I sighed deeply letting my body relax even further into her. "It isn't the same without you, Sam."

I ran my hand up her back as I laid my head on her shoulder. I was sure people must have noticed us standing there wrapped in each other's arms but at that moment it truly didn't matter. Nothing did.

CHAPTER 27

I COULDN'T SLEEP that night. The linens of my bed felt heavy against my body, causing me to feel as if I were fighting for each breath while trapped beneath them. I kicked at the material until the sheet and duvet became a crumpled mess on the floor. The red numbers of the bedside clock mocked me as they very slowly clicked from one minute to the next. It was one o'clock in the morning and my eyes had yet to know sleep. Thoughts of Sam's body lying across mine sprung into my sight the moment I closed them. They were so vivid . . . I nearly felt the warmth of her body and breath against my skin.

I sat up and swung my legs to the side of the bed. "This is ridiculous."

I had left the window cracked but even the breeze flowing in wasn't enough to shake me from my frustrations. I stood up, exhaling a large grumbling sigh, and picked up the jeans that lay across the foot of my bed.

A few moments later I was driving aimlessly under the city's street lights . . . no thought or direction, just an innate need to escape the four walls closing in on me. Of course, the radio stations sucked at that time of night, their choice of song selection grated on my nerves even more. I shut the irritating noise off with a forceful turn of the knob and gripped the steering wheel tighter as my thoughts ran freely. Was there ever to be any escape from the vision of Sam's body? Frustration could spurn fear, anger, or in this case . . . bravery. I decided to face Sam and finally rid myself of these thoughts.

"Who in the hell is ringing my buzzer at this time of night?" she called through the outdoor entrance speaker after only a few buzzes.

"Sam, it's me. Can I come up?"

"Rayne? What's wrong? Are you okay?"

"I need to talk. Will you buzz me up?"

The door clicked, signaling the lock had been released. My

heart jumped up in my throat as I climbed the last stair to see her standing in the doorway waiting for me. She was in a pair of cotton shorts resting across her upper thighs and a white V-neck shirt one size too large. Its opening around the neck had slid down exposing her chest. Her hair was tossed lazily over to one side. She looked . . . sexy as hell.

"What's wrong, Stormy?" she asked.

I said nothing. For a split second, I could do nothing . . . but stare. Then I walked slowly toward her through the doorway, sliding my hand within hers to pull her inside behind me. Hearing the door click closed behind us, I turned to face her—yet still said nothing. No words came to my mind. There were no words to say. Our clasped hands were suspended in the air between us.

"Okay, Stormy, you're starting to scare . . ."

I placed my finger against her lips and applied enough force with it and my body stepping closer to cause her to rest her back against the door. All I wanted to do was look at her—absorb every curve of her into my mind. I watched the questioning in her eyes as they darted back and forth. I felt the twitch of her lips against my finger, the softness of them as I ran my thumb across her lower lip.

Her palm began to sweat as it remained held within my hand. I bit the corner of my lip as I traced my finger down her neck. Its pulse quickened to my touch as my finger passed down over the skin and slowly across her collar bone. I slid the tip of my finger under the V-necked rim of her t-shirt and pulled the edge of it down along one side to uncover her as much as I could without removing it. A swirl of heat seared through me, starting deep in my belly and shooting straight up to my head when the hint of her breast was first bared.

The grip of her hand tightened within mine. I slid my hand underneath its perfect form . . . the weight of it cupped in my palm. Her head hit hard against the wooden door as I gently traced my thumb across her nipple. The sound distracted me and I looked back up at her face.

Her lips were parted. The expression in her eyes no longer held the questioning they did a few moments earlier. They held something different now . . . something more. Her pupils were dilated wide, causing her eyes to seem black. The knot in my stomach curled tighter. I felt a twinge of strength in her arm pulling my hand toward her. I followed her silent command and took her lips within mine. My hand squeezed against the weight of her breast as our kisses deepened. Our lips parted, allowing the first touch of our tongues.

The electricity between them caused me to sit straight up in the bed. The breeze through my bedroom window ran a chill across me as I felt a bead of sweat run down the small of my back.

"What the fuck?" I screamed into the loneliness of the night.

CHAPTER 28

I WAS HAUNTED by the night time visions of Sam. The dreams came more frequently as time passed. I didn't seem any closer to a resolution or explanation of my feelings now than I had that last night at the cabin. At this point it was more suppression than understanding. My dreams were invaded by her night after night, most of which were of an intimate interlude between us. Never, not once in those dreams did I stop her or myself like I had the night at the cabin. Often I would lie awake at night, cursing myself for stopping her. I would try to find reason for why I had stopped but the answers never came. Thankfully the hours of my general surgery residency helped to occupy the day. Normally, I was scheduled for sixteen hour shifts but rarely left any earlier on days I wasn't.

"Hey . . . have you been waiting long?" Grant asked, plopping down hard in the booth across from me.

"Waiting?" I said.

"Yeah. How long ya been here? Sorry, I got held up in a case. The attending broke the damn suture when he was tying the knot so we had to redo the whole graft again. Idiot. Anyway, you been here long?"

I looked down at my watch. Actually I had been waiting for thirty minutes but I had hardly noticed. The lack of sleep last night had numbed my brain for the day. "No. Not too long."

"I ran into Paxton on the way out of the case," Grant continued to ramble, barely taking a breath. "Man, I was cussing up a storm. He said that attending is always screwing stuff up. How he ever made it to be an attending beats the hell outta me." He stopped long enough to order a Coke from the waitress as she brought me a fresh Diet Coke to replace the watered down one in front of me. "Oh, yeah. He wants us to go to dinner with him and his wife Saturday night. Think you can swing it? I have some studying to do but should be able to break away for a few hours."

"Who's breaking away from studying over here?" Sam asked, walking up to the table.

The sight of her immediately caused a heat to flush my cheeks as my mind pictured her backed against the door gasping at my touch.

"You should come too, Sam?" Grant said, looking up at her.

"Come where?" she asked, motioning for me to slide over so she could sit down.

"I don't know where yet, but knowing Paxton it will be some swanky restaurant. Think you could round up a date on such short notice?" He teasingly waggled his eyebrows at her.

She gave him a sarcastic smirk and a tilt of her head. "Oh, I think I can manage." She looked over her shoulder at me. "Sure. Sounds good to me. I could use a night off with friends." She nudged me with her knee under the table. "What's up, Stormy? Cat got your tongue today?"

My mouth turned dry as I thought of our tongues sliding over each other's in the kisses of my dreams. I had to swallow hard before answering. "No. Just tired. Long hours, you know?"

Her face turned serious. "Yeah, I know . . . but you don't look like you've slept at all in days. Maybe you need to pull back on those volunteer hours."

"How do you know I've been volunteering?" I asked in surprise.

"Oh I have my sources," she said, winking at me. "Seriously, are you sure you feel up to this Saturday night? Maybe you should get some sleep instead."

"Oh, Gawd, no," I said.

Another night alone was the last thing I needed right now. Maybe a night out was what would bring me a good night's rest again. Sam had been as busy as I in her rotations, pulling any extra hours she could get as well. She felt she needed to play catch-up to those who had been in the OB/Gyn rotations longer than she had. We managed to fit in a couple of Sunday brunches here and there but the time never seemed long enough. I missed the hours we used to get to spend together. She had started dating and going out again. I wasn't a part of this side of her life as I think she found it just as hard to include me as I found to be included.

"No, she's right," Grant said flatly. "It's okay if you are too tired to go, Rayne. We can do it some other time."

"No, I'm fine. I want to go. Besides, I don't have to go in on Saturday. All I have planned is to clean my apartment. I'll sleep in that morning."

"How about you sleep in and then sleep some more. Do like I do." Sam stole a grape off of my fruit salad. "Hire an undergrad to clean it while you're at the hospital."

I laughed at both her suggestion and the look on her face as she chewed the stolen fruit. "No, I will have time but thanks for the suggestion."

"Great. I'll text Paxton and tell him it's on." He leaned over the table to kiss my forehead. "Sorry, babe, gotta run but I will come by your place tonight after rounds. Maybe we can get some takeout? See you Saturday, Sam." He tossed a twenty dollar bill on the table and turned to walk out of the restaurant.

"Who's Paxton?" Sam asked, stealing another grape.

I couldn't help but laugh. "Oh, you'll see."

FRIDAY NIGHT MY feet felt like they wore shoes of cement instead of the tennis shoes I had put on seventeen hours ago. My scrubs smelled stale with sweat, betadine, and latex. I unlocked the door to my apartment and only hoped I had enough strength to take a shower before collapsing onto my bed. There was no way sleep would escape me tonight. Exhaustion would surely win the battle. The door swung open, giving way to smells of lavender and vanilla. The shock of the foreign scent caused my eyes to spring open.

The apartment was spotless—not just clean, but immaculate. No clothes were strewn on the floor, no dishes scattered the counter top, and no towels hung from different hooks in the bathroom. There was a sheet of paper on top of one of the pillows on my bed. I picked it up and pressed the pillow against my nose to smell the fresh linen. One word was written in quite a familiar handwriting, "Sleep!"

Text message to Sam at 11:43pm: "Thanks!"

Text message to Sam at 11:47pm: "Can't believe you did this!"

Text message from Sam at 11:52pm: "Knew that key would come in handy one day."

Text message to Sam at 11:54pm: "I'll give you ten more copies :-)"

Text message from Sam at 11:56pm: "Nah, I'll never lose this one. Go to sleep."

Text message from Sam at 11:57pm: "Now!"

Text message to Sam at 12:00am: "Good night. Thx again."

Text message from Sam at 12:02am: "My pleasure. Sweet dreams."

CHAPTER 29

"HELLO," SAM ANSWERED on the fourth ring.

"Did I wake you?" I asked.

"Uh . . . no." She hesitated.

"Oh, sorry. Are you alone?"

She chuckled. "Yes," she said in a very drawn out manner. "What's up?"

"Nothing much. I didn't get to talk to you at dinner; so, I thought I'd call to see if you were still up." My stomach still ached from being over sated and my inhibitions slightly lessened with the four bottles of Chianti the six of us had shared at dinner. Upon Paxton's suggestion we went to a family-owned Italian restaurant downtown. The food was the most authentic I had ever tasted. The couple who started the restaurant still managed the affairs on the weekends even though they were well into their seventies by now.

"Yeah, the guys dominated the conversation something terrible. And damn if they weren't loud. Hell, I couldn't even talk to you across the table." I heard shuffling noises across the line.

"What are you doing?" I asked.

"Sorry," she said in a muffled voice. "You caught me getting ready for bed. I was trying to take my shirt off. Hold on a sec." I heard more shuffling as her voice drifted away from the phone. "Don't peek."

My eyes rolled back in my head with the thought of her undressing in front of me. A grumbling sigh escaped my lips.

"Okay . . . I'm back," she said. "So does Grant really want that guy as a partner?"

"Who knows," I said, fumbling with the sheet across my lap as I sat with my back against the headboard of the bed. "So, where's your overnight company? Not opening a new toothbrush tonight?"

She paused. "Where's yours?"

"He didn't stay. He had to get up early to round. Besides I was too beat for that anyway."

"That? Hmmm . . ." she murmured in the phone. "Interesting way of phrasing you have chosen there."

I hadn't completely thought through how Sam would perceive my meaning. Sex with Grant was the farthest thing from my mind. I wasn't in the mood for the pull and push of him trying to instigate what I knew was not happening.

"Yeah, I s'pose. So . . . where's . . . *Zoe*?"

I knew the question came out more sarcastic then I had intended but I was taken aback when Sam walked in with her date for the evening. I hadn't seen many of the women Sam dated since we decided to keep our relationship as a strictly platonic friendship. Yet this girl was a far cry from Claire. I would never describe Zoe as a woman with class. Her makeup seemed too done up and her shirt seemed not done up enough. I didn't think it was legal to come to a restaurant showing that much cleavage. Apparently Sam met her at one of the surrounding, off-campus hospitals where she had pulled some extra clinic hours.

"Ha. Why do you say her name like that?"

"I don't know. But honestly. Sam, she didn't seem your type."

"What do you mean?"

"Nothing bad. I only meant she didn't seem like someone I thought you would be attracted to."

"Why, Stormy, you almost sound as if you're jealous."

"I'm *not* jealous. I just meant I thought you could do better is all."

She sighed deep enough to where I could hear it through the receiver. "Yeah, well . . . the good ones are always taken, aren't they? Look, it was one date. I'm not interested so I took her home straight after."

"I'm sorry, Sam. I didn't mean to upset you."

"You didn't, Stormy. It's just frustrating sometimes."

The silence across the line grew between us. "Want me to let you go?"

"No, please let's talk some more. I don't want to hang up like this. And I'm sure you called for some other reason than to find out if I was alone or not."

I chuckled. "Yes, there was another reason."

"So . . . shoot."

"Really it was just to talk." That was a lie and I knew it before

I said it. It was the safest answer to give. The truth was I couldn't stop thinking of my dreams while I sat across from her at dinner. It seemed every moment I saw her now I was plagued with the vision of her lips against mine. I yearned so badly to feel them again.

"Tyler seemed nice enough, didn't she?"

"Huh?" I asked, pulling myself away from my thoughts. "I'm sorry . . . what?"

"Tyler. She seemed nice. I can't believe she is married to Dr. Dick."

Tyler was a very nice woman. She had been pleasant and engaging, joining in the conversation when she could add something. However Grant and Paxton truly dominated the entire evening. They talked of their rotations and cases they had gotten to perform. For the majority of the night, neither of them seemed to notice the table had four other people sitting at it. Paxton was the definition of obnoxious. He was rude not only to the waitress but also quite condescending to Tyler and interrupted her every time she spoke. Sam and I had heard about the infamous Dr. Dick during our rounds on the floors. We both agreed the staff named him fittingly enough.

"I know. He definitely married up," I said.

"You can say that again."

I stared up at the ceiling as I ran one hand through my hair. "Hey, Sam . . . can I ask you a question?" I paused, not really waiting for an answer but rather waiting for the words I would choose. "How did you know?"

"How did I know what? That he was a dick? Hell, I knew two minutes after meeting him."

"No, not that." I rubbed the cotton sheet in between my fingers before patting it flat across my lap. "How did you know you were gay?"

She was silent.

"You don't have to answer if you don't want to," I said quickly, afraid I had overstepped the boundaries of the conversation.

"I've always known," she said softly a few seconds later.

"Always? What do you mean always?"

"Ever since I was a kid. I was never like the other girls. I never really fit in when they wanted to gush over boys. Heck, I was friends with boys more than I was girls. Girls made me nervous. I don't know, Rayne, I've always known . . . like it was never anything I questioned."

"But didn't you have a boyfriend in school?"

"Nope."

"Never?"

"Nope," she said again.

"Have you ever kissed a boy?"

She laughed quietly. "No, I've never kissed a boy."

"Huh?"

"You seemed surprised."

"Yeah, I guess so. I can't believe you've never . . . ever kissed a boy before."

"Had you kissed a woman before me?"

"Well, no," I said.

"Then why the big surprise? You grew up attracted to boys so it was natural for you to kiss them. I grew up attracted to girls. It's the same thing really. So why would I kiss a boy? Besides I can't imagine it would feel any better than kissing a woman." She paused, then whispered, "Not for me anyway."

Not for me either. Now I was the one silent. I thought about our kiss on the dock. My fears had gotten the better of me that night at the cabin. The fear of finally feeling what I had always dreamed of feeling only to have it taken away. *Sex is sex*. Afraid of what a label would mean to my life. What it would change in my life? The fears and questions of the unknown had kept me from feeling the searing energy her kiss had sent through my body. It was fear that caused me to push her away. It was clear to me now. Yet the fear was absent in the subconscious of my dreams when I found myself pulling her back to me.

"So, Stormy . . . now I have a question," she said.

"Yeah?"

"Why do you ask?"

"I don't know." I ran my finger across the speaker of the phone as if it was her lip resting softly against my cheek. "Curious, I guess."

"Are you sure?" she asked, barely audible through the phone. Her voice had grown raspier. "Are you sure that's all it is . . . curiosity?"

"I think about the night at the cabin a lot, Sam."

She was silent.

"We never talk about it," I said. "There is so much unsaid between us. So much I question."

And still she said nothing.

"Please talk to me."

"Stormy . . . would those answers change anything about us. I mean, would it change who we are to each other next week? Would finding those answers change our relationship at all?"

"I don't know, Sam."

"I can't discuss them or that night until you do know. I'm sorry. I just can't."

CHAPTER 30

THE SLEEPLESS NIGHTS seemed to be intensified after the phone call with Sam. The sadness in her voice plagued my mind until the nights of unrest flowed continuously. I decided to volunteer for more call hours. The extra hours gave me vital experience and surgical skills but it was the distraction I found most rewarding. The fluorescent hospital lighting didn't seem to cast the shadow of Sam's face the way the moonlight streaming into my apartment did.

A Saturday night call in the UAB emergency room had never failed me in the way of distracting my thoughts. Weekend night call was brutal for a general surgery resident. Yet there she stood in front of me. I knew it was Sam the moment I saw her. She was standing at the coffee station with her back to me. Her hair was pulled back in a ponytail, exposing her long, delectable neck. I stood in silence, watching the scrub shirt shuffle over her back as she fixed a cup of coffee. The visions in my head betrayed me once again as I imagined my hands replacing the cotton fibers to flow across her skin. I was lost in the moment of envisioning the warmth of her skin against my fingertips.

She turned around. "Holy shit."

Her arms flew up, spilling the freshly made cup of coffee down the front of her shirt.

"What the *fuck*, Stormy?" She pulled the shirt away from her chest with one hand while slapping away the excess fluid with the other.

Normally in a situation like this I wouldn't be able to prevent uncontrollable laughter. I loved being the practical joker that scared everyone. I had ever since I was a child. A few of Memaw's white hairs were no doubt the result of my shenanigans. One of my favorites as a child was when I would awaken before Memaw could come into my room to get me. I would lie in bed as still as I could until she leaned down to kiss me. At the moment her face was next to mine, I would shout something or raise up quickly to

C. D. Cain

kiss her on the cheek. Memaw would lose composure every time. It was quite hilarious.

But this time, this time I wasn't laughing. My mind had not been free of thoughts of Sam in some intimate way since the dreams had started. Tonight, alone with Sam in the women's break room, was no exception. In fact, I believe my mind was wandering all the more rapidly.

"I'm sorry."

"It's okay," she said, laughing a little as she swiped again at the front of her shirt. "It is eerily quiet in here tonight. I had probably already gotten a little spooked even before I saw you standing there."

"Yeah, it's pretty quiet in here tonight," I said.

"I think we are the only two women residents on call."

"Looks that way." I didn't move.

"Is Grant on call tonight too?"

"Yeah," I said flatly. "He's still trying to get that vascular fellowship. He practically lives up here now."

"Are you okay with that?" she asked.

"Yeah."

Sam studied me for a few minutes longer before again stretching the scrub shirt away from her chest. "Damn, this thing is getting cold now. Was hot as hell a second ago. Come in here with me while I change tops." She motioned toward the door that led into the locker room. "And then you owe me a cup of coffee." She winked at me before walking toward the door.

I followed her into the small changing area and tensed as she raised the soiled shirt over her head to expose the red satin bra she was wearing. Quietly I backed myself against the opposite wall but was unable to focus on anything that wasn't red satin. I watched the flicker of her chest muscle as she tossed the shirt over into the linen basket. Either she was genetically blessed with a toned abdomen or she found a few minutes in her day to do crunches. I didn't know which . . . and I didn't care. The bright orange drawstring of her scrub pants was tied snuggly below her navel. The sight of it begged my body to trace its circular pattern through my fingertip.

"Ahem." I looked up to see her eyes holding me with a quizzical expression. "What's up with you tonight, Stormy? You seem so out in left field. You okay?"

"I haven't been sleeping much."

"Oh? Do you wanna talk about it?" she asked.

"It's nothing. Just dreaming a lot these days."

"Mmm . . . hmmm, are they the ones where you're the only person left after the zombies attack?"

I didn't laugh. I didn't even smile. I couldn't. All I wanted was to rip my shirt off to feel her skin against mine. "No."

Her smile faded. "Rayne, you sound serious. What's up? Are you really okay? Do you want to talk about it?"

"No," I said, finally taking my gaze off of her to look down at my shoes. "And no."

She took a step toward me. The clean scrub shirt still in her hand.

"No . . . don't come any closer," I said, putting my hand up in the air between us.

"What?" She stopped and rocked back on her heels to stand again in front of the wall of lockers. "Why?"

"Because . . ." I felt the line of tears wetting my lower eyelids.

"Because why, Rayne?" Her voice was unsure—timid even.

"Because I'll do this." I took two fast steps toward her and put my hand behind her neck as I got close enough. My actions were without thought . . . without inhibition . . . without reservation. My lips were upon hers before I had even sensed my body had moved of its own accord. I didn't care. In that moment I knew kissing her was as fundamental to my life as the very air I breathed in.

I felt her lips pull abruptly apart from mine. Her eyes searched mine for a few seconds before she put her arms around me to pull me in closer to her. Feeling her moan against my lips caused my head to spin. She took my breath with the first touch of her tongue against mine. I had felt Sam's kiss before but this was different— *entirely different.*

I couldn't feel her enough, couldn't get her close enough. I tightened my arms to pull her body against me. The excitement of her kiss continued to steal my breath, making me dizzy in her arms.

I pulled my lips from hers to draw in a deep gasp of air. She whispered my name as she leaned in to continue her kisses along my neck. The contrast of the softness of her lips and tongue against the nibble of her teeth as she brought the skin of my neck into her mouth caused my head to fall back as I gave in to the ecstasy of her. The pounding of my heart deafened nearly every sound around me.

I was lost in the feeling of her. There was no room around us . . . no walls . . . no lockers . . . just us. I could hear only the sound of her breath in my ear, see only the curls of her hair falling across my face, smell only the eucalyptus mint flowing from her skin, feel only the warmth of her against me, and taste only the leftover kiss upon my lips. There was nothing else. My fingers trickled down their own path, causing her to once again return her lips to mine. She sucked my bottom lip between hers as my fingers coursed over the satin-covered breast. Her moan vibrated against my lips as my thumb traced quickly over her nipple. Her abdomen quivered under my touch as my hand slid down her waist and slowly underneath the edge of her scrubs pants.

Sam grabbed my wrist as I intertwined the drawstring between my fingers. "Wait . . . wait . . . wait," she panted. "Not like this . . . Rayne. Not . . . here." Her breath was labored as she fought to speak.

"Please, Sam . . . *please*," I murmured raggedly against her lips. "I have to touch you." I kissed her softly. "I *need* to touch you."

The grip of her fingers loosened from around my wrist, then they ran up my arm to my neck and pulled my lips back to hers. We shared a deep moan as our tongues touched once more. My heart beat faster and my hand shook as I pulled the bow of the drawstring loose. The material was no longer bound tightly against her waist and exposed the feeling of more satin against my fingertips. My mind envisioned a red panty line fitting snugly over the top of her hip. I slipped the tip of my finger over the top of the satin band to pull it toward me before sliding my hand between the fabric and her skin.

My breath became short—rapid. I feared I would pass out if one more sensation swarmed my body. Twinkling lights flashed sporadically in the darkness of my closed eyelids. My chest rose and fell heavily with the warmth of her against my hand. I had never felt softness like this before . . . had never had my excitement heightened this intensely simply from knowing what my touch was doing to another. We both groaned loudly in unison as I felt the essence of her upon my fingers.

Beep . . . Beep. The pager chirped and vibrated between our bodies as they were pressed together. *Beep . . . Beep.* I froze until the pager once again vibrated against me.

Sam's head fell back against the locker. "This is so *not* happening right now."

I looked down dazedly to read the flashing numbers—*6704* illuminated on the screen. It was the emergency room.

"I guess I have to take this," I whispered, still fighting for solid breath.

I stepped away from her to the phone on the wall. Her body was slumped against the lockers. Her scrub pants dangled enticingly from her hip, exposing the red underwear. She didn't move to adjust them back over her waist and I didn't take my eyes from her.

"This is Dr. Storm. I was paged."

"Sure, Dr. Storm, one sec. Got Dr. Storm on line one," the ward secretary yelled as she put my call on hold.

"Dr. Storm, this is Angie a nurse down here in the ER. We got a trauma coming in. EMT's called it through. Fifty-two-year-old unresponsive male lateral T-bone MVA. He's tubed and bagged. They're coming in hot. ETA five minutes. Wanted you to be aware."

"Thanks, Angie. I'm headed your way."

Sam opened her eyes and slowly rolled her head toward me. I could only sigh as I gave her a small shrug.

"No problem, Doc. He'll be in Trauma 12."

Hanging up the receiver was the only time I took my eyes from her beautiful body. I cursed the timing under my breath before walking back to stand in front of her. She cupped her hands around my face.

She inhaled deeply and let out a long exhale. "I know you have to go, but please tell me what this was. Please tell me *this* isn't over."

"I don't know what to call it." I looked up at the ceiling but was pulled back to stare into eyes of blue as she rubbed her thumb over my bottom lip. Her touch was soft. "I wanted to feel what my dreams had been telling me I needed. And no. This isn't over."

Her smile was shy, yet pleased as she leaned in to kiss me once more. The kisses before had been hungry in our need to explore.

This kiss—this kiss was perhaps more intimate than those. I felt everything from her in that moment. The way her lips and tongue caressed mine screamed she too had as much need for me as I did for her. I couldn't have understood what she felt for me any clearer than if she whispered the words into my ears instead of letting them flow in our kiss. My knees weakened and I fell further into her arms . . . further into her.

She pulled her lips away and rested her forehead against mine. Her breath was short and quick. "What time do you get off? Please tell me you didn't sign up for a double shift."

I smiled. "You know me too well."

"Dammit," she mumbled.

"But this is the second shift. See you at seven," I said, smiling, and kissed her quickly before turning to go.

"Oh, thank God!"

THE ELATION SPRINTED my body and I took to the stairwells two steps at a time. I felt alive. My body finally found the truth for which it had always yearned. Never had I felt the excitement in another's touch. Never had it felt so right. I had to force my mind to return its concentration back to the trauma awaiting me in the emergency room. Maneuvering the stairwells, I tried to focus on the clinical pearls of differential diagnosis common with injuries found in motor vehicle accidents.

"Look for injuries to the abdomen and chest," I mumbled as I remembered the lectures. "Ask if a seat belt was worn or if an airbag deployed. The force of a seat belt can cause serious soft tissue injuries and if there wasn't an air bag, watch for trauma to the chest from the impact against the steering wheel." Words flew freely from my mouth with hardly an effort in my train of thought. "Of course there could be a head injury or broken bones. Will need to get X-rays and a CT scan if he is stable enough. Oh crap. She did say only one victim right?"

The automatic entry doors to the emergency room opened in front of me as a team of paramedics wheeled a gurney toward the triage room to the left of where I stood.

"Right this way, Doc," a short woman with even shorter bleached blond hair shouted as she followed the gurney.

The scene around me was organized chaos.

The EMT pulling the head of the gurney was calling out his report as Angie hurriedly recorded the information on her clipboard. "Fifty-two-year-old male per his driver's license. Unresponsive at the scene. Patient was involved in a MVA of lateral T-bone. Victim was hit at a high rate of speed. Air bag deployed. Seat belt intact." His hand was constantly squeezing the Ambu bag in a steady rhythm providing breaths through the endotracheal tube that had been inserted in the patient's mouth for an airway. "He's hypotensive and tachycardic. Heart rate has been holding around one-hundred-and-twenty beats per minute. Two liters of normal saline were given with a bump in blood pressure but dropped again as we pulled in."

The gurney stopped and I began my examination. His abdomen was exposed as his shirt had already been cut open. It was hard, rigid, and distended against my palpation. I heard no bowel sounds through my stethoscope. I noticed the classic seat belt sign of bruising across his abdomen. His skin was pale, cold, and clammy. Pulses in his wrists and feet were faint and barely palpable.

"Angie, grab me an ultrasound STAT." I looked up to take in my ever-changing surroundings. "You," I pointed to a nurse standing next to the paramedic, "hang two units of O positive blood now. Draw a CBC, chemistry panel, toxicology screen and type and cross. We will start with O positive blood but we need to get his blood type. Tell the lab to stay two units ahead of us."

I noticed Angie wheeling in the ultrasound machine. "She's ready to go, Doc."

"Great. Quick insert a Foley catheter now. Tell me the urine output and for God's sake yell if you see blood."

Within seconds I heard the sound of denim being cut and pulled away. I ran the ultrasound wand through the conducting gel over the left upper quadrant of his abdomen. I noted an increasing dark rim of fluid around his spleen which meant he was bleeding from or around it. With the rigidity I found in his belly, I feared he may also be bleeding from his liver.

"*Shit.* He's bleeding." I called out orders in succession to whoever was available. "Call the OR. Tell them we have a STAT exploratory laparotomy headed their way. Somebody get Dr. Rapsner on the phone. Tell him we're headed to the OR. I'll meet him up there."

"Fifty cc's of urine but clear," Angie said.

"Good, let's hope that means his bladder is intact."

"Mean arterial pressure just dropped below sixty. Blood pressure dropping fast. Heart rate one-hundred-forty-six beats per minute," the paramedic called out.

"Christ! He's crashing. Get that blood going now. Hang it on the way. Let's go people. Let's move. Angie call the lab. Tell them to send up a unit of fresh frozen plasma and platelets ten minutes ago. We've got to get him some clotting factors," I said as I started to help push the gurney out of the room. I knew we had to get him to the operating room fast. The only way to save him was to open up his belly as quickly as we could to stop the bleeding.

The operating room trauma team ushered us into an open operative suite. The scrub techs were already in their sterile gowns preparing the table of instruments that we would need for his surgery. The patient was wheeled next to the bed as the anesthesia team counted out, "On my count . . . one, two, three, move!"

I continued to bellow out orders without conscious thought. "We need to get this room warm. Turn the thermostat up. Push all fluids through a warmer. Get a warming blanket across his arms and chest. Then another one below the thighs. He's a bleeder. We'll need to prep him from the sternum to mid-thigh. Let's get a cell saver in here STAT." I knew with this amount of blood loss we needed to keep him warm and to try to salvage as much of his own blood as possible to give back to him. The cell saver would come in handy for that but only if there wasn't an underlining injury to his bowel. If the bowel was disrupted or open then the blood would be contaminated and unable to be used.

"Let's hope the lab has those units ready," I said.

"What do we have here, Dr. Storm?" A deep voice sounded from behind me. I turned to see Dr. Rapsner, my attending chief of trauma surgery enter the room.

"Fifty-two-year-old unresponsive male MVA. High velocity T-bone. Hypotensive. Tachycardic. Ultrasound showed bleeding around the spleen but with the distention of his abdomen I fear further hemorrhage. Possible hepatic. He hasn't been stable enough to get a CT scan. I'm unsure of bowel injury at this time but ordered a cell saver until we find out. Lab has been notified."

"Go scrub in, Doctor. We have work to do," he said.

Nervousness had not yet filtered into my roaring emotions. The magnitude of running my first trauma from start to finish had not fully registered yet. I was acting on adrenaline alone. Standing at the scrub sink, I let my thoughts escape to the feeling of Sam's wetness moments earlier on the fingertips now held under a flow of running water. I held her there for a fleeting moment before finishing my scrub and returning to the operating room.

Dr. Rapsner walked to the assistant side as we approached the table dressed in sterile gown and gloves. "You got us this far, Dr. Storm. Let's see what you can do."

I made a large incision across the middle of the patient's abdomen to get the best visualization. I needed a large open field to be able to see the organs of the upper abdomen like the liver and spleen as well as inspect the bowel and bladder. Once I reached the lining covering the internal organs, I warned anesthesia of the possibility of excessive blood loss. Some abdominal injuries which resulted in a significant amount of bleeding could actually tamponade, meaning that the bleeding was slowed due to the increased pressure in an enclosed belly. But once this was opened the blood loss could be quite significant and quite fast.

"Let's get some laps ready," I said to the scrub tech as I made the incision in the lining.

I packed lap sponges in all areas of the abdomen, particularly around the spleen and liver to soak up the blood. I elected to remove the spleen due to a large laceration across the surface. A few small tears were in the superficial lining of the small intestine but these were easily closed with a simple suturing technique. The liver on the other hand was persistent with oozing of continued blood loss.

"Dr. Rapsner, I think we need to apply new packing and a layer of Surgicel around the liver. Otherwise I don't think we'll get adequate hemostasis." I had used Surgicel in many previous operations to help stop oozing blood loss, particularly along a wound or organ bed. The fine material was coated with medications to stimulate clotting and could be manipulated around any surface.

"And how do you plan to close the abdomen, Doctor?"

"Actually I don't. I want to leave the packing in with plans to return to the OR in the next twenty-four to forty-eight hours for re-exploration. I'm concerned for increased abdominal pressure leading to Abdominal Compartment Syndrome. So, I would elect to apply a sponge-based negative pressure device. This would allow for uniform suction of the peritoneum and easy access for re-exploration." If an abdomen was closed while bleeding continued inside, the pressure could increase, causing reduced blood flow to the viable organs which could lead to damage or death of the tissue. Instead of suturing the belly closed, I could apply the device that would allow both the suctioning of excess fluid as well as an easy means to reopen the belly.

"Strong work, Dr. Storm. Very strong work. Be sure to let me know if you change your mind about plastics. You would be a welcome addition to my team."

"Thank you, Dr. Rapsner. You'll be the first to know."

Beep . . . Beep. My pager chirped and vibrated across the metal table of the nurse's station. *Beep . . . Beep.*

"Looks like you aren't getting much sleep tonight, Dr. Storm."

"Heather," I called to the circulating nurse, "that's my pager. Would you mind checking it for me?"

"It's a long distance number, Dr. Storm," Heather said.

"Probably a transfer from one of the smaller hospitals. That's the life of a Level One Trauma Center. Go grab it. I can put the wound vac on from here," Dr. Rapsner said as he took the negative pressure device from me.

I felt a smile spread across my face under my mask as I stepped away from the table. *What a rush!* I walked to Heather who was dialing the number displayed on my pager as she handed the receiver to me.

"This is Dr. Storm. I was paged."

"Rayne? It's Mom . . ." Charlie Grace's voice cracked. "She . . . she's suffered a stroke. You need to get here right away. I've got you a ticket waiting at the airport. Your plane leaves in two hours. Honey, I don't think you'll get here in time if you drive."

Static crackled on the line between us.

"Baby girl, are you there? Did you hear me, Rayne?"

The words . . . phrases . . . commands . . . that had come so easily a few moments before were now lost to me. No answer nor response entered my mind. I had comprehended her words, yet could utter not one sound.

Silence.

"Rayne?" Charlie Grace said louder.

Heather's fear-filled eyes searched my face, waiting to hear the reason for the emergency page. The stare in her eyes shook me back into the reality of the room and my surroundings. I couldn't imagine what I must have looked like to her in that moment. In the moment that words spoken on the phone changed everything about me.

"I heard you, Mother. I'm on my way," I said.

CHAPTER 31

"ARE YOU CHECKING any luggage?" the airline ticket operator asked.

I stood before her, dressed in my hospital scrubs. A single suitcase haphazardly thrown together was clutched tightly in one hand with a cell phone held in the other. "Yes, one bag."

Being a physician allowed direct access to talk with other physicians. I used my standing to discuss Memaw's condition with the doctor who was taking care of her. Memaw had been found unconscious on the floor of her kitchen. An initial CT scan of the brain showed bleeding. The timing of the stroke was unknown. Unfortunately repeat CT scan showed the hemorrhage to be increasing in size.

At some point during the incident she had also suffered a compounding heart attack which resulted in significant muscle damage to the heart. Further life-saving measures were not able to be performed due to her Living Will and Do Not Resuscitate orders on file with the hospital. They did not expect her to regain consciousness. Comfort measures only were ordered at this point. She was considered unstable and in heart failure. Her prognosis was grave. His monotone and dissociated words of medical terminology played over and over in my head, carrying me through to the security check point. A faint, distant calling of my name caught my attention as I was about to enter the security check point.

"Rayne! Rayne! Stormy!"

I turned to see Sam with outstretched arms running toward me and slowing only as she captured me in her embrace. She held me tightly. The small shield of strength I had managed to form fissured in the warmth of her arms. My head was too heavy to hold up any longer and fell on her shoulder. The feeling of her in my arms a few hours earlier burned in my brain.

"Oh God, Rayne. Your mom called me. I'm here, sweetie. I *am* here." She held me tighter in her embrace. "Let me see if I can get a ticket to come with you."

"No," I said, shaking my head with the same meaning. "No, don't do that."

"But I want to come with you. I don't want you to be alone."

"I won't be alone. Jacques is picking me up at the airport. I'm fine."

"No, you aren't. How could you be? If you won't let me fly with you then I'm going home, getting my car, and driving to Louisiana. I should be there by morning. You hang strong until I get there." She pulled away to look me directly in the eyes.

Tears filled my eyes and blurred the vision of her until they broke to run down my cheek.

"Do you hear me? I'll be there. You won't be alone. No matter how hard you fight to push me away. You won't be alone."

I STARED OUT into the blackness from the airplane window. Two lights along the wing of the plane, one red . . . one green, flashed in rhythm—their illumination barely bright enough to light the darkness of the night. Grant was stuck in an aneurysm repair when I left the hospital. I had seen his name on the surgery schedule board hanging on the wall across from the front desk. The case was scheduled to take seven-to-eight hours and had only begun an hour earlier. I sent him a brief text after I boarded the plane. I wondered if he would have come as quickly as Sam had done. I wondered if I would have found the same comfort in his arms as I had hers. I wondered a lot of things.

How long had it been since I'd last seen Memaw? I was having trouble remembering the last time I'd been home. I was absorbed in my rotations, focused only on mastering my surgical skills. What time was not spent on those was concentrated on my struggling feelings for Sam. It had been far too long since I thought of home much less visited. The self-loathing was nearly to the surface before my memory returned me to Memorial weekend. *It was Memorial weekend with Sam at the cabin.*

CHAPTER 32

"DO YOU HAVE any bags?" Jacques asked. He had volunteered to pick me up at the airport.

"Just one."

We stood silently, watching the luggage float by on the baggage claim belt. I grabbed my bag and he took it from my hand. He was quiet for several minutes in the car. Jacques had never been one to say too much, which made him the perfect fit for mother. She didn't have to compete for the attention. He was satisfied to sit in the corner of her life and merely observe.

The night was as dark as the rapidly growing hole inside of me. Its ravenous hunger consumed the remaining light I desperately clung to. The stars above us had been robbed from the thievery of a cloudy night. Rain fell in a steady drizzle, keeping a consistent stream of water dripping down the car window. Their drops ran along the smooth glass, crossing paths until they collected in a puddle along the rim of the door. I watched the rain's stream of water along the window, knowing it was a mirrored reflection of the tears on my cheeks. My heart ached with fear as to what the night held for us. My mind was numb of rational thoughts and filled with unwanted images.

A flash of oncoming headlights caught my reflection briefly in the glass. The gold cross shined brightly in their beams. My memories took me back to much younger versions of Memaw and me. We sat on her bed, looking at old photos of Papaw. Her thumb lingered and slowly rubbed a photo of him dressed in his army uniform. He stood in front of a motorcycle, smiling broadly. Even as a child I realized the smile she carried was masked with a sadness . . . a longing. She rubbed the black leather cord around her neck with her other hand.

"Memaw, what's that you wear around your neck?" I asked.

"Why, honey, this is your pa's wedding ring." She pulled the *gold ring from under her shirt. "I wear it to keep him close to my heart until the day I'm a gonna be with him again."*

"But he's gone."

"Yes, baby girl, that right. But I'm a gonna be with him one day. We gonna be in heaven together."

"But . . . how will I see you when you're in heaven?"

"I'll wait for you just like he's waiting for me. But you gonna live a full life while I do."

"I don't want to be without you, Memaw," I cried and she took me in her arms to rock me back and forth.

"One day I'll go be with Papaw but . . ." She looked around the room, rose to her feet, and walked to her dresser. She pulled out a tiny box hidden under her clothes. She returned to sit beside me with a small gold cross and chain. "Here, Sis. You take dis. Your papaw gave me dis the day your momma was born. I want you to have it." She reached around my neck to fasten the clasp. "And on the day I do go to be with him, you hold onto this here cross. I want you to know'd how much I love you each time you look at it."

"Rayne," Jacques said, breaking the flood of memories.

I looked at Jacques. I found comfort not to wipe away my tears as they were surely hidden from him in the darkness of the car.

"May I talk with you for a minute? You know, before we get there?"

"Sure."

"After tonight I'd like for you to try to never think of this night again. My mother passed away when I was a young man. Cancer had eaten away at her until she was nothing but a shell of the woman I'd known. To this day, when I think of her that's the first gosh damn image I see. She deserves more than that. She deserves me to remember the young, vibrant woman she was . . . not the one that disease made her be. Who you'll see tonight is not Addie. Try to forget this image of her that you're going to see or at the very least suppress it. Let your first thought of her be the one she deserves."

My throat was dry to the point I could hardly swallow, much less speak. The glowing, red emergency sign of the hospital illuminated the dark in front of me. At this hour of the night, it was the only open entrance.

"She's in room two forty-two. The room was pretty full when I left. Flossie and Cora were there. Your mom of course. Addie's brother and sister with their kids had just made it in from Mississippi."

I looked down at my watch. *11:28.*

Jacques directed us through a maze of hospital hallways until we reached one filled with a group of people. I vaguely remembered some of their faces from my youth. Our approach silenced their quiet chatter. Slowly each of their heads turned in our direction. Silently they stepped to each side of the hallway, creating a walkway toward the room.

The numbers, 242, were carved into a brown plaque hanging on the wooden door. The door was cracked open, giving sight to the end of a bed with a silhouette of two feet lifting the mauve blanket from the mattress. I continued toward the door along the path I did not want to walk. Uncle Joe, Memaw's brother, was the last I passed before reaching it.

He clasped my arm with his strong hand. "She's been waiting for you. She stirs every time someone says your name." His voice was coarse with years of tobacco smoking. I had seen him a few times throughout my life as he was the one to visit Memaw the most out of all of her siblings.

The room appeared much like the outer hallway. People stood and sat in various positioning.

Their eyes focused on me as I entered the room. The quiet chatter once again hushed in my presence. Outstretched hands squeezed my own as I passed by them. Some even placed a hand on the small of my back, encouraging me forward to the bed.

I saw Memaw in full view. She was a form, lying on an impersonal bed—in an impersonal room. Nothing of her was visible there. Nothing of her was visible anywhere. Her face was pale and blank of expression. Her long white hair was tame as it lay across the pillow. Her brilliant blue eyes were hidden under closed lids. Short, shallow breaths were inhaled and exhaled as her hands lay motionless across her chest. Charlie Grace's hand rested gently across her mother's arm. She sat on one side of the bed. Flossie sat on the other.

Short . . . shallow . . . breaths.

Flossie stood slowly, stretching an old body stiffened from

sitting too long. "She's been waiting for you, Sis." She squeezed my shoulder as she walked from the bed to stand next to Cora who was still sitting on the love seat. I stared down at the now empty area of the bed next to Memaw.

Mother leaned over to whisper into Memaw's ear. "She's here, Mom. You can go now."

Short . . . shallow . . . breaths.

I sat on the side of the bed to still the spinning room. I cupped Memaw's hand with my own. It felt foreign to me. Her hand didn't hold any warmth to its skin. Her hand was cold, lifeless, and gave no return caress. Her touch was empty of the comfort I had always found within them before.

Short . . . shallow . . . breaths.

She made no motion to look up at me. Her eyes were void of flickered movement. I wanted her to see me. I wanted her to know I was there. I kissed her forehead lightly, letting my lips linger to inhale her scent. A faint wisp of honey and brown sugar soothed me, reminding me she was still with me.

Short . . . shallow . . . breaths.

I bent over to whisper into her ear. My words were strangled within me as I fought to capture my own breath. "I love you, Meems, with all of my heart and soul." Those were the words I managed to say to her. But inwardly I screamed, "I'm not ready. Don't leave me! I'm not ready!"

Again she gave no hint of a response. She made no movement at all. She gave not one single flutter of her eyelids.

Short . . . shallow . . . breaths.

My inner screams quieted as I felt the change of the hand held within mine. Its temperature was cold with the warmth draining from her fingertips, leaving behind a purplish hue. An icy chill crept further up her hand and arm. I watched her chest rise. My own breath halted as I waited for her chest to fall. I stared at it, wishing for evidence of air's escape but none came—nothing but silence . . . nothing but stillness.

Charlie Grace had been looking down at the sheets and twirling a loosened string from the blanket in her fingers. I suppose it was her way of giving Memaw and me our final moment or maybe it was her escape from the reality of the night. She raised her head to meet my gaze as if she had felt my eyes searching for hers, searching for her to notice what it was I could not speak. A look of panic, fear, and sadness washed over her even before looking toward Memaw's still body. We sat there in the silence of the room, watching the body her soul left behind.

Mother took my hand. "She needed you with her to make the final step," she said through a slow steady stream of tears.

Crack . . .

Fissure . . .

Break . . .

Those were the feelings of my heart being ripped apart inside of me, sucking the last drop of remaining strength from me. I fell across Memaw's chest, broken and weeping from a place I did not know existed. The tears came from a blackness deep within me. A blackness that now consumed me.

"Oh, dear God," I heard Flossie say in the distance—an echo in the darkness.

Her words rang faintly in my head before the black overtook every inch of me. My soul was shattered and screaming, "I'm not ready! I wasn't ready!"

CHAPTER 33

"SWEET GIRL, IT'S time," Flossie said from over my shoulder. Her hand gently traced circles on my back. "We need to let her go now."

My body flinched again with the remembrance of her words. I'm not sure how long I had lain across Memaw's still chest before Flossie came over to get me. When I finally raised up and opened my eyes, I realized all that remained in the room was Mother, Cora, Flossie, and me.

Flossie's eyes were red from crying. Her voice was broken as she spoke to me. Cora had not changed her position from sitting on the small couch across the room. Her hands were clasped together on her lap. Her fingers were so tightly wound they were white from the strength of her grip. Her big, round glasses had fallen down the bridge of her nose. Both fresh and dried tears were present on her face, streaking her makeup in the path in which they fell.

Mother remained sitting on the bed across from me. She stared blankly at the form lying in between us. The vision of Memaw's body seared my thoughts and burned my eyes.

My body stirred again as I realized a warmth with the stinging of the vision behind my closed eyes. Eucalyptus mint filled my senses as my mind slowly awakened from the painful memories to recognize the touch of a hand lightly stroking through my hair. Warm arms held me in an embrace as she lay next to me on the bed. Sunshine peeked through the drawn curtains to give evidence that another day had come. The sun had risen. The night had passed. Life had not ended even though my soul ached in death's calling.

"Hi," Sam said softly.

"Hi," I said with a morning's first spoken raspy voice.

"Sweetie, I don't have the words to say to ease you one bit. I was never good at times like this. Always wanting to fix it . . . but you never can. All I can do is not pretend to know what you feel or what you need." She was half lying half sitting against the headboard. She continued to brush her fingers through my hair. "Can you tell me anything at all I can do for you?"

"Right now this is good."

"Then here is where I'll stay."

I'm unsure how many minutes passed before I felt her hand slow in its movements through my hair. Her breath became rhythmically deepened. Of course, she was exhausted.

I realized time had slowed since I left Memaw's side. It had only been a few hours since we left the hospital. A few hours since I had seen men in white scrubs one on each end of a stretcher enter room two hundred forty-two.

Sam must have gotten to my house in the early morning hours. I felt a brief smile form as I thought of the woman whose arms I was lying in. She had traveled the night to be by my side, undoubtedly coming straight into my room the moment she arrived rather than waiting for me to awaken.

"SAM," I SAID, lightly trying to wake her, "I think I should probably go downstairs now."

"Yeah . . . yeah . . . I'm awake." She ran her hands through her hair and shook the tousles out along the sides. "Damn, sorry, Stormy. Think I passed out on you."

"Yes, you did. You must've been exhausted."

"No point arguing that now that I have drool all over my face. How long was I out?" she asked.

"I'm guessing about three hours."

"So . . . you're ready to go downstairs then?"

"No," I said quickly, "but I s'pose I have to."

"Alrighty then. Follow me. I know the way," she said, standing up from the bed and reaching her hand for me to take it.

We walked hand in hand down the hallway and stairs to the kitchen. Her hand in mine was such a comfort and took away a hint of the loneliness the night before had left in me. Nevertheless underneath the comfort lurked unsettling thoughts I had not yet allowed to surface.

She held my hand lightly enough to feel her caress but not so strongly it was all I noticed. That was until we came to the doorway of the kitchen. I heard whispers of conversation behind the walls as we walked closer. I began to pull my hand from hers.

She tightened her grip and kept our hands together as we came into view of those in the kitchen.

Jacques and Grant were sitting in the middle of the long island bar. They held coffee cups in their hands as they rested their elbows on the countertop. Flossie and Cora stood opposite them with their backs against the unused stove, each holding cups. Mother sat alone at the breakfast table. Her back was to us as she stared out the bay windows. The table was bare in front of her. Jacques, Grant, Flossie, and Cora all looked up when they noticed us in the doorway. Grant's eyes immediately focused on our held hands. Mother never turned around.

"Morning, Rayne . . . Sam," Jacques said. "Can I get you girls a cup of coffee?"

"Yes, please. That would be great," Sam said.

Grant didn't speak nor rise to greet us. He sat, still staring at the joined hands. His stare made me more and more uncomfortable with each passing second.

"How you doing, honey?" Flossie's voice startled me in its proximity. She now stood less than a foot from me.

"I'm fine," I said.

Sam squeezed my hand before releasing it to walk around Flossie toward Jacques.

"How's she holding up?" I heard Jacques whisper to Sam.

Sam looked over her shoulder at me before turning back to Jacques and whispering, "Not sure yet."

Flossie cupped her hands along both sides of my face. "Uh huh. Sure you are. You know's I don't say much but I'm here for you. You know'd that right?" She examined my face for several seconds before looking deep into my eyes. She was one of few who knew how to read my thoughts and feelings by studying my eyes. My eyes were my giveaway. They were that one feature I couldn't mask, couldn't hide. If you learned to read them, you knew me. Besides Memaw, Flossie was the only one who could do this.

Memaw.

"I know, Flossie. I just . . . I just . . . I'm sorry. I can't right now."

"And you don't have to. Why don't you and Sam take your coffee outside?"

"No, I need to stay in here with everyone," I said.

"Honey, they 'bout to discuss the arrangements needing to be made. I don't think you wanna hear that."

I looked over her shoulder to see Sam staring at us. Jacques was talking but she kept her focus on me. Making eye contact, she lifted her chin in the air and smiled, giving me the strength I needed. "No, I'm fine. I'll stay."

Grant stared at his coffee cup.

Mother had yet to look away from the window. With coffee in hand, we all joined her at the breakfast table. Grant and Jacques stood with their backs against the opposite wall.

"I think I'll use Mulhearn and Bonner. They have the nicest wake service. Of course our church will do the funeral. Brother Dan does a nice sermon for times like these. She already has a plot next to Dad." Charlie Grace's tone was distant—separated from the words she spoke. "I'll get dressed and go up to the funeral home to get everything arranged."

"I'll go with you," Jacques said.

Mother looked at him with a half-hearted smile.

"Why does it have to be your church?" I asked.

"Why wouldn't it?" she said.

"Maybe because she never once stepped foot in that church."

"And just where would you have us hold the service? What spread her ashes over that damn bayou of yours?"

"Why not? Or why not graveside? She would like that better than having it done by your Brother Dan."

"Rayne Amber, do not bring any form of blasphemy in my house on this day. I'll not have it. Not have it one bit. You aren't the one who lost her mother."

The words hung in the air between us. I pushed my chair against the wall as I rose to my feet. I held her in my glare. Sam and Grant stood looking at each other as if they too held surprise and uncertainty.

"I'm sorry. I'm really sorry," Mother said. "I didn't mean it. Honey, please . . . sit back down."

"No, Mother. I'm fine. Do what you will." I stormed out of the kitchen.

I heard footsteps coming up from behind me to quickly close the gap.

"Rayne, wait up."

My heart sank a little in the deepness of the voice. Hadn't Grant come to be by my side just as Sam had? Hadn't he driven all night to support me? Yet it was her arms I awakened in. It was her arms I remained in long into the morning hours. It was her voice I wished to hear racing toward me. But it was *his* voice I knew I should be wishing was the one following me.

"Rayne, where are you going?" he said.

"I don't know. Away. Out of here."

He put his arm around me as we walked out the front door. The large circle drive was empty of cars except for ours. This would not be so in the days to come. The cars would be bumper to bumper of those coming to pay their respect to our loss. Thoughts of people coming and going, bringing casseroles of every variety, staying to share their stories of Memaw, or discuss her in some way drained me of the energy to continue to move. I sat down hard where I stood at the edge of the porch and let my legs hang off of its side. The railing was a sturdy support to my arms as I rested them across the wooden beam.

"Rayne? You okay?" Grant asked in a whisper.

"I'm fine."

"Well, I know that isn't true. But what I meant was . . . is there anything I can do?"

"No, Grant. Thanks though. Really, I'm fine."

If I had known something he could've done, I surely would have told him. But there was nothing. Nothing entered my mind as to what could possibly take away the blackness, the coldness that filled me. She was gone. There were no thoughts beyond this.

"But Sam can help?"

"What?"

"I can't help . . . but Sam can. I'm your boyfriend for Christ's sake." His tone was filled with bitterness.

"Please, Grant. Not now. Please don't do this now." I couldn't fathom having to deal with another emotion.

"Don't do what? Act upset when you walk into a room holding a lesbian's hand?" He stood, staring down over me. His eyes were darkened with anger—an anger I had never witnessed on him before. "No, I want to know right now. What the hell is going on that you are holding her hand?"

I didn't answer.

"Just forget it, Rayne."

I watched him storm into the house before I turned back to rest my forehead against the porch railing. I knew he was right to question what he had seen but I was too emotionally drained to deal with it right then. All I could think of was Memaw—the loss of Memaw. How I would never again see her face . . . never again talk to her . . . never laugh with her. A life without those things wasn't one I had envisioned much less prepared for at this juncture in my life. My shoulders tensed at the sound of footsteps walking up behind me. As the steps silenced, I felt a soft tickle on my cheek. I turned to see Flossie standing next to me, a black leather band was dangling from her hand.

"Hey, can I sit with ya?" she said as she pointed toward the empty spot next to me.

"Yeah . . . sure."

"I thought we might'n could keep each other company." She slowly sat down next to me and let her feet dangle off the porch. Even at her age, she was taller than me so her feet hung lower than mine. "I wondered if'n maybe you wanted this for yo' cross?" She lifted the black strap in front of my eyes.

I grabbed for the gold cross and held it between my fingers as I slid it slowly back and forth on the chain. Tears welled in my eyes as my thoughts took me back to the day Memaw had given it to me.

"Aw hell, Sis." Flossie exhaled deeply. "Addie loved you something fierce."

Her words broke the invisible wall that was giving me strength to control my tears in front of her. Streams ran down my face and ended in puddles on my shirt. "Did she . . . ?" My words were stuttered with gasps of air in an attempt to catch a breath in between the violent sobs. "Did she . . . ever . . . at any time . . . tell you I had disappointed her?" The question had been burning, boring through me the moment she passed in my arms. I had failed her. I wasn't there when she needed me. I had let my dreams—my wants fail her.

"What?" she asked, collecting me up in a strong hug. She buried my head under her chin as she rocked me gently in her arms. "Good heavens, no!"

"But . . . but . . . I failed her. I wasn't . . . wasn't there when she needed me."

"You can't think like that. Not at'oll, you hear me? Addie loved you as her own child. She 'bout burst with pride over you. You never once . . . not *once* . . .done disappointed her."

I continued to cry against her neck. "I don't know what I'm going to do without her. I don't know how to go on without her."

"Sure you do. And she would a wanted you to. You know'd that right? You know'd Addie would hunt you down from her grave if'n she had one notion you gonna try to give up." She tried to force out a laugh. "You gonna see her one day, Sis. But until you do, she gonna watch you from high above."

I pulled away to look at Flossie.

She must have seen the surprise in my eyes. "What? You don't think'n I believe in heaven. Just cuz I don't go to that Bible-thumping, Holy-roller church yo momma go to don't mean I ain't a believing in heaven. Addie is up there right now lookin' at us."

I found a quiver of peace, enough to stop the tears, as I thought of Memaw watching us from above.

"So what ya think?" Flossie asked, holding the piece of leather in the air.

I took the black string from her. "I would like that very much."

She reached around my neck to unclasp the delicate gold chain, slid the cross from it, and threaded the black leather through its loop. She had fashioned a clasp by making a loop on one end and a knot on the other. I felt her tighten the strap before patting my shoulders. "There now."

"Thank you, Flossie," I whispered, again holding the gold chain between my fingers.

"Lawd, child, watching you holdin' that chain brings yo' pa to mind. I remember the first day I met him. Addie done met him a few weeks earlier. Had done had them some dates, I reckon. Anyway she and I slipped off and got us in some moonshine one night. That juice was makin' us feel real good real fast. We walked up on a swimming hole and thought we best jump in. Wasn't nothin' back then to jump in a watering hole bare as the day you were born. So there we wuz splashing around in our birthday suits. Damn if yo' pa didn't walk up on us. Addie was fit to be tied.

She yelled at him to throw her something to cover up with. That man done reached up and throwed her a handful of moss from the tree. She was mad as a hornet, strolling out of that water with the moss covering up her girlie parts." Flossie chuckled and so did I. "I swear I couldn't catch a breath from laughing so hard. But you wanna know the funniest part?"

I nodded. I smiled as I envisioned Memaw wrapped in moss and walking bare bottom out of the water.

"The funniest damn part of the whole thing was Addie got some kind of chiggers from dat dere moss. Her girlie critter itched her something vicious. I told her she done look like one of them dogs scratching their butt 'cross the ground. Oh Addie, could give a good cussing if'n you rubbed her the right way. I tell you I got me a good'un that day!"

I couldn't help but to laugh a little.

Her face lit up in a smile. "There now, that be the smile I was hoping for."

CHAPTER 34

NUMB . . . VOID OF any feeling or recollection of myself—that was a good description I would use. I was a mass of emotionless movements, dressing for the day I had not expected for years to come. Had I truly not expected it or had I never honestly considered it would be? How did one anticipate the day her own heart stopped beating?

Black . . . that was the color of the material of my clothing reflecting back at me in the mirror. It was the color of the proper attire of the day's event. It was the color of my existence without her. Black—the color that was now my soul.

Proper . . . it had all been so proper. Charlie Grace arranged the details required of a proper funeral. The wake was a learned lesson in the etiquette of death. Memaw's makeup and hair had been professionally styled. Her body was adorned in a fashionable dress of black with pearl buttons. Her lifeless body was a stranger to me with nothing of her anywhere to be found. Yet it was oh so proper.

As I lay broken across Memaw's chest in room two hundred forty-two, I felt the strength slip from my body. It was a strength made fragile with escape of her last breath. Without the strength I once knew, I fell into conformity of Charlie Grace's will.

Dutifully I attended the wake the night before the funeral service. I stood in the corner of the large room, apart from the crowd, to provide some separation but not enough to cause scorn from those orchestrating the services. I stared at the casket that held the body of the stranger inside of it. Memaw looked nothing like herself. Charlie Grace brought in her hairdresser to fix Memaw's makeup and hair. Her dress was a style unlike any Memaw would have picked out. Most people at the wake had seen Memaw in nothing more than blue jean Dickie overalls and a t-shirt.

She looked like a stranger to me too. Then again, maybe it was easier to see a stranger lying in the casket instead of the woman I loved and already missed dearly. Nonetheless, I gave no conflict

to Charlie Grace. I stood in the corner, responding to those who
came to greet me. I used the same four phrases over and over:
"Yes, she was a wonderful woman" "Yes, she will be missed"
"Yes, it is a loss" and the most common, "Thank you for being
here." Charlie Grace seemed pleased with my performance.

The tension between Grant and Sam grew. He hardly
acknowledged her presence at the visitation. Sam was either
oblivious to it or she simply didn't care. Her focus seemed to be
solely on me. The tension between Grant and me wasn't much
better. He was supportive to a degree but his distance remained. In
fact he left to stay with his parents shortly after our argument on
the porch. I didn't mind his absence as I was still not prepared to
finish our earlier conversation.

The morning of the funeral, I stood alone in front of the mirror,
staring at my reflection. I saw as much of a stranger to me as the
body of the woman lying in a shiny, mahogany casket the night
before. I was wearing the ensemble Charlie Grace had left lying
across my bed. The dress was solid black with pearl buttons along
the chest and wrist. My eyes focused on the pearl necklace around
my neck—a neck void of the single gold cross. The site of its
absence shocked me into a reality, resurrecting a portion of my
failing strength.

One strong pull of my hand was all it took to break the string
holding the beads together. I watched pearls bounce across the
granite counter top and spill onto the hardwood floor. I grabbed the
collar of the dress with the same force I had used on the necklace
and ripped the thin material from my neck and shoulders.

"One last stand together," I said to the woman staring back at
me.

I STOOD OUTSIDE the huge oak doors of Charlie Grace's
Northside Baptist Church and stared at the brass knobs as I tried
to decide if I truly wanted to open them. The weight in my arms
was growing heavier by the minute. Through the doors I could
hear Brother Dan giving his sermon masked as a funeral service.

I quietly cracked the door to peek inside. Brother Dan was a
man rich in Biblical verse as he preached his doggerel to the loved
congregation. Charlie Grace sat in the front row. Her head was
bowed but her body was erect—a prideful posture. Jacques and

Grant sat on either side of her. My contempt for the spectacle being displayed grew with each "Amen" and "Preach to us brother" shouted from the church members crowding the pews.

There was nothing of Memaw anywhere within those four walls or among the rows of those attending. There was nothing of her within the words being expressed as a last testament to her. A shifting body caught my attention. I turned to see Flossie squirming in her seat next to Sam.

As if sensing me looking at her, Sam turned toward the doors. She saw me and cocked her head. "Where have you been?" she mouthed in silence.

"Now, brothers and sisters, won't you join me in the singing of Adelaide's favorite hymn." Brother Dan's voice boomed across the church. He ran his hand over the strip of hair resting above his ear, smoothing the strands that had become displaced during his exaggerated mannerisms.

The choir behind him stood to sing in unison, "Amazing grace . . . how sweet the sound . . . that saved a wretch like me . . . I once was lost but now am found . . . was blind but now I see."

Her favorite hymn? That was not *her favorite hymn!* A voice inside of me screamed as the anger toppled over and coursed through me.

I let the oak doors slam forcefully behind me as I entered fully into the church. My entrance was sure to be grand no matter the timing, albeit this may have been a masterful interruption.

Everyone turned in my direction. I swallowed hard as the gawkers of the congregation focused their eyes on me. The choir stood in a trance-like state. Their song abruptly silenced. Brother Dan stood behind the podium looking back and forth between Charlie Grace and me. A sight I surely must have been.

My footsteps down the center aisle were made heavy with nerves and shoes caked with Louisiana mud clay. Sweat had formed at the small of my back, causing a coolness from the dampness of my gray t-shirt. Perspiration continued to bead my brow and neck as I lugged the heavy pot. Trails of dirt spilled from the rim and dropped down the front of my heavily soiled blue jeans to leave a trail along the well-traveled red carpet.

I met Brother Dan's shocked expression as I came to stand next to the casket. I inwardly snickered and wondered if he was

C. D. Cain

enlightened yet. Had he recognized the return of the girl who felt out of place in his church?

But this time, I *was* dressed the part. This time I *felt* the part. This time I was the granddaughter remembering and respecting the woman that lay before him. I would honor her in the way she lived, not in this masquerade put on by Charlie Grace.

I placed the pot containing the freshly dug up Hibiscus next to the coffin. I leaned in to kiss her cheek, breathing in her scent as I did. She had become the epitome of the beautiful flower void of scent. She no longer smelled of brown sugar and honey.

"My heart will beat for the both of us, Memaw," I whispered over the body, hoping the soul would hear.

I grabbed a fistful of soil and sprinkled it lightly across her hands and chanted the Cajun French phrase she had taught me long ago. "Be one with the earth. Be one with nature. Grow, flourish, live in this new world before you."

I let the canvas cooler bag slip from my shoulder. The melted ice sloshed against the sides as it came to rest on the floor. I unzipped the top and folded back the lid. Someone sitting in the front row gasped. Faces holding scrutinizing eyes turned quickly to those with gaping mouths as I loosened the cap from a bottle.

"Schweesh." I raised the bottle high in the air. "To you Memaw." I took a long swallow of the ice cold beer. I wiped the excess liquid that had escaped my mouth with the back of my hand.

Charlie Grace stood up. "Rayne Amber Storm. How dare you show blasphemy to the Lord in this way?"

I turned on my heel and took another deep swallow of the brew, my eyes casting their disdain for her over the amber-colored bottle. "How dare you show it to her? This is not Memaw." I waved my arms in the air. "None of this is her. You know this is not what she would want. How dare you use this to put on a show for your social snobs! You had no right." I stepped toward the casket and placed a bottle of Pabst Blue Ribbon in Memaw's clasped hands. I turned around and walked back down the center aisle. The tears threatened to break free but I was determined to hide them from those around me.

Charlie Grace sat down hard in exasperation. A loud sigh or possibly even a gasp escaped her lips.

Loud over the crowd I heard Flossie yell, "Amen!" as she stood and pumped her fist high in the air.

Those who knew Memaw stood from their seat as I passed. Our eyes met, and I received a smile or a nod praising me for my actions. Mrs. Imogene Bell started to rise but then quickly sat back down. I noticed Singleton's hand gripping her arm in disapproval of her support. She looked him squarely in the eyes before shrugging her arm free.

She stood and grabbed my forearm as I passed. "She would've been proud, Sis. That old broad is dancing a jig up in Heaven right now."

Flossie stood in the aisle at the end of a pew. "Toss me one of those, huh?" I lobbed a bottle to her. Cora watched with an approving smile.

I felt strong hands on my shoulders before hearing Grant's voice from behind me. "What say we blow this joint and finish off those cold ones you brought into Brother Dan's house of God?"

"I second that," Sam said as she walked up beside me. "Damn girl. I've never been more proud of anyone in my entire life." She wiped a fallen tear from her cheek. "Damn proud."

My strength wavered with tears sprinkling down my own cheeks. I parted my lips to speak but only sobs escaped.

Sam slid her arm around my waist. "I know. I know."

We didn't attend the graveside service during the burial of Memaw. I had already said my good-byes in the best way I knew how . . . in the only way I knew. I had taken Jacques' advice and made a memory I would be proud of when my mind traveled back to my life's darkest of times. Memaw had always told me mine was an old soul living in two worlds. Those two worlds had all new definitions now—one having been shared with the bluest eyes I had ever known and one that had to learn to live without them.

I spent the next few hours with Sam and Grant at the old shack on our family property. In all honesty, I drank the most of the remaining beers in the cooler. The brilliant white of the low-hanging moon illuminated the trail through the pecan orchard back to the house. Grant whispered an apology to me as he hugged me good-bye at the door. Sam turned her back and entered the house to give us our apology. He kissed me softly on my lips before he left for the evening.

The house was dark, quiet. Charlie Grace's church had hosted a fellowship hour in the main social hall that began directly after the graveside service. Their idea of an hour was far different than mine. Those events would go on well into the night. Sam gave me a questioning look as we walked into the living room. The room would have been completely darkened if not for the moonlight shining through the tall paned glass windows. The curtains were left drawn back to display Charlie Grace's decorative tiebacks.

"They are probably still at the church getting their fellowship on," I said sarcastically.

"Oh," she grunted as she nodded. "Hungry?"

She grabbed my hand, pulled me with her toward the kitchen, and stopped next to the bar stools lining the center island. "Sit." She turned to rummage through the refrigerator. "Do you know I make one helluva mean omelet?"

"I did not know that."

She stopped spreading the ingredients out on the counter long enough to smile at me. "Well . . . I do."

I hadn't realized I was hungry until I smelled the sautéed mushrooms, peppers, and onion. It occurred to me I hadn't eaten since sometime the day before. Any other time that would have been a recipe for disaster considering the number of beers I had drank earlier. Unfortunately I felt no buzz at all from the alcohol. I would have welcomed it tonight, a numbing distraction from the pain pulling at my heart.

"Hey you." Sam softly rubbed my forearm. Lost in my thoughts, I had rested my weary head on my hand. "You still with me?"

"Oh yeah . . . sorry."

"Good, because dinner is served." She held up the two plates in front of me. Cheese billowed out from the folded edges of the omelets causing a spontaneous growl of my stomach. "Let's go eat upstairs on the balcony."

"Sounds good."

I FOUND THE quiet to be fitting, if not slightly unsettling. It was either that or the fact I was standing in the middle of a cemetery for the first time in as long as I could remember. Beautiful would never be a word I would use to describe the monument splattered piece of land before me. Although if there was any spot which could reach for such a description, it would be Meem's.

I vaguely recollected where Charlie Grace had described Papaw's plot. Yet once I saw the large oak's shadow over a weathered stone sitting next to a dome of fresh dirt, I knew the whitened marker must hold Memaw's name engraved on it. I sat at the foot of the pile and picked up a clump of dirt, praying my mind could trick my hands into feeling her hand within mine again.

I sighed deeply. "Aw, Meems. I miss you so much."

I looked up into the brightness of the blue sky, all but for a few thin, linear clouds hanging in streaks just above the tree line that bordered the cemetery.

"It's not right. It was too soon." I pinched a clump of red clay into dust between my fingers. "I don't know how to go on without you . . . who to be. Everything centered around me coming home to you. Now what do I do?"

Surely I didn't expect an answer to appear from thin air but I did expect something. Some sound of life among the cold tombstones. There was nothing—no breeze to rustle the leaves, no insects singing to one another . . . nothing, just the quiet.

I stood, facing away from the headstones. At some point a large low-hanging branch of the tree had been cut away. Most probably part of the caretaker's maintenance to avoid damage to the stones. I placed the palm of my hand flush against the center of the stump. Here alone I still fought to choose my words.

"Did I do it? Was all of this my fault? You know I would never have done anything to hurt you. I would have given or sacrificed anything to keep you safe." My thumb circled the drying wood. "If Brother Dan's teachings are right then all of this could be my fault. You could've suffered for my sins. Losing you would have been the best way to punish me." I laid my forehead against the tree. "If you believe."

I walked a full circle around the tree, letting my fingers trail along the bark. Off in the distance I heard the hum of a leaf blower and was aware that I wasn't completely alone under the afternoon sun. I sat on the ground and leaned against the back of Memaw's headstone.

"I struggle to believe it, Meems. Kissing Sam that night . . . being in her arms . . . it's the first it ever felt right. How can something

so wrong that it takes you from me feel so right? For the first
time in my life, I didn't feel regret or disgust being in someone's
arms. How can that be so wrong? I just don't understand but they
say we aren't to question God's will or ask for His reasoning." I
closed my eyes to the tears falling from them. "And what if I don't
believe it, then what? It's not like Sam has promised me anything
whatsoever. She's never even been in a relationship. What makes
me think I'm so special she would change that for me? She's never
even insinuated she wanted something permanent. Even if she did,
she sure as hell doesn't want to live in a small town. This is my
home. I don't know anything else but this. So what would it end
up being anyway? My guess? Heartache. I can't do casual . . . not
with her . . . not when I love her."

The gas-powered whistle of the leaf blower grew stronger. I
saw a man walking along the asphalt path sweeping his arm back
and forth as the leaves scattered before him. I ran my hand across
the soon-to-be-cut grass.

"I go back to school tomorrow, Meems. I came to tell you
good-bye." My voice cracked as it strained against the lump in
my throat. "I love you." I roughly wiped a tear from my cheek
with the palm of my hand. "Oh, how I wish I could feel you hug
me just one more time."

I stood and felt a breeze seemingly lift from the ground to flow
across me. It was strong enough to raise the cotton material of my
shirt from my skin and then quickly it subsided, letting the cloth
gently fall back against me.

MOST OF THE passengers had left the terminal at the end
of the airport. The small commuter airplane had taxied to the
farthest row of glass before we were allowed to deplane. I walked
slowly in the mix of them. Their idle conversations echoed in my
ears somewhere between legible understanding of their words to
nothing more than mumbles. I let them walk ahead of me and
stopped to sit in the black vinyl and metal seats of the terminal
waiting area. It was the same terminal I had flown out of two
weeks earlier.

School had allowed me two weeks excused absence for
bereavement. Sam and Grant had to return the day after Memaw's
funeral. Both of them asked to stay with me but I couldn't let

either of them jeopardize their residencies. I delayed my return as long as I possibly could, which was why I found myself sitting in a nearly deserted airport terminal at eleven o'clock at night. The day after the funeral, I moved out to the cabin. I knew it would give me distance from Charlie Grace but I had hoped it would also give me comfort to be in the place filled with so many memories of the time we spent together. It didn't. It only made the pain of losing her that much greater. The morning I left, I locked the double locks of the door not knowing when I would return . . . *if* I would return.

"I was beginning to think you didn't make the flight."

I jerked the last remaining piece of luggage from the carrier belt before turning to see Sam standing behind me.

"I would've left if I hadn't noticed your bag," she said, reaching for the handle I was holding.

"I got it," I said, pulling it behind me. "How did you know when my flight was?"

"Flossie called me. I gave her my number before I left. Been checking on you."

"Oh."

Sam reached to hug me but pulled her arms back to her sides after I took a step away, deflecting her affections. "Stormy . . ." She sighed deeply. "We need to talk. You've hardly spoken to me since I left Louisiana. You barely answered my texts and only returned one phone call."

"I know, Sam. I know," I said. "But not tonight. Okay?"

"Sure." Her voice was flat. "I understand."

"Thanks."

"I can drive you home," she said.

"No, that's okay. I left my Jeep in the airport parking lot."

"Are you sure? I could keep you company. You know so you won't be alone."

"No, it's late. I'm beat. I'll talk to you tomorrow." I turned to walk out of the sliding glass doors. I didn't hear her come up behind me nor did I look back to see if she still stood there watching me.

CHAPTER 35

SINCE THE FUNERAL, I had dreaded the day I would have to come face to face with Charlie Grace's wrath. I knew it was only a matter of time before she would make it known to me. I had already learned through Grant that folks three parishes over had heard tale of the anger she harbored over my toast to Memaw in the middle of the funeral service. The miles between Louisiana and Alabama had given me ample distance from her, yet I still knew the day was coming when I would have to stand in front of her. The longer the time stretched between us, the more I feared the depth of her plotting.

"We will have two pulled pork sandwiches, an order of sweet potato fries, an order of regular fries, and two sweet teas, please, ma'am," Grant said.

He and I had met at our favorite barbecue joint across the street from the main hospital entrance. Even though I avoided time with Sam, I forced myself to find time to share with Grant. This had become one of our favorite choices for lunch. Usually we spent the time to catch up on how our residencies were going. It felt good talking to him about school. It felt . . . comfortable.

"So, have you heard from your mother yet?" Grant asked before taking a long sip of his iced tea. "Pop says Charlie Grace is fit to be tied. He said she has been holed up in her house for weeks because she is," he changed his voice to sound like a woman's, "too mortified to show my face in public."

"Gawd. Does that ever sound just like her. No, I haven't talked to her yet. I have no doubts she is waiting for me to call and apologize for my heathen ways of embarrassing her. I s'pose I will . . . eventually." I used the straw to swirl the ice around in my glass as I thought of Charlie Grace's antics. "We are at the uncomfortable impasse where each of us feels the other should call to apologize. Honestly, right now, I don't feel I should apologize at all. Even when I do break down and make the call I probably still won't feel I was the one who should do it. I'll give her a ring in the next few days or so. I'll let her bask a little while longer in the sympathy of having such a disgraceful child."

"I think you are safe unless she has discovered a way to physically reach you through the phone. If she ever does that, none of us are safe." He laughed, although the fear of her discovering such power sent a small shiver down my spine.

"God help us all if that happens."

"I have actually been giving your dilemma a great deal of thought."

"Oh, have you now?" I asked. "Any brilliant ideas come to mind?"

"As a matter of fact one pretty freakin' awesome idea came up. A solution that will have her so disoriented she will forget your twenty-one swallow salute."

"Well, technically it was only two swallows in front of Brother Dan. But please . . . go on. My curiosity is peeked."

"Seems Charlie Grace needs a reason to come out of hiding. What better way than shopping?"

"Shopping?" I said.

His smile broadened. "Yes shopping. It's Christmas or haven't you noticed."

"I've noticed. I just don't get how her Christmas shopping is going to get me off of the hook."

"It will if she gets to have a lavish weekend of it. Mom and Dad have rented one of the condos in the Mountain Brook Country Club area. It's a mansion on the eighteenth hole. This thing is always photographed in *Southern Living Magazine*. Mom is beyond excited. Dad agreed to let her have the entire weekend catered even down to the mimosas on the cabana. I'm sure he plans on being on the course for most of it. But all Mom has to do is shop." He paused as the waitress brought our food and reached into my basket to grab a hot sweet potato fry. "Anyway . . . they asked me to see if your mom and Jacques wanted to ride over with them. I thought a weekend of plush catering would be right up Charlie Grace's avenue."

"That sure does have Charlie Grace written all over it. But what makes you think she would come. It would mean she would have to see me." I popped a fresh fry into my mouth.

"Yeah, but how do you feel about it? Would you want that, if she agreed to come?"

"Sure. Seems like the safest option to be surrounded by people when I look directly at Medusa."

"Good, I was hoping you would say that." He took a large bite out of his barbecue sandwich and chewed incompletely before grabbing his glass of tea. He swallowed hard through the straw. "They'll be here next weekend."

"*What?*"

He laughed almost smugly. "Mom had already asked her. She jumped at it. It was you I was worried about."

"Are you kidding me? Next weekend? As in next weekend . . . next weekend?"

"Yep. That be the one." His smile had not yet faded though I was feeling anything but humor. "Sam is coming too."

"*What?*" I felt my heart flutter in my chest. "What do you mean Sam is coming too? I didn't think you two talked anymore."

"We don't really. I ran into her up on the floor when I was doing a consult on a pregnant woman with gallstones."

"Why on earth would you do that?" I knew my tone was cold and bitter but I didn't care.

As if I wasn't angry enough with him taking charge in arranging this whole event with Charlie Grace, I was mad as hell he included Sam in it. I hadn't talked to Sam the next day as I had promised at the airport. Truth be known, I had barely spoken to her since returning to Birmingham two weeks ago. We had shared a few brief texts and calls that contained not much more than a simple hello and rarely spoke about anything other than school. I had thrown myself back into the long hours of residency and volunteered for as many call hours as the program would allow. The few hours of freedom I allowed myself were spent with Grant. Now thanks to Grant, I would have to face both Charlie Grace and Sam at the very same time. This was going to be a wonderful night.

"Why wouldn't I? Ya'll are friends, right?" He paused briefly. "Or is there something else I should know about. You haven't talked about her much since you got back."

"Of course we're friends. Why wouldn't we be? We've just been busy is all."

"You don't seem too happy that I invited her."

"It's fine." *Actually it was anything but fine.* I didn't have the strength to push the argument. "A shock is all."

"Good." He took the last bite of his sandwich and pushed the plastic basket lined with wax paper toward the center of the table. "This'll be an epic weekend of celebration."

Yeah, epic.

THE LAST THING you want to hear coming home from a long sixteen-hour shift when you have to turn around and be on call the very next day is a knock on the door. Nonetheless, there it was with its incessant noise. I willed my body to stand from the couch as it was obvious whoever was knocking wasn't going away anytime soon. A thousand needles pricked the bottom of my feet when I first put weight back on them. I was exhausted to the point I couldn't remember the last time I had showered much less when my head last hit a pillow.

"What?" I pulled the door open wildly without looking to see who was there first. I didn't care. I just wanted them to go away.

Sam flinched and took a step back. I saw indecision flash across her face as she must've realized quickly this may not be the best time for an impromptu visit. She hesitated a moment longer. "Stormy, I know you're tired. I can see it on your face. In fact, sista, you look like pure hell. But we need to talk."

"Can't it wait."

"It has waited."

"Then call me tomorrow or something."

Sam pushed passed me. "That would be a novel idea if you actually answered your phone every now and then."

"I've been busy. Have been pulling a lot of hours lately." I followed her inside and fell back onto the couch.

"Yep, that's what you do." She didn't sit but rather stood there staring down at me.

I got her meaning but didn't let it be a segue into our conversation.

"Rayne . . . why have you been avoiding me?"

"I haven't been avoiding you."

Sam arched her eyebrow. "The hell you say. All I'm asking for is a few minutes. I mean . . . damn, Stormy. We haven't spoken at all about that night in the locker room. You said . . . you told me that it wasn't over just because you got the page and had to go."

"Yeah and then I got another page."

Sam shook her head. "I know. I know, okay? I just mean you acted as if you wanted what we were doing in the locker room too. Hell, you started it. I thought you wanted that to happen between us as much as I did."

"Sex? You mean I wanted sex as much as you did?"

Sam grunted and then sighed deeply. "Come on. You know I don't mean that. It wasn't . . . it wouldn't be like that."

The needles pricked my feet with a vengeance as I stood to face Sam. "Then what would it be like? Hmmm? What would happen if we hadn't been interrupted that night? Where would we be then . . . now?"

Sam took a step back as if caught off guard by my directness. "I . . . I don't know. I mean, what do you mean?"

"I mean where would we be? What would we be tomorrow or the next day or next year if we went back to my bedroom right this minute?"

"I can't answer that, Rayne. No one could. We would see where this goes." She motioned her finger between us. "I guess we would find out what could be between us."

I pursed my lips together. "Hmmmm . . . *what* could be between us. Well, I'm not the toothbrush queen so I wouldn't know how all of this is supposed to go."

Sam's eyes widened and her face dropped.

I plopped back down to sit on the couch and pinched the bridge of my nose. "Look, I'm sorry. I shouldn't have said that. I don't want to fight."

Sam rested against the arm of the couch and sighed deeply. "God, it's not like I want to fight either. I just wanted to know what was going on with you . . . with us. Why you've pulled away from me so much. Now maybe I have an idea."

"It's not just you. I haven't wanted to be around anyone."

"Obviously Grant doesn't fall into the same category. Apparently there's a big party this weekend."

I looked up at her for the first time. "I'm sorry about that. I didn't know he invited you. You don't have to come."

Her eyes widened. "So that's your response? You're sorry I was invited."

I took in a deep breath. "No. I meant I didn't want you to feel obligated to come to dinner is all. It's just to appease Charlie

Grace because she is still wallowing over Memaw's . . ." A lump formed in my throat around the word "funeral." Hadn't the long hours at the hospital kept that word far from my vocabulary? Yet here within minutes of being home it finds its way back. I pressed my palms firmly against my eyes before the tears could roll. "I can't do this right now, Sam."

Of course, I heard the crack in my voice and apparently so did Sam. She sat down on the couch next to me and took in a couple of breaths.

"I can't pretend to know what you feel," she said, rubbing circles on my back.

"I don't think I feel anything. I'm numb," I mumbled softly unsure if she could hear me. "Just numb."

Sam patted my back. "You're right. This isn't a good time. I'm sorry. I've been so confused about us." She blew out a breath. "If there even was an 'us.' I couldn't decipher the mixed signals."

Mixed signals. Yeah, that's on point.

Sam stood from the couch and ran her fingers through my hair. I had yet to look up from keeping my face hidden in my palms. "I'm going to go. I'll see you later, Stormy."

The tears rolled freely after I heard the door open and gently close. I let them fall along my cheeks without wiping them away. At this point, I knew there was no way to stop them. I let my body sink into the cushions of the sofa. My eyes drifted closed only to spring open by the sound of the door opening again.

Sam. I sat up to look over the arm of the couch. Grant stood in the doorway.

"What was Sam doing here?"

I shook my head. "What?"

"I asked what Sam was doing here at one o'clock in the morning."

"What are *you* doing here?"

"I'm your fucking boyfriend that's what I'm doing here."

I stood up and stepped toward the hallway leading into my bedroom.

"I asked you a question, Rayne." Grant met me before I rounded the sofa and put his hands on my shoulders.

"I'm not doing this right now, Grant. I'm tired and going to bed. You can stay or go. Makes no difference to me."

He dropped his arms to his side. "Just tell me what's going on between you two. I think you owe me that."

I looked at him with harsh eyes.

"Are you cheating on me? I mean like in a . . . in a . . . gay way?"

Gay way. I rolled my eyes. "No." I pushed passed him and walked into my bedroom.

GRANT HADN'T EXAGGERATED when he described the weekend. Ned's hired staff had planned a weekend of elaborate dining of three meals a day, eighteen holes of golf with a personal caddy for the men, and a day at the spa for the women. Unfortunately, I missed the Friday night dinner because of my call shift. And after little to no sleep the night before there was no way I had the energy to spend Saturday with Nadine and Charlie Grace even if it was a spa day. I doubted there was a masseuse capable of working out the knots I mass produced in my shoulders. By the time I got to the house Saturday, everyone was gone but the staff. Secretly I hoped the different environment would help me sleep. I hadn't been able to shut my brain off since my visitors surprised me the other night.

It was nearly sunset before I awakened to seek out Charlie Grace. I watched her for several minutes before making my presence known by stepping into the purplish hue of the setting sun. Charlie Grace sat perfectly still as she stared out over the eighteenth green. Her stare didn't flicker to look in my direction as she brought her cocktail up to her lips for a drink.

"Penny for them," I said.

"Would cost you a great deal more than that," she answered dryly as she brought the glass to her lips once more.

"I don't doubt that." I sighed and looked out at the flag flapping in the gentle breeze. The numbers flowed effortlessly in the wind, rippling the one and eight in synchronicity. How I wished this particular conversation could flow as easily. "Thanks for coming, Mother."

"I came for Grant."

"And again I say . . . I don't doubt that." I turned to walk away but stopped before I was out of earshot. "You know I was right in what I did."

She turned so quickly toward me that her drink sloshed over the rim of her glass. "You were *right?* It is *right* to bring alcohol . . . *beer* . . . into God's house. On what planet do you think that is excusable behavior, Rayne Amber?" Her voice was thick with hostility.

"Okay . . . so maybe the beer wasn't the best idea. I'll give you that. But neither was putting on that spectacle of a show with Memaw. She never would have wanted it and you know it. You put her in a dress, Mother. She had her hair rolled and styled like some old lady. *That* was *not* her."

"She was my mother," she said through gritted teeth, "not yours."

She was a far better one than you were. Dammit, why couldn't I say that to her? Instead I stormed away surprised in her coldness and angered in my cowardness.

Was it really being a coward or did I have this insanely innate belief I still owed her respect because she was my biological mother? Besides, I knew what relationship Memaw and I had. I'm not sure what I expected to see when I looked back over my shoulder. Perhaps a part of me thought she may have been chasing after me to apologize. This was not the case. She merely sat there staring out across the course slowly sipping the remaining cocktail.

"DR. SAMANTHA LEJEUNE," the young man announced.

Oh, dear God. The breath caught in my throat as Sam stepped around him. She was exquisitely dressed in a black halter knee-length cocktail dress. I waited to see who would step in behind her—waited to see the date she had invited to be her escort.

"I hope I'm not too late for cocktail hour?" Sam said as she maneuvered the two stairs down into the room.

"No, not at all," Jacques said as he rushed to hold his hand out for her. "You're just in time. So nice to see you again, Sam."

Her smile spread infectiously across her face. "Such the gentleman."

"How could I not be when a beautiful woman walks into the room?" He walked her around the front of the pool table to introduce her to Ned. "This here is Ned Thibodeaux, Grant's poppa. Ned, meet Dr. Sam LeJeune. She goes to UAB with the kids and has become one of Rayne's closest friends."

Sam's eyes shifted slightly over to where I sat before returning back to Ned. "Please call me Sam." She extended her hand out to him.

"It's a pleasure to meet you, Sam." Ned held the end of Sam's slender fingers in the grip of his much larger hand and brought them to his lips to kiss them. "Stunning . . . absolutely stunning."

"Thank you." A blush colored her cheeks. "And thanks for letting me crash your party."

"What? No date tonight?" Grant asked and then leaned over the dark green felt of the pool table.

"No, no date," Sam said dryly.

Grant pushed the pool stick forcibly forward and sank the eight ball on the break. "Woohoo. Good thing I am not losing my touch like Sam over here. I believe I'm up another fifty bucks now."

"Dammit to hell, boy," Ned said, looking away from Sam to Grant. "When on God's green earth are you going to stop costing me money?"

Grant smiled. "Oh . . . sometime after I start my practice." His smile fell as he watched Jacques walk Sam over to the bar.

My heart thudded nearly as loud as the click of her heels on the walnut wooden floor.

"And this is Ned's better half . . . Nadine Thibodeaux."

"You've got that right, Mister," Nadine said.

"Hey!" Ned shouted from across the room.

The loudness of his voice echoed off of the walls of stone and wood. Gray slate stone like that on the exterior of the home adorned the wall and formed the bar where Charlie Grace, Nadine, and I sat. The stone was broken up by shelves of matching walnut nearly completely filled with bottles of wine. I halfway expected the bottles to vibrate with the boom of Ned's voice.

"Mind your business over there," Nadine said.

She patted the empty bar stool that stood between us. Charlie Grace had sat at the end of the bar on the other side of Nadine when she came in earlier, keeping the distance between us.

"Come, dear," Nadine said. "Sit with us. Let the men play their silly game and smoke their stinking cigars."

"Miss," the man standing behind the bar called, "may I get you something to drink."

Sam looked at the variety of drinks at the bar. Nadine and

Charlie Grace were drinking martinis and I was having a beer. "Hmmm . . . I think I'll have something red. Got any suggestions?"

The bartender smiled. "I think I have the perfect wine for you." He turned and shuffled through the bottles in the wine cooler behind him. Its dark glass door hid the bottles from plain view. Once he opened it I could see it was well stocked.

"Ah, here it is," he said and stood back up at the bar. He poured an inch of the red wine in a long-stemmed large-bowled wine glass. "Try this."

I was mesmerized as I watched the delicacy in Sam's hand as she swirled the wine glass on top of the marble bar. She brought the glass quickly up to her nose to breathe in its scent before taking a sip. Her eyebrows danced upwardly in approval of the wine.

"Mmmmm," she purred. "That's very nice. What is it?"

"It's a one of my favorite pinot noirs. I find it to remind me of timeless beauty, eloquence, and grace. All qualities I see in the woman I am serving."

Sam arched an eyebrow. "Going for a nice tip are you?"

He chuckled lightly before filling her glass with the wine. She turned to me and smiled as she tucked a strand of hair behind her ear. The curls were loosely placed in a bun positioned low and to the side of her head. I scolded myself for having to fight the urge to brush another strand off of her face.

"Hey you." She nudged me with her shoulder.

Sam peered around Nadine. "Good evening, Charlie Grace. It's nice to see you again."

"Yes, Samantha. It's always nice to see you," Charlie Grace replied.

Her tone implied the conversation need not go any further. In fact, she hardly made eye contact with Sam at all when she spoke. Obviously, I was not the only one going to be punished but everyone who knew me was to be as well—everyone except Grant.

I sat at the bar, listening to Nadine getting acquainted with Sam. I could tell she was already fond of her. Why wouldn't she be? Sam was polite, entertaining, and charming . . . oh, how she was charming. I let myself drift into their conversation as I listened to the articulations of Sam's raspy voice.

She shifted her positioning on the bar stool when the

conversation quieted. "I'm sorry about the other night. I truly am. Please don't shut me out any longer. Can we please talk again? There's more I want to say. More I should've said." I felt and heard her whispered breath in my ear.

I stared into her eyes and gave her a small smile before blinking several times to pull my eyes from the lull of hers.

THE DINNER CONVERSATION was with much the same experience. The eight-person table seemed small within the large dining room. The caterers placed Jacques and Ned at the heads of the table, their wives to the right of them. Sam seemed alone on the side opposite me.

"See, Sam," Grant said, looking at the empty chair that rested between her and Charlie Grace, "you should've brought you a date."

"Not dating much, Grant. But thanks."

"I don't know how any of you find the time what with your schooling and all," Nadine said. "I just thank the good Lord in Heaven my baby boy has Rayne to help him through all of this."

"Is that it, Sam? You've been too busy to find you a honey?" Grant asked.

His cockiness was starting to get on my nerves. I was sure his demeanor was due to his leftover anger from the night a few days earlier. Yet I had much rathered he direct that hostility toward me instead of Sam.

"No." Sam looked down to adjust the linen napkin in her lap. "Nothing like that."

The main caterer entered the room with four attendants following closely behind. "Dinner is served."

Thank goodness. I didn't think Grant was ever going to drop it. What had I expected? Had I too wondered why she came alone? Wasn't she the woman who never dated seriously? After all, hadn't she coined the phrase "sex is sex"?

Grant rose to his feet. "I want to thank ya'll for coming here tonight. I couldn't think of anyone else I would rather share this night with. Mom . . . Dad . . . you've both been such an inspiration to me. For all of my life, you have been there encouraging me to never give up on my dreams. To chase them with every bit of strength I have. For that I'm so thankful." He held his glass up to his parents at the end of the table. "I hope I've made you proud."

Nadine's eyes glistened with tears. She shook her head at Ned as he looked at her as if asking him to speak for them.

"Of course you have, son," Ned said. His deep voice cracking. "Of course you have." He put his arm around Nadine.

"Mr. and Mrs. Doucet," Grant raised his glass to Charlie Grace and Jacques, "thank you for coming to share this night with us. It has been a pleasure having you with us. Your daughter has become a vital part of my life. I hope you know that."

"We do, Grant," Jacques said. "We're so happy to be here with you and your family."

"Sam," Grant began.

I was compelled to look at Sam after I had avoided looking at her as much as possible, fearing direct eye contact would break all resolve I desperately tried to muster up. She sat like a child being scolded. Her head was drawn to her lap while her hands fiddled with the napkin.

"Sam?" Grant said again.

She looked up at him, not once letting her eyes drift over to me. "Yes?"

"Thank you for coming. I know it probably wasn't the way you would have ideally spent your Saturday night. What . . . with no date and all." He smirked.

She returned a smile—a smile that didn't reach her eyes. "It was my pleasure."

"You have become Rayne's best friend. I knew she would've wanted you here for this."

For this? What did he mean for this? What this?

My inward questioning was swiftly answered with the sound of screeching wood on wood as he pushed the chair away from the table and knelt on one knee where it once sat.

"Oh, my God," Nadine cried out.

"Shush, woman," Ned whispered, patting her arm.

"Rayne, I have loved you from the moment I delivered your Jeep to you. I had never seen a more beautiful woman than the night I watched you walk toward me. And to this day you still captivate me each time I look at you." He reached into his jacket pocket to pull out a blue velvet ring box. He opened it to show a beautiful two-carat vintage diamond engagement ring. "Will you marry me, Dr. Rayne Amber Storm?"

My head spun as if alcohol had taken its effect. *Gawd, why didn't I drink more at the bar?* I tried to focus on something— on anything. At that moment, it seemed the anything would be Charlie Grace.

For the first time all evening, she was looking at me. An element of happiness sparkled in her eyes. It was slowly evolving into concern as my hesitation continued. I closed my eyelids much longer than the time for a normal blink and opened them to see Sam's eyes fixed on me as well. Hers held anything but the same expression Charlie Grace's did.

"Rayne?" Grant said. "Will you make me the happiest man alive? Will you vow to live your life with me?"

"I . . ." My head spun out of control until I saw her.

Sam sat motionless in her chair. Her eyes unwavering as they held me. I couldn't look away, nor did she loosen me from her stare. My body screamed questions without a spoken voice. *What? What should you have said? Do you love me? Is that it? Could you promise me a future? A future I could live with?*

"Rayne?"

Grant's voiced ripped through my ears but my eyes never released Sam. *We don't want the same thing? You want big cities and flings and damn toothbrushes. I'm not that kind of woman. I want, no, I need stability. I'm scared of the unknown.*

"Rayne, honey, don't leave the man down on his knee," Charlie Grace said.

Sam looked at her, stood from the table, and walk out of the room.

SOMETIME AFTER ELEVEN o'clock that night I slipped away to walk the grounds. The night was stifling with humidity, shortening my breath as I walked in search of calm for my restless heart. I sought solitude under the moonlit sky, hoping its stars held the answers I was seeking.

I stopped when I noticed a large river birch tree along the path. Its base was made up of three separate trunks—each a separate entity of one another and each large enough to be a tree all on its own. Yet here they stood considered to be anything more than one. Its bark was peeling in clumps with each layer of it edged and frayed, leaving beneath it three pale white trunks untouched by the warmth of a summer sun as they lay hidden under the mass of shimmering green leaves. Or had the bark possibly separated because it had felt the warmth? Had it ever felt the light filter in only to have it shadowed once again? Perhaps its fraying edges reached away from their foundation to know the warmth again? I wondered if I was one of those trunks.

I walked to the cabana where I had found Charlie Grace sitting earlier in the day. Resting against the arm of the outdoor sofa, I stared out into the night. Inner reflection had been the only company I had on my walk . . . until now.

"Stormy?"

I heard her voice but was powerless to look behind me in search of her. She had already taken my breath once this evening. What would it do to see her now after the big proposal?

She stepped in front of me still dressed in her cocktail dress except now her high heels dangled from her fingertip. The gold buttons fastened from the end of the V-neck cut to the wide waistband of her dress sparkled under the brightness of the moon. Its light filtered in between the sweep of the sheer drapes caught in the night's breeze. She kept her eyes fixed on me but didn't close the distance between us.

"Stormy, aren't you going to say anything? Aren't you going to talk to me at all?" She rested her back against the post of the cabana.

I looked down at my shoes, afraid the tears would fall if I searched her eyes again. They had nearly started when she first walked under the light of the chandelier hanging in the center of the outdoor room. The strip of eyeliner on her bottom lid was much broader than I had noticed before. The edges of it smeared along the creases of her bloodshot eyes.

"Please," she said. "Please talk to me."

"I don't know, Sam. I don't know what to say."

"Do you love him?"

"Yes."

"Are you *in love* with him?"

I looked up at the ceiling and closed my eyes briefly to the light before looking at her. I couldn't answer her question.

She walked to me and put her hands on the sides of my neck. A butterfly caught in my stomach. Her fingers slid into my hair as her thumb traced my lip.

"Don't do this," she whispered. "Please don't do this."

I cursed my body for the sensations shooting through me with the closeness of her. The warmth my body craved with the feeling of her standing between my legs was a betrayal to everything my mind had told me I had to be—to what I could no longer feel.

"I can't."

"You can't what?"

"I just *can't.*"

"Rayne . . ." She removed one hand from my neck to wipe away the tears streaming down her cheeks. "Don't say that. Please, don't say that."

"I'm sorry."

"Don't be sorry. Don't say that to me," she said, gritting her teeth at the last word.

"I told you," I said. "I don't know what to say."

"I have loved one woman . . . one . . . *person* my entire life. In all of my life, just one. And it's you. Always . . . only . . . you. I'm begging you not to do this." Her tears flowed freely and salted my lips as she leaned in to kiss me gently. *She loved me. She said it, but how can we be together?*

Immediately my lips became hers, wanting to be hers. My body yearned to pull her into me fully but I forced myself to push her away. The ache I felt in my heart once my lips lost the touch of hers was nearly as painful as the one I felt a while back.

"Please, Sam . . . I can't," I said through a cracked voice as my tears joined hers. "I can't be like this. I can't do this to people."

"Can't be like what? Do what to people?"

I looked up at the ceiling to see anything but the tears streaming down her face.

"Don't you know I feel everything you feel for me when we kiss. It's like . . . it's like I'm a part of you when we kiss. It has been like that from our very first kiss. I've never felt this before. I know you care for me too. I know you do."

"Of course I know. But it's wrong." I kept my eyes focused on the ceiling.

"Wrong?"

"Yes. Wrong," My words became fractured as the force of my crying choked my breath. "The one time . . . the very first time I let my body feel what I had for so long fought not to feel. The first time I let myself fall into you. The first time I felt completely free in my entire life . . . that one time, she was taken from me."

Sam took a step back, focusing her eyes on me. I could tell she wanted to say something but all she did was rock her head back and forth as if in disbelief of what I was saying.

"He took her, Sam. God took her that night."

"He punished me for my sin by taking her from me. He changed my whole life!"

Sam continued to shake her head slowly. "Rayne, no. No, that . . . that isn't it."

"Oh, yeah? Then what is it? How do you explain it then? Tell me it isn't true. The very night I give into my feelings for you . . . my desires to touch you, she's taken. Hours, Sam . . . in hours after that she was ripped from life. What was it, if not a punishment for giving in to my feelings?"

"Honey." She caressed my neck with her hands. Her face was a definition of shock. "It doesn't work like that. God doesn't work like that."

"Oh, really? And you know this how? Because I can sure tell you I spent enough time at that damn church of Mother's, listening over and over on how this was an abomination to God and all homosexuals would have to answer for their sins. I heard the scriptures Sunday after Sunday after Sunday." I pounded my fist against my thigh.

"They preach through fear. They preach using fear not love. God doesn't punish like that. There are two paths into Heaven . . . love God with your whole heart and love your neighbor as yourself. Rayne, those two. Just those and both of them use love. God is about love . . . not anything else. Memaw passed. She passed, honey, and as painful as it is that is *all* it is. It wasn't your fault. Nothing is your fault. Please, don't ruin your life because of this. Love is real. *I am real.*" She placed my hand over her heart. "*We are real.*"

I shook my head. "Don't you know I want you to be right? But even if you are . . . then what? What's best for our lives?"

"Best for our lives? To live our life not theirs, not anyone's but ours. That's what is best."

"Okay. Then what's right for my life . . . for your life?"

"What do you mean?"

I pointed my finger into my chest. "My life. I want to go home, Sam. I want to go back to what I know . . . what I'm comfortable in."

"You really think you'll be happy moving back home?"

"I want to try. It's my home. All I ever wanted was to get out of school and move back home to be with Memaw. She isn't there but at least her spirit is. And you're a woman who wants culture and fine dining in some far up northern state. So what . . . you're going to move to a small town in central Louisiana? You talk about happiness. Would you be happy then? Would you give up what you want just to be with me when you haven't been with anyone for any length of time? And even if you did . . . Do you honestly think we would be accepted? Do you think either of us could practice in my hometown as the lesbian love couple? It doesn't work like that."

"Looks like you've got it all figured out," she said, shaking her head. "I know you, Rayne. Living a lie no matter how you sugarcoat it will destroy you."

I let my head fall, feeling defeated in my own remembering of reality. "I'm not strong like you."

She gazed at me with sad, heartbreaking eyes. "Yes, you are, stronger even. It's just too bad you don't know that."

AN HOUR OR more passed since I watched Sam walk away, carrying her high heels draped over one finger. In fact, I watched her silhouette until I could no longer see it, even then I stared aimlessly in the direction it had disappeared.

A pang was in my heart as I truly didn't know if the good-byes were meant for the evening or for something more lasting. Did I believe there was any way possible to maintain a friendship? I hadn't told her I loved her. I hadn't been able to voice it even though my body screamed it loudly. What good would come of her knowing I loved her as much as she had confessed to loving me? Then she too would have to suppress the knowledge as much as I was going to have to do. No, it was better this way.

I watched the stillness of the eighteenth flag as it lay against the pole. It was motionless without the night's breeze. A part of me wondered if my future was to be as stagnant without the breath of fresh air Sam's presence had given me.

About the Author

Although CD Cain now loves living in South Georgia, she does miss days spent on the bayou behind her family's home. It was through her daydreams of longing to once again feel her toes dampened in the cool water that characters began to awaken in her mind. She soon realized they weren't going to quiet their chatter in her brain until she gave them life. Thus the Chambers of the Heart Series was born.

Beyond writing, CD enjoys spending time with her partner of twenty-two years, their four-year-old son, and multiple furbabies. She is the happiest when outdoors either simply relaxing on her porch or camping with her family. When she is not writing, she works as Physician Assistant caring for patients with spinal disorders. Many times she refers to her patients as her second family.

She hopes the Chambers of the Heart Series connects with her readers by creating characters who make them laugh, remind them of a happy time in their lives, give them renewed strength in trials once faced and conquered or let them bask in the newness of love. She enjoys hearing from her readers so please contact her through: Twitter (@cdcain1019), Facebook (C.d. Cain), Goodreads (Cdcain), E-mail at cdcain1019@yahoo.com or on her webpage www.cdcainauthor.com. Her next goal is to become a better web-page designer and blogger . . . perhaps after a couple of glasses of a nice smooth red.